Praise for

The Jacq of Spades

"A mystery, a damn good one … your characters are still living in my head."

— DAVID BRIDGER

"The Jacq of Spades hooked me immediately, almost against my will, and pushed me through a story that both captivated and puzzled me."

— LILYN G, SCIFI AND SCARY

"Jacqui is no Sherlock Holmes, but she is a delight ... The world feels very much like the dark underbelly of Victorian fashion and style, with a gritty mafioso vibe."

— HEIDI ANGELL

"... this mystery kept me guessing up until the very end."

— BARGAIN BOOK REVIEWS

"... a stunning example of steampunk and noir combined. The main character is a perfect combination of femme fatale and private investigator ... I loved seeing her come to life on the page."

— E.G. STONE

"This was the first steampunk book that I've read that I actually really loved."

— GABBY'S HONEST BOOK REVIEWS

For more reviews, visit JacqOfSpades.com

BOOKS BY PATRICIA LOOFBOURROW

RED DOG CONSPIRACY

MAIN SERIES

The Jacq of Spades

The Queen of Diamonds

The Ace of Clubs

The King of Hearts

The Five of Diamonds

The Two of Hearts

The Three of Spades

The Knave of Hearts

The Four of Clubs

THE PREQUELS

The Alcatraz Coup

Gutshot: The Catastrophe

Brothers

Vulnerable

THE COMPANIONS

Drawing Thin

THE JACQ OF SPADES

Patricia Loofbourrow

ISBN-13: 978-1-944223-04-5

Published by Red Dog Press, LLC
Printed in the USA

To my children, who have taught me so much.

The Letter

A domed city, split by four rivers, an island at its center. In the southeast quadrant, a taxi-carriage pulled up to a shop on 2nd Street. In the gutter lay a card:

BRIDGES: 500 YEARS OF CULTURE

THE JEWEL OF THE GREAT PLAINS

The postcard depicting an elegant couple crossing a golden bridge lay in horse manure. A carriage-track ran through it.

I stepped over the scene as I climbed from the taxi-carriage, my borrowed boots grating on the rough concrete sidewalk. Trash flew past in the wind. The air smelled of rain, clouds hanging dark in the afternoon sky. "How much to wait?"

The clocks chimed half past two. The driver, in his sixties, pushed his goggles up on his forehead. His horse tossed its head and shifted. "Here? Penny now, penny when you done," he paused, leering, "cause I like you." He made no attempt to hide his survey of my person.

Unimpressed, I handed him the penny, entering the white wooden storefront as large drops fell.

The floorboards squeaked. The front room, lit by a bulb hanging from the ceiling, smelled of mildew. Grayish-green paint flaked off the walls.

The woman behind the counter, pale with graying brown hair, wore widow's brown. "Welcome to Bryce Fabrics. How can I help you?"

Eleanora. When I last saw her ten years ago, she screamed curses and wept. How could she be here? What would she do? I felt an urge to run.

I took a deep breath. A child changed more in ten years than a woman. Her face held no recognition. "You sent for assistance?"

"Oh! Yes!" She grabbed my hand, her relief plain. "I'm Eleanora Bryce. I'm so glad you came."

She led me behind the counter and into their back room. Three beds and a rickety desk lined the walls. A small table with two stools sat in the center. A rusty hat-rack stood in the corner close by: three thin, battered coats hung there.

A tall, thin adolescent with dark hair sat on a stool in the far left corner. He pointed when I entered the room. "That's her!"

He was six when last I saw him. How did he recognize me?

He held up the newspaper with my portrait (among others) on the front page. Emblazoned across the top, it read:

GRAND BALL EXTRAVAGANZA

Bridges Family Meeting Countdown

Mrs. Bryce grabbed the paper from his hand, then peered at me. "Herbert, you're right, it is her!"

Mrs. Bryce appeared astonished to see me in my disguise: a shop maid's uniform, black with a white apron. "Mrs. Spadros herself!" She curtsied. "I would never have called if I would have known such a fine lady would answer!"

I felt sad. Would she be glad to see me if she learned my true identity? Would she curtsy then, or would she strike me?

Rain beat against the windows and lightning flashed, the rumbling of thunder close behind.

Herbert didn't bow.

Those same eyes.

The same pale serious face.

"Jacqui, don't go."

The moon hung high overhead. The frigid air smelled of dirt and sweat. Thirty children trained at knife-fighting by lamp-light a few yards up the narrow alley. "Please don't go. This feels bad. Men don't want little kids for nothing good."

Mrs. Bryce said, "My boy's gone missing."

Startled at her words, I jolted out of the memory. "What?"

"My son. He's missing. It's why I called you." Several portraits sat upon a tiny dresser in the corner across the room to the right. Mrs. Bryce went to it and handed me a tintype photo: a boy. Light skin, dark hair, dark eyes, round face. She claimed he was twelve; he looked closer to ten.

Sitting with Ma at her trestle table in the cathedral, eating warm bread with butter. The sounds of moaning and panting down the hall behind the tan linen curtains. Telling Ma our story and laughing at escaping the police. The smells of sex and baking in the air. His big dark eyes happy, his pale face flushed with the liquor he tasted and the candle-lit warmth. His little legs kicked under the stool …

I shook my head, trying to clear the memories of that terrible night. "This is a recent picture?"

Mrs. Bryce nodded. "Yes, mum, taken before Yuletide. Maybe three weeks ago? Right after we moved here."

"And you're sure he didn't run off?"

Mrs. Bryce's brown eyes filled with tears. "No, mum, I swear. David was a good boy, in the midst of his chore-work. 'Off to sweep the stair,' he said, 'I'll be right back.' He never came in."

Thunder pealed. Harsh light illuminated the barren room.

I called myself an investigator, but I investigated minor matters: a missing dog, renters who moved without paying. So this case violated rules I laid for myself.

I avoided police affairs …

"I can't pay you …" Mrs. Bryce said.

… and I didn't do a case without payment in advance. Not even this one.

"… but I'll do whatever you like, anything, if you'll help me."

I never liked Eleanora. She never liked me. When she realized who I was ….

"Please, mum, I know how it looks. The police said he run off, but I know he was taken and they all ignore me."

This woman lived most of her life a dozen blocks from this very point, well on the other side of that spiked wrought-iron fence encircling the Pot. Why would she expect the police to help an out-of-town widow with no Family connections and no bribe money? Had she really forgotten?

My borrowed corset pinched at the hips; it chafed with every move. I wanted to change into my own clothes, get away from this room full of bad memories and guilt.

I regarded the portrait, feeling melancholy: David looked just like him. "Show me where you last saw the boy."

The Bryce's back stair appeared much like any two blocks from the Pot: rickety wooden steps with rusty metal banisters leading down to a rat-infested alley.

Clouds loomed dark across the sky. The only real light came from an oil lamp far down the alley to our right. We took refuge from the downpour under the eaves, out of the wind.

A dark figure moved in the shadows twenty yards to our left. Something about him frightened me. I hoped the rain would hide our words and send him away.

"When your boy disappeared, did you find anything amiss?"

"Everything was as it should be, except I found his little broom on the ground," her voice broke, "and him gone."

I surveyed the alley. It appeared normal … except …

I crossed towards a red spot on the far wall, near waist level. "Was this here before he went missing?"

"No, mum, at least, I don't think so."

I leaned over to examine the spot, Tenni's corset stabbing at my midsection. A solid red silhouette of a dog, ink-stamped onto the wall.

The tower clock chimed three. The man began walking towards us.

"I must go." I might be Jacqueline Spadros, but that would hardly stop a scoundrel from committing robbery or worse before he learned of it. We hurried back inside, and I breathed a sigh of relief when the door locked behind me.

Then I remembered I carried weapons, and felt silly.

Mrs. Bryce said, "You're going to find him … right?"

I shook my head and kept walking through the room. The situation frightened me. "This is a police matter, and I can't be involved. No quadrant-lady can, but especially not me."

"But —"

I turned to her. "Do you realize who my father-in-law is? What he would do to all three of us (I gestured at Herbert) if he learned I came here?"

She turned even paler than she was, and nodded.

"Don't ever contact me at my home again. It's much too dangerous. If you wish to hire me in the future, send a note to Madame Biltcliffe. Address it to my maid Amelia Dewey."

Mrs. Bryce stared at me, mouth open. "I — I never sent anything to your home, mum! I swear!"

I put my hand in my pocket, touched the letter hidden there. "I'm curious. Why did you contact Madame Biltcliffe?" My dressmaker Marie Biltcliffe owned a shop in downtown Spadros quadrant; she sent me cases from time to time.

"When I went to the police station, mum," she said, "a couple sat nearby. They must have heard me talk to the constable. The lady told me I might find help there."

A couple so certain of Madame Biltcliffe's association with an investigator that they told others of it? "Did they give names?"

"I didn't ask," Mrs. Bryce said. "I was so upset …"

"I understand. What did the couple look like?"

Mrs. Bryce smiled like a young girl. "Nice looking, especially the man!" She fanned herself with her left hand. "They were about your age, and the lady had red hair."

This didn't help much. "If you meet them again, please let me know." I felt like a traitor. "I'm sorry, I really am. But I can't help you. Leave this to the police."

Walking through the front room of this shop, I knew the right thing to do, even then. But I felt too afraid.

I handed the taxi-driver his penny. "Madame Biltcliffe's dress shop on 42nd street, please."

His mother Eleanora, in Bridges, her youngest gone missing.

David looked just like him.

"Jacqui, you shouldn't go."

Heedless of the pedestrians and carriages beside me in the street, I wept.

* * *

I entered Madame Biltcliffe's dress shop through her back door. A warm glow and the smell of fresh linen greeted me. Madame's shop maid Tenni handed me a hat box. "For tonight."

I smiled. Quite clever, Madame.

Tenni was just seventeen, yet appeared much like me from behind — curled reddish-brown hair, light brown skin. We wore close to the same size, and I often used Tenni as a decoy when on a case: I would wear her clothes, and she mine.

We went to a fitting room. Tenni helped me change into my original dress, a peacock blue walking gown. My husband Tony said he liked it because it matched my eyes.

I sighed with relief on removing Tenni's new maid's corset, which left a red mark on my hip. "Did anyone inquire for me?"

"No, mum. And I stayed out of sight, as you asked."

"Good girl." I gave her a penny.

Tenni curtsied. "Thank you, mum."

"Ask Madame to return."

Madame Marie Biltcliffe entered: a tall, handsome, middle-aged woman with perfect black hair.

"Have either of you spoken to anyone about my business? Someone who decided not to contact me?"

They both shook their heads.

"I have never had anyone refuse your help who I referred," Madame said. "And I never speak your name before the meeting."

"Mrs. Bryce said a young woman with red hair told her to contact you."

Madame Biltcliffe frowned. "I know of no such woman."

"I feel confused, Madame. When Mrs. Bryce wrote you, why did you not contact me?"

She seemed surprised. "I never contact you until I speak with the woman myself. I didn't know her, and she merely sent a note. If she would have waited —"

I shook my head. "She says she didn't write to me."

"How strange." Madame Biltcliffe appeared as perplexed as I felt. "I suppose I am glad she is no forger."

I laughed at that thought. "No, that she is not."

I remembered my sore midsection. "Would you make a maid's corset for me to keep here for future use?"

"I would be happy to." Madame Biltcliffe smiled and went to the curtain, holding it open for me. I emerged from the dressing room, and she curtsied as I passed by.

I breezed out of the shop and onto the street. My black and silver carriage stood ready, drawn by black horses with silver tackle. As I took my day footman Skip Honor's hand to enter the coach, I glanced to my left.

A man wearing brown stood several doors down, turning away at my glance. I didn't see his face, but he seemed familiar. I felt certain he had been watching me.

I turned to Honor. "That man. How long has he stood there?"

But when Honor and I looked again, the man was gone.

While in the coach on the way home, I pulled the letter from my pocket.

> Dear Mrs. Spadros —
>
> I hate to impose upon you during the holiday, but it would be of much help if you could find time to call on me today. My maid Tenni will, of course, be ready to assist you. It is a matter of some urgency.
>
> Your servant, Marie Biltcliffe

The letter, on Madame's stationery, scented with her perfume, in her handwriting. Madame claimed she never sent it. Mrs. Bryce claimed she never sent it either. Then who did?

A puzzle. I moved the pieces around in my mind and could make nothing of it.

The Ball

The Grand Ball. The one night this town of thieves and liars pretended they weren't ready to stab each other at the slightest provocation. I anticipated an interesting time.

Stars studded the night sky as we alighted from the coach. My husband Tony took my hand, and we moved through the crowds lining the wide marble stairs to the Grand Ball House.

Tony's men scanned the people and rooftops for danger, and the crowd parted before them. We stopped on occasion to allow the newsmen to take our photos with a flash and a puff of smoke.

Fireworks boomed above us. In the distance, cheers went up after each fiery blossom.

Boom. Cheer.

Boom. Cheer.

Fireworks reminded me of him. Every New Year's Eve, we played with his wind-up automatons, made from bits of junk he found. When we were eleven, he set them all walking around his flat roof while we watched the show and laughed. He never saw fireworks again.

I felt Tony's solemn blue eyes upon me; I had stopped on the stair. I took a deep breath to clear my head, to smooth my face for the cameras, and continued on. The lamps threw strange shadows behind and between our paid admirers.

I imagined the other Families climbing their own staircases. Why have our own photographers, our own toadies throwing hothouse flowers? Why this fragile ceasefire, which required separate entry to the building to ensure peace?

A magnificent building once, the years had not been kind to the old Ball House. The occasional coat of whitewash did little to hide the cracks in the foundation as the island the Ball House sat upon sank under the weight of so much falsehood.

We reached the top of the stairs without incident. Armed men in black and silver Spadros livery opened the brown paneled doors for us.

Inside lay a rosewood-paneled antechamber, smelling of lemon polish. To our left, brown leather attached with brass tacks covered the top of the coat-counter.

"Take your coats and hat?"

Tony handed over his top hat and overcoat, then brushed a strand of black hair back into place.

"And your weapon, sir."

Tony hesitated, then retrieved his holstered revolver from his left pocket.

Tony helped me out of my floor-length forest green over-coat. It was my favorite: trimmed, beaded, and embroidered in black. I took Tony's arm as he led me to the Ladies' Room.

A woman dressed in black and silver opened the door, and the scent of cut flowers billowed towards me. The Ladies' Room glowed yellow in the lamplight. Mirrored in front of me and to my left, the room overflowed with flowers and glittering ladies. These ladies were the most trusted wives and sisters of Tony's main men.

The women beckoned me to the center of the room past a small table and ottoman. They took my new green velvet hat, fussing over my hair. Then they brushed off mud and blotted out wet spots on my gown. I sat on the ottoman, where they exchanged my muddy boots for soft green dinner shoes. When I presented myself to the Ballroom, I must appear flawless, or they would face questions as to why.

Every so often, a loudspeaker blared to my right announcing each group. The words were incoherent, muffled by distance and closed doors.

My lady's maid Amelia brought my cigarettes. Short, plump, her black hair turning gray, Amelia Dewey wore a uniform like my disguise a few hours earlier. I let her light me up and took a long drag.

The golden lamplight reminded me of home. Not my gilded cage in Spadros Manor, but my real home in the Pot, Ma's cathedral.

Ma was beautiful, the owner of the finest brothel in the Pot. Her hair was curly and dark; her skin, soft and brown. She taught me how to make deals, how to run the business, how to smile at a mark. I missed her so much it hurt.

Was she safe? Was she happy?

Had she learned to live without me?

Amelia rose. "It's time, mum." Entering the Ballroom at the scheduled time kept us from meeting another Family in the hallway without our men to protect us.

I went across the room, through the door, and to the right, down a long red-carpeted hallway to the Ballroom entry. Jazz music played far in the distance, growing louder as I approached: a dance tune.

Tony waited at the closed doors and smiled when he saw me approach. "Into battle."

I laughed in spite of myself as the doors opened.

A golden railing lay before us. A long sweeping stair led down along the wall to our right. Beyond and far below, at least two hundred people danced. The polished oak floor gleamed.

A great red pillar stood in the center of the room, rising to a white and gold vaulted ceiling. A large raised area surrounded it, bordered by four long steps and large enough for a whole party of its own. Rectangular tables stood on this dais. Here the four Family heads sat with their Inventors, one group to each table, on all four sides.

Bridges had a Mayor, a Chief of Police, but the Families ruled the city.

The platform rotated with clockwork precision. When a group appeared at the appointed time, their Family heads faced the stair to greet them. A jazz orchestra sat at the far left of the dais, the members sorting their sheet music.

An announcer stood by a podium to our right, a loudspeaker in hand. He glanced at us as we came through the doors, checked his pocket-watch and a list, then nodded. "MR. AND MRS. ANTHONY SPADROS."

We descended into the Ballroom, accompanied by applause. The room smelled of cooked meats, candles, perfumes, flowers, and floor polish. It smelled of a party trying to be fine, and it looked the part.

The Ballroom walls were white paneling, edged with gold, with red velvet inlays. But our Family colors decked the room as well. Black velvet with silver embroidery covered the tables; silver candlesticks sat upon them. Tacky, but it got the point across: the Spadros Family hosted the Grand Ball this year.

Tables lined the walls, laden with trays of cubed meats, candied fruits, cheeses, and small sandwiches. Waiters wearing black and silver brought drinks and cleared tables.

Tony's parents already sat at their table on the raised area. Crossing the hall, we went to the steps to greet them.

Glittering strands of snow now crept in among his black-ice hair, but the name Roy Spadros still turned brave men into statues of frozen terror.

I remembered the frigid night I first saw him. He stood on the cobblestones in that moonlit intersection composed, as if in complete control as people died around him.

Roy smelled of cold hard cash; his tuxedo, black as a clear winter's night. Blue-ice eyes stared out from a pale uncaring face, yet he could pretend courtesy when he wanted.

"Hello, Anthony, Jacqui." He spoke with no emotion as he shook Tony's hand and kissed mine. "Good to see you."

"And you too, sir," Tony said.

Molly Hogan Spadros was beautiful, buxom, and raven-haired. She wore heavy makeup and a long-sleeved red gown which showed her figure to good advantage.

She hugged each of us in turn and didn't flinch when I hugged her back. "I am so glad to see you."

"And you." Her nose had healed, and she no longer wore her cast. Matters in Roy's empire must please him these days.

The orchestra began to play, dancers swirling around us. Our Inventor, Maxim Call, closed-lipped and eccentric as most on the Board were, didn't rise. He scribbled in a notebook, glancing up to nod at us.

After our visit with Tony's parents, we circled the dais as it rotated, visiting the heads of each Family in turn. I didn't know them well, but we were only expected to offer brief greetings. Politeness dictated we should be off the dais before the announcement of the next guests.

Charles and Judith Hart were both red-haired, although silver battled red. It was clear Charles enjoyed his meals — and if rumors told true, his vodka — much more than he should. The couple wore forest green trimmed in silver, which suited them.

Roy Spadros despised Charles Hart; any mention of the man's name threw him into a rage. Roy placed the orchestra in front of the Harts as an insult, so their people would have to walk around it to greet them.

I believe Roy intended me to kill Charles Hart one day. But Roy did not excel in persuasion. At the time, I saw more reason to kill Roy Spadros than Charles Hart, should the choice ever appear.

For I remembered the glint on Mr. Hart's cheek at my wedding. It would not surprise me if Roy knew of Mr. Hart's soft-hearted nature, and let him attend just to watch him cry. Roy's motivation for any action was to cause pain; it seemed to be the only thing which gave him real enjoyment.

Mr. Hart held our hands in his and smiled at us as proudly as if we were his own children. "How are you?"

"Quite well, sir," Tony said, and I nodded.

Mrs. Hart fixed her eyes on Tony. "A pleasure to see you." In all the times we met, she never once looked me in the eye.

I smiled. "A pleasure to see you too."

She flinched and set her jaw. So disdain, not shyness, kept her from greeting me.

Get in line with the rest, sugar.

The Harts' Inventor (and heir) Etienne Hart never acknowledged us, so engrossed was he in his book. His thick spectacles had a multiplicity of lenses for closer magnification.

Julius and Rachel Diamond, so dark of skin and hair, were the most attractive and the youngest of the Family heads. They gained their title when the elder Mr. Diamond turned his cards in six years ago.

Rumor had it the father's death was not natural, but who expected a Family Patriarch to die in peace?

Julius wore a black tuxedo with a white cravat. Ironic, since Tony wore the same. Rachel wore a beaded, embroidered silver-gray gown. One of the Diamond sons (they had seven in all) stood across the table. We waited at a discreet distance until the man finished conversing with his father.

The man, just past thirty, glared at Tony when he saw us, then left. We came forward.

"Hello," Mr. Diamond said, but he didn't offer his hand to either of us. A powerfully built man, but a fiercely suspicious one.

"Hello, sir." Tony didn't offer his hand either.

Julius Diamond had never spoken to Tony in my presence otherwise. Something deep lay in his eyes, close to outrage, as if Tony once gave him a terrible insult which felt fresh, which he could never forgive. Tony had never revealed what sparked his wrath; he accepted the anger as if he deserved it.

"One of these days we must get together." Mrs. Diamond spoke in a childlike tone. Could she be unaware of her younger son's vendetta against our Family, the glares of her older son, the open hostility of her husband?

They say Rachel Diamond was once a brilliant woman, who never recovered from the death of her father-in-law. I felt it a pity not to have met her before then. "Yes, we must."

Their Inventor, a thin man with a face to match, tinkered with his pocket-watch there at the table, unaware of our presence.

Alexander and Regina Clubb had bright blue eyes and golden hair. Lean and athletic, they appeared much younger than the truth, by all accounts. Some whispered Regina must be at least seventy, her oldest daughter being over fifty. Whatever her age, Regina had smooth skin and a fine figure. Her royal blue gown matched Alexander's cravat.

Alexander Clubb had a mechanical left arm, a memento from the Bloody Year long before my birth. Rumor said his arm was a marvel, made by a master craftsman, and all the fingers worked. Just a glint of bronze and leather showed between his white glove and shirtsleeve when he greeted us.

"We're launching our new yacht next month, assuming the weather holds warm," Mrs. Clubb said. "Would you like to visit for a week in the Spring?"

We glanced at each other. The invitation seemed genuine. "Certainly!" Tony said. "Please send word when you're ready."

Their Inventor, a young brown-haired woman, smiled and shook hands without rising. To speak with another Family's Inventor raised suspicion. So our duties completed and the music waning, we descended to join the real party.

I glanced back at the dais. "What do you suppose the Clubbs were about?"

Tony smiled for the first time since entering the ballroom. "We'll learn soon enough. Neither of them breathe without it being part of some intrigue."

The loudspeaker blared, the applause died down, and the music began. Tony and I danced a slow waltz, deliberately circling the dais. This gave us the opportunity to survey the room. Couples from all four Families danced around us. Since the Bad Times, much of the city's population had Family ties, even if "under the table."

"Fled, dead, or in a Family bed," so it was said.

Lance Clubb, a shy blond man of three and twenty, chatting with Julius Diamond? A more unlikely pair I couldn't imagine.

"What do you find funny?"

I gestured with my chin, and Tony peeked at the two.

Julius Diamond beamed, shaking Lance Clubb's hand with enthusiasm.

"I have a guess as to that."

"Do tell."

"You like puzzles, solve it yourself."

Lance was Alex and Regina Clubb's youngest child, only son, and the Clubb Family heir. But what could he have said to please Julius Diamond so much? I needed more information, so I put the matter aside.

The music ended, the loudspeaker died away, and we turned to promenade the room. "A drink?" Tony said.

"Will they serve anything stronger than port?"

"It's unseemly for you to drink liquor in public."

I laughed. "You mean to drink a 'man's drink.'"

He continued on with the same pace, his face and body not showing his emotions. He was a master at it. "No, Jacqui, you drink too much. The amount you drink at these events is commented upon."

I patted his arm. "I am always in perfect control of my faculties. I would never cause you embarrassment."

"We shall see." But he brought me to the bar anyway. Tony could never deny me anything back then.

The bar did have some proper drinks after all. I chose a rum and soda. Tony chose a table across the room where we could see the staircase, the dais, and the dancers.

"The perfect place to sit," I said, and Tony smiled.

Our rather long table filled with sycophants, Tony's main men, and their dance partners.

Major Blackwood, white-whiskered and round, classified in the first group. As always, in uniform, which I suspected was custom-made well after leaving the service.

Major Blackwood made his living by being amusing at parties. He then secured invitations to luncheon, dinner, and tea the rest of the year. I imagine this saved him quite a bit of money.

The Major began regaling the ladies at the far end of the table with a bawdy story from his days in the military.

"... I had a time when I was shot in the leg when I was in the Army, and I learned to use a cane," he brandished it, "to get around, and began to rely on it for fetching other things near to my bed ... pretty nurses, for example!"

The ladies giggled.

"The use of a cane is like a habit to me, and I was walking along once ..."

Since they were at the other end of the long table, the music was a bit too loud for me to hear him properly. I spent the time watching the orchestra.

"They play well," Tony said. "I'll have Michaels send a note of congratulations to the leader." Jacob Michaels was Tony's manservant, like my Amelia. The idea of servitude is abominable, but few people care what I think.

"That would be lovely." I drank more of my rum.

"... why, it wouldn't have been gentlemanly for me to just let her lie there ..." Major Blackwood said.

A fair quality rum, but they served better the year before. Had Roy Spadros taken up economizing as his new hobby?

"I remember when I was in the military," Major Blackwood said, "the scrapes I got into ..."

I wanted a cigarette, but it annoyed Roy when women smoked. I didn't need to attract his attention tonight.

"... and we hoisted the horse onto the ROOF!"

Gales of laughter came from the other end of the table. Tony and I grinned at each other.

When the set finished and the applause died down, the announcer said, "MASTER JOSEPH KERR, AND HIS SISTER, MISS JOSEPHINE KERR."

I sat, mouth open in shock, my heart beating painfully. I could hardly breathe.

Joseph Kerr.

When I saw him on the stair after all those years, I knew he was going to be trouble.

Dark brown hair, green eyes, golden skin, stylishly and immaculately dressed, his body toned and taut. Sensual as a cat, a large, dangerous cat, exciting and sleek, languid yet fierce.

Still the most handsome man I have ever seen. He knew he was handsome, and from the rumors, used it to good advantage.

Arm in arm with his twin, Joseph Kerr acknowledged the applause all the way down the stair. Josephine was as blond as Joe was dark, beautiful, and single. I heard many stories of their exploits over the years. Every young man wanted her; every young woman wanted him.

Josie refused every man who asked for her hand, a source of constant discussion and speculation. As far as I knew, Joe never asked anyone for her hand since the night we last met. This sparked less controversy and more speculation as to who would tame him. No one ever asked my opinion, for which I felt grateful.

I watched Joseph and Josephine Kerr descend the stairs. The unmarried set gathered around them, laughing and talking.

Joseph Kerr was only a year older than I, yet had a reputation as a gambler, a womanizer, a dandy. Some accused him of worse. But most people defamed the Kerrs since they lost control of Bridges four generations ago.

A waiter approached, so I finished my drink and exchanged the empty glass for a glass of champagne on his tray. Tony took a glass too, and asked the waiter to bring some for the whole table.

Tony stood, addressing his men. "This has been a good year for the Spadros Family, and it's because of you. To greater success in the New Year."

I paused, remembering a magical night long ago, then smiled up at Tony. This time, it was genuine, the smile of a woman who adored her man, a woman in love. Tony, confident in his triumph, gave me the same smile in return. If I thought about it too long, it might break my heart.

In my whole life up to then, I had only loved one man. I had given my whole heart to this man, my very soul, if you (unlike most) should think I owned one.

"To greater success in the New Year," the rest of the table said, and sipped at their glasses.

That man …

… was Joseph Kerr.

The champagne tasted bitter, but I drank my glass dry.

***

I went to the Spadros Ladies' Room just off the ballroom and found Amelia to get another smoke.

"Are you enjoying yourself?" Amelia said.

"Certainly." I sat and let Amelia light my cigarette, while the attendants fussed with my gown and hair.

Why was Joseph Kerr here, now, tonight, of all nights? Where had he been all these years? Why had he never sent one word? I took a drag, and tried to blow away the melancholy in smoke.

The wind blew chill beside Benjamin Kerr's statue, broken upon the ground. Burns and ax-marks and hateful words decorated it.

Joe stared at the ruin. "My ancestor." He surveyed the shattered plaza. "One day this place could be good, like he made it. No more cold, no more rags." He took my hands in his. "I love you, Jacqui. I want you by me when all this is set right. Will you have me?"

"I will." I kissed his hands. "But how can I? I'm to marry his boy."

Joe turned away. "My daddy's old man has money, I seen it. We can go on the zeppelin, far from here. Just think, Jacqui … we'll be free."

That was six years ago. I believed Joe, and gave him all a girl had to give a man.

That night, my mother woke me. She put me into a carriage with people I had never met, to live with people who had only disdain for me.

Roy Spadros said if I set foot in the Spadros portion of the Pot again, he would burn Ma's cathedral with everyone in it.

I never saw Joe again, until tonight.

I still loved him.

I put out the cigarette and went to the door.

"… smoking again … shocking behavior … not sure why the Family puts up with it … what do you expect from a Pot rag …?"

I opened the door; a few old biddies stood along the wall. One hushed the other, but I strolled to the closest table as if I heard nothing.

A handsome, brooding man sang, while the orchestra played a slow song of young love thwarted.

I listened to the man sing, desperately trying to hold the pain back. A waiter passed with a drink tray, and I took a glass, not caring what it held.

The music died away, and there was applause.

"I'm sorry, Jacqui." That beloved voice behind me held true sorrow, but I dared not turn, not even for my dearest friend.

Jonathan Diamond walked around to face me, and bent to gaze at my down-turned face. "What's this?"

I brushed at my eyes. "Nothing."

He took my left hand and kissed it. "You knew this would happen sooner or later. I'm sorry it was tonight." He took a step back, the ever-present small brown velvet bag of vials at his left hip clinking. "You look absolutely beautiful."

Jonathan Courtenay Diamond was a tall, handsome man of twenty and six. The youngest of the Diamond sons, Jon had an easy air and fine manners, so unlike his father. He wore a forest green tuxedo and a black cravat pinned with his Family's symbol. His normally tight-coiled hair he wore neatly pressed, parted just right of center. "You look quite dashing, Jon."

He beamed at me, and I do believe he blushed. "Thank you!"

For some reason, his blush made me feel better. I raised my glass to him and drained it. "I wish I could get drunk and forget everything, like everyone else seems to."

Jonathan chuckled. "It's not as fun as it sounds, sweet girl, especially the next morning."

His tone of voice made me smile, just like always.

"I wish I could chat, dearest. But I must make the rounds." He winked. "Duty calls."

I set the empty glass on the table and returned to my seat. Perhaps I could survive this night after all.

***

After some time, Joseph and Josephine Kerr arrived at our table. We rose to greet them. Joe wore a dark burgundy tuxedo, while Josie wore a burgundy gown trimmed in white. They took dressing alike as a challenge; when we were young, they would do (or steal) anything to match.

Josephine's blond curls cascaded down one side of her perfect face beneath a rose-colored half-veil. I took her hand. "The goddess approaches! Radiant, as always."

She blushed. "You look lovely, too, Mrs. Spadros," emphasizing my title, "And I would love to get the name of your dressmaker!"

"I will have my maid Amelia send you a card."

"I would be delighted!" Josephine clapped her white gloved hands. I thought this played the ingenue a bit too far, considering she was a year older than I.

Joe took my hand and kissed it, his eyes meeting mine. "Charmed to see you again."

Oh, my … he was stunning.

"I didn't know you were acquainted," Tony said.

I smiled at him. "Childhood friends."

Tony paused, puzzlement on his face. "Ah, yes."

Evidently he had forgotten my past. No one else seemed to.

Tony shook Joe's hand. "Then you're most welcome here."

The twins beamed at him. Josephine had a gorgeous smile, but Joe's lit the room. His smile held happiness and freedom, life and contentment, a smile usually only seen in small children.

No one who smiled like that could ever be false.

"It's so grand to be welcomed," Josephine said. "We adore these parties, don't we, Joe?"

Joe gazed fondly at his sister. "We do." He turned to Tony. "We meet such fascinating people."

Tony seemed at a loss for words. I took Tony's arm, heart pounding, and spoke to Joe, trying to keep my tone light. "Is your grandfather well?"

Joe focused on Tony, yet spoke loud enough so anyone could hear. "He's 87 now. Putters around in his garden, his library. Josie takes care of him these days."

Tony put his arm around me. "The old have earned relaxing afternoons. I suppose we'll see those if we live long enough."

The rest of the table laughed. The twins excused themselves, promising to return once their "duties" were through.

"They seem a pleasant pair," Tony said.

One of his newer Associates came to the table. Reeking of alcohol, he laughed in derision, his words slurring. "A couple of gods-damned Pot rags, daring to show their faces around decent folk. Shameful."

Tony frowned. "That will be quite enough."

All eyes were on me, except for Major Blackwood. "Well, if they're Pot rags, they're certainly delightful ones."

I laughed at the Major's oblivious cheek. Everyone followed.

Tony turned to me. "I will have that man gone."

I shrugged. "I find his honesty refreshing."

Tony frowned and shook his head. "I won't have such a man in my service. He insults you, or your friends, he insults me. He insults the Family that raised him up."

Tony turned to his right-hand man, an imposing fellow they called Sawbuck, and spoke in his ear. Sawbuck stood, whispered to a couple others, then gestured to the new man. They all left.

This new man would be found floating in the river. He probably wouldn't even learn why. Such was life in the Business: fast to rise, just as fast to fall.

Every time Tony did something like this, though, I found it disturbing. "Why should a man die for having an opinion?"

"My men must be devoted to this Family." Tony's voice was pitched to carry. "All of this Family. If he can't be loyal there are many others who will."

It seemed no one wanted to speak first after that.

After the next song completed and the loudspeaker died away, I said, "I could use some air."

We moved down a red-carpeted hall to the Spadros train platform. Two of his men, watching everyone and everything but us, followed at a distance. This train entry allowed us private entry to the opera, government areas, and so on.

Mighty columns held the level above us, with large copper pipes running overhead. We sat at a table in the black and white tiled area. Tony had my cigarettes with him, and he gave me a light. "I apologize for my man's conduct."

I waved it away. "I told you, it was nothing."

"I want nothing more than for you to be happy."

This surprised me. "That is very kind of you."

The buzz of the other tables echoed in the platform, the music and loudspeaker faint in the distance.

"I hope we can someday live without violence." Tony's voice was tense, as if he were in pain. "My greatest aspiration is to leave our children a peaceful future and a business worthy of respect."

I had never heard such words from him before.

"If I show mercy it's seen as weakness, by both my father and my men. But with each act of cruelty and retribution, I fear I'm signing my death warrant."

I put my hand on his. Talk of death always brought my situation — or rather, my probable situation — to mind. I hoped a paying case presented itself soon.

The danger to Tony seemed ever-present. Most men in the Business met a violent end. Should Tony die, his estate would revert to his father, Roy Spadros, who would have no further use for me. I would be without protection. It was part of what drove me to go out on a rainy New Year's Eve to secretly meet a client.

I took a deep breath and let it out. I had to prepare for when the inevitable occurred. If I became an independent woman of means, I could hire bodyguards until I left the city. I had saved a small amount from my household allowance plus my business over the past few years. But not enough to hire guards or even buy a zeppelin ticket, should the worst come to pass.

I hoped it never would. While I didn't love Tony, except perhaps in a platonic manner, I wished no harm upon him.

Tony stood. "Enough of this. You're too beautiful for me to spoil the evening with melancholy. Want to return to the party?"

I put out my cigarette. "I would love to."

Our table had been abandoned. Major Blackwood sat at another table, laughing with a different set of ladies. Tony's men sat at various other tables with their dance partners.

We sat at the end of our original table, which held a few Clubb retainers at the other end. The waiter came round, and we ordered more drinks.

"I fear this will be the last drink for me," Tony said.

"We have a carriage to take us home."

"Yes, but I would like to be taken home alive."

I chuckled, patting his hand. He smiled, face flushed, and pulled my chair closer as we watched the dancers. He put his arm around me and began kissing my ear.

I found this quite intriguing.

We had been back about ten minutes when the announcer said: "MASTER JACK ROLAND DIAMOND THE THIRD"

The room went silent. I turned to face the staircase, and my heart was pounding with fear, my mouth dry.

Black Jack.

The man in my nightmares since that terrible evening ten years ago descended the stairs, head shaven, dressed in white. His glare cut across the room to settle on me, and my blood froze at the malevolence in his eyes.

My stomach knotted; my hands began to shake.

Jack Diamond was Jonathan Diamond's identical twin, but all similarity stopped at skin level. Where Jonathan was kind, Jack spoke harshly. Jonathan was warm-hearted; Jack, bitter and grasping. Jonathan wore whatever fashion dictated. Jack only wore white, even to the soles of his shoes, no matter what the event or the weather.

Black Jack was not named so for his black hair and eyes. Nor for his skin, which, like all in the Diamond family, was such a dark brown as to be close to black. He earned this name from childhood for his rages, his cruelty, his mysterious disappearances and the terrible rumors which followed them: girls murdered, men tortured, a head found on a pier.

All sort of evil was attributed to Black Jack Diamond: whether truth or fiction, few knew. All I know is he promised if he ever laid hands on me, it would be my last painful day.

And I believed him.

"I feared he would be here tonight," Jonathan Diamond said.

Tony stood, shaking hands with a smile. "Jon! How are you?"

"Well enough, but the weather has inflamed my joints. I carry this these days." Jonathan brandished a black walking stick topped with silver.

How had I not seen his cane before this?

"My poor benighted brother fears he is forgotten," Jonathan said, compassion in his voice, "so he makes his appearance. I sincerely hope he doesn't cause you alarm."

Tony pulled a chair away from the table. "Please join us." So Jonathan sat.

A waiter came up. "Some wine, sir?"

Jonathan said, "Tea and milk, if you please." Jon never drank alcohol, and I often wondered why.

By this time, Jack Diamond had descended the stairs and disappeared into the crowd.

***

I danced several turns with Tony (the first few, rather unsteady on his part) and a few with Lance Clubb while Tony and Jonathan sat talking.

Though Lance was a year older than I, he seemed younger somehow. Like most this season, he wore a dark brown tuxedo with brass buttons.

Lance Clubb appeared intrigued at my conversations with Jonathan. During the second set, he asked if he might one day be introduced to Jonathan's younger sister, Gardena …

… who was both beautiful and unmarried.

After Lance Clubb escorted me to my chair and moved on, I whispered to Tony, "Mystery solved."

Tony seemed pleased his guess had been correct.

After sipping wine with Tony (who seemed to have forgotten his earlier words), I took a lively turn with Charles Hart. Although portly and seventy, he was a excellent dancer. Roy had left the room, which was probably why Mr. Hart chose this time to dance with me.

"You were a good pick for Anthony," Mr. Hart said. "I'm glad you two are happy."

"Why, Mr. Hart, we've been married three years now. Of course, we're happy."

"So why no children?"

Turning my head, I glimpsed Jack Diamond across the room watching me. His eyes met mine: I shuddered at the hate in them.

The music was ending. I felt unsure of how to reply to Mr. Hart. "Is that proper to ask a married woman?"

Mr. Hart roared with laughter; everyone standing nearby turned and stared. Then he put his hand on my bare shoulder. "My dear, you are magnificent. You honestly don't know. It's a sincere pleasure to finally get to know you. I hope Anthony realizes what a prize he has."

"Why thank you, sir." I wondered what he found so funny. At the time, I thought the man was drunk.

As Charles Hart escorted me to my seat, a shout, then a loud commotion came from behind, drawing ever closer.

I didn't turn or give any other sign I heard, but I marked the sound's passage as we strolled along. When we neared Tony, he stood, gazing past me with concern. I turned to see Jack Diamond storming towards us from halfway across the room. My stomach churned, although I steeled myself not to show it.

The music, which had begun again, stopped.

Ten paces away, Jack Diamond struggled to free himself from the men from various Families who restrained him. "Let me go!" His voice, deeper than his brother Jonathan's, carried well.

Tony said loudly, "Let the man have his say."

Jack Diamond approached to three paces away. "You may have forgotten, Spadros, but I have not. I will never forget. I will not be ignored, and I will not be mocked. I call vengeance on your house and on the scum you shelter and protect, who murdered my own."

A brown-haired man I didn't recognize dashed towards us, shouting urgently. The gunshot echoed down the street; the man collapsed, ten yards away.

Jack Diamond galloped up bareback on one of his father's white horses. Rushing to the brown-haired man, he held him in his arms, shocked and disbelieving. Jack's face crumpled in grief, kneeling in the frozen mud and filth. He laid his head on the man's chest, sobbing.

They say though he was cruel and reckless before, that night drove Jack Diamond mad.

Tony shook his head. "Diamond, this," he waved his hand to encompass the hall, "is neutral territory. Ten years has passed since your man's death. Has there not been enough suffering?" He paused. "Do you really want war between our Families? Is that what you truly desire?"

Jack Diamond hesitated, then took a step forward, pointing at me. It took every ounce of courage I had not to shrink from his approach. I would not give him the satisfaction.

"I want her father, dead! I want her family to pay for my brother's murder —"

"He was not our brother," Jonathan said mildly, standing next to and a bit in front of me.

"And you — you drink with his murderers! Look at you! Traitor! Scoundrel!" Jack lunged at Jonathan, who took a step back, eyes widening in alarm.

"No!" I felt horrified at the thought of Jack hurting him.

Tony pulled me out of Jack's path and advanced upon him. "You dare threaten my wife?"

Joseph Kerr drew Jack away, whispering to him. Jack Diamond's demeanor changed at once; he smiled and let himself be led off.

Jack Diamond had quite a different look when his father and five older brothers dragged him from the room.

I found that most entertaining.

Tony turned to me, shaken. "Are you all right?"

I nodded, but I felt my voice trembled more than it should. "Perhaps the man has had too much Party Time."

Party Time: colorless, odorless, tastes like cinnamon sugar. The one thing still illegal in this rat-hole, yet the one thing everyone wants. The fact it's illegal let us live like kings.

Jack showed no signs of being on Party Time. Rather, he seemed a coward and a bully. Jack hated my father, who he couldn't touch, since Roy protected him. So he shouted at me and at his brother. It was shameful; he would never have dared such a display with Roy Spadros in the room.

The music resumed. I got another drink and leaned back in my chair, trying to calm myself. My hands shook as I drained the glass. I set it down and turned away to hide my stinging eyes.

"I apologize for my brother's outburst," Jonathan said. "Thank heavens Joseph Kerr was there to calm him. I wonder what clever words the man found to turn his anger."

I wondered about this as well.

How did Jonathan come to meet Joe, or Joe to meet Jack?

"I owe Master Kerr a debt," Tony said.

"Indeed," Charles Hart said.

I forgot the man stood there and witnessed everything.

I felt embarrassed at him seeing our trials and glad for a chance at hospitality. "Mr. Hart, please join us."

Charles Hart glanced at Tony, who said, "Yes, please do."

Mr. Hart sat; a servant brought him some wine.

"Are you enjoying your evening?" Tony said.

"Come to mention it, yes!" Mr. Hart said. "The evening has been most entertaining."

We laughed, and the thudding of my heart slowed. I thought I might not get another chance to ask, so I did.

"Sir," I said to Mr. Hart, "forgive me, but this brings to mind something I saw today: a strange stamp on a wall, a silhouette of a dog, all in red. Since your Family's color is red, I wondered if you had knowledge of it."

Mr. Hart shook his head, his eyes not meeting mine. "Some childish prank — think nothing of it."

Tony turned to one of his main men, a distant cousin who appeared when we seemed to be in danger. "You know anything about this?"

"Yes, sir. It looks like a new gang. We caught a boy the other day putting their marks around, sent him packing with a bit of a beat-down for his —"

"That will be enough," Tony said. "A lady is present."

"Yes, sir," the man said. "Sorry, sir. My apologies, mum. But … they call themselves Red Dogs … or something like that. Mostly slum boys."

Tony said, "Where did this happen?"

"We caught them around 80th."

80th street? Those boys were miles from home.

"Well, I don't need riffraff marking up my quadrant," Tony said. "Makes the place look bad. Send a couple of Associates to find out who's behind all this nonsense."

This made me think of David, suddenly missing from his back stair. Did he get involved with these boys?

"Yes, sir," the man said, "I'll have them get one of their stamp cards to show you."

Tony tucked a curl of hair behind my ear. "Let's forget this unpleasantness and enjoy our party."

When Roy Spadros returned to the room, Charles Hart moved to another table, as did Jonathan. I must have danced with every man of note in Bridges before the New Year's toast and the midnight dinner.

As we crossed the lofty pale bridge from Market Center to the Spadros quadrant, Tony pulled me close. "The moment I first saw you, I thought you were the most beautiful girl I had ever seen."

I remembered his wide innocent eyes as he sat in Roy's carriage that cold, terrible night, and let him kiss me.

He was a good kisser.

Tony was more than a bit drunk, so it didn't surprise me that when we reached home he asked for his husband's prerogative.

The common advice to young women about to wed is "lie back and think of England," a true absurdity during these enlightened days in the New World. But my task was much more pleasant. I thought of Joseph Kerr these many years, remembering those stolen moments in his arms, his too-skillful attentions upon my body. It made me as satisfied with my duty as any husband might wish for.

This might sound cruel, it might even sound scandalous, but who did it harm? My spouse had his pleasure, and I had mine. We were both content.

Seeing Joe there … ahhh, he had grown into a fine figure of a man. Too fine. I wanted more than thoughts. I wanted him, in my arms, in my bed.

If I had listened to Air and stayed home that terrible winter's night, I would belong to Joe.

What would our lives have been like?

The Editorial

The gun went off.

The light left my best friend's beautiful dark eyes. His little body slumped to the ground three feet away, blood pooling around him.

I struggled, I tried to scream, but no sound came out.

David Bryce raised his head. "Help me."

I woke, my face in the pillow, heart pounding.

The bed lay empty in the pale dawn light. I felt a pang of loneliness, my eyes filling with tears.

A firm knock at the door.

I took a deep breath, let it out. "Yes?"

"Your tea and wash-water, mum."

"Thank you, just leave it on the table."

My day footman Honor came in, set the tray on my tea table, and left, without once glancing my direction.

I pulled the covers over my head. I didn't want to think of my dream. Did it mean David was dead?

Some said the dead sent messages to the living; the idea frightened me. If anyone should send a message, why hadn't Air sent one on his brother's behalf?

Air and I were born the same day. We went everywhere together, as far back as I can remember. Air's real name was Nick, but he could jump much higher and farther than anyone his size should be able to. Joseph Kerr, one of our gang leaders back then, called him the air boy, and the name stuck.

Amelia had been in to open the curtains. It looked to be another drear, overcast day. Although weary, I got up to wash my face and hands before the water grew cold. Sitting by the window, I sipped my morning tea.

My room held white furniture trimmed in pastel blue, with pastel blue rugs over gray tiles. Portraits of strangers and landscapes of places I'd never seen hung in pale frames. I hated pale colors, but no one cared what I thought.

Snow lay in dirty piles, torn up by the feet of horses and servants milling around in the courtyard. The effect was bleak.

The tea's bitter taste reminded me of last night's discussion with Charles Hart. If Charles Hart dared approach me about our childlessness — why him, and not Molly Spadros? — then it was already being discussed amongst the Families.

Three years. I thought I had more time.

I stared into the clear brown liquid in my teacup, one of the things my mother taught me after that horrible night. She tried her best to protect me, to prepare me for what lay ahead.

I would have children when I wanted to, not whelping on command like some Spadros broodmare.

Should I have agreed to find David Bryce?

The idea of Air's brother gone missing twisted my heart. But what could I do? Even if I took the case, I had no idea where to look for the boy.

The morgue might seem a reasonable place to begin, but I had no connections there. A woman inquiring after a child's body might alarm the inspectors, who might contact the police, who would want to speak with her. I couldn't risk that sort of attention.

I felt sure the Red Dog stamp on the wall was a clue. Perhaps if I learned about this gang it would help.

Amelia entered with my provisional tray: "regular" tea and toast, jam and butter, newspaper and mail. "Did you sleep well?"

I thought of my nightmare. At least I hadn't screamed and wakened the household, like most nights. "Well enough. We were up later than usual."

"Yes, I suppose we all were. My little ones were so excited by the fireworks they did not want to go to sleep!" Amelia and her husband Peter's three children, two girls and a boy, helped Peter in the stables.

I smiled, picturing their bright eager faces. "Amelia, how did you and Peter come to Spadros Manor?"

She turned away and chuckled, but it seemed forced. "Ah, that would be a **long** story, mum, and I need to prepare your bath, or you won't be dressed in time for breakfast."

What favors must these people give to earn such high positions? I shook my head and turned to the paper.

NEW YEAR'S DAY, 1899, the *Bridges Daily* screamed. Flattering and appropriate photos from the night before graced the front. The articles spoke of the color of a dress, the hairstyle, the cut of a suit.

People hungered for diversion. The Families encouraged this attention to the frivolous. It distracted from real questions, like why they struggled to survive while we feasted.

The paper mentioned minor incidents in the Clubb quadrant: horse-tackle cut, shops egged, windows broken. With each event, the police found a Red Dog stamp on a wall or card afterward. While most gangs kept their activity to the slums, these incidents in the fair parts of Clubb had been occurring for some time.

The Clubb merchants demanded "something be done," and the Mayor promised increased patrols. The article called these incidents pranks, but a brave reporter printed an editorial:

Year End Violence A Symptom

An Editorial By Thrace Pike

> Once again the year ends with malicious acts towards the betters of this city. One might point out that merchants are of a lesser class, just as most readers of the news. However, to the majority who shiver in their homes, Yuletide feasts consisting of bread and soup — and a thin soup at that — the fat merchants strolling among them must incite dismay, if not anger.
>
> And why should the merchants not charge?

> They have fees to pay, just as do those they sell to. We all have fees to pay, but to those hanging at the bottom rung, these fees are a lead weight threatening to pull them to the utter desolation of the Pot.
>
> These acts of anger are symptoms of a greater ill. Perhaps it is time to make changes to the current state of affairs before the illness becomes serious.

Those who couldn't be bought … fascinating.

Amelia came in with a package. "Rocket already sniffed it, never fear."

Rocket was a black pit bull terrier, the best bomb sniffer dog in Bridges. He could smell when you had fired a gun hours before, and would bark.

"I found some messages in your coat, mum. I'll put them in your study."

"Thank you, Amelia." People often passed notes, flowers, or trinkets to others at the Ball, and this year was no exception.

I knew what the package was before I opened it: today's *Golden Bridges,* the local tabloid. Its byline read, "Fuck the Fairy Tales, Get the Real Story."

One of my contacts sent me a copy when she could get one: they sold thousands of copies within hours of publication.

Their lead story:

Mad Jack Rampage At Ball

> The notorious Jack Diamond was at it again: shouting at the Spadros heir in the Grand Ball. Why? Who knows why 'Black Jack' does something, or his next target? Our inside reporter caught a glimpse of the scene as he followed the Diamond men dragging the culprit from the Ball: 'Master Diamond

> flailed, offering excuses as he struggled to free himself from the wrath of his father and brothers, who suffered embarrassment at his antic. Unamused, they stuffed him into a carriage forthwith.' Perhaps Master Jack will refrain from intemperance next time, but we doubt it.

I laughed aloud.

"Why do you read such trash?" Amelia said.

"I must know what people are saying. The *Bridges Daily* tells me what the Family Patriarchs want people to say." I passed over a detailed account of the gang wars raging through the slums and came across this:

> Ball Happenings: An Inside Look
>
> We sit with our inside reporter, who gives us the scoop on the real news.
>
> GB: What tidbits did you glean from the night's events?
>
> IR: Other than Jack Diamond's outburst? The Grand Ball was another spectacle of indulgence. The jewelry and beading worn by the ladies alone could carpet the room.
>
> GB: It's interesting you mention Jack Diamond. Was this his first Grand Ball?
>
> IR: Indeed. I felt impressed with the restraint of Mr. Anthony Spadros, who had partaken quite a bit of wine prior to Master Diamond's display. Not to mention Jack had the effrontery to threaten violence.
>
> GB: Restraint in a Spadros? This is an unexpected development.

> IR: He's always been an unusual one; we're noting his progress. I did see a bit of kissing the wife, but you can't fault a man for that.
>
> GB: Well, if I was married to Mrs. Spadros, I'd dare the scandal of a public display too.

Really! Shaking my head, I set the paper aside. "Amelia, do we have any callers scheduled?"

"On New Year's Day? I don't believe so, mum. Oh, wait … when Mr. Anthony took his tray just now, out on the veranda … the poor man, he had the bottle of salicylate with him … he told Michaels you and he were calling on the Kerrs for luncheon."

When did he arrange that?

Tony took Joe's assistance more seriously than I thought.

This would be interesting …

***

Bathe, dress, hair done, then downstairs for morning prayers with the staff. Tony insisted on doing this daily.

It reminded me of the one unbroken stained glass window in Ma's cathedral. Beautiful ladies walked in flowing gowns, Card symbols surrounding them.

We never did prayers in the cathedral. We might be the Dealers' daughters, but the knowledge they held passed long ago.

The flat area still remained where the Dealers laid their Cards before the Bad Times. Our elders held a reverence for that place, and never allowed us to play on it.

After prayers, Tony and I went up to a full sideboard in our breakfast sun-room at the back corner of the house. I looked forward to this time: Monsieur made the most excellent sausage, and I loved the view of the gardens. After breakfast, we then went to the morning meeting, back downstairs in the staff room.

Spadros Manor was shaped like a U. The parlor and entry lay on the right arm, the breakfast room and dining hall on the left. Our study rooms lay between, our quarters and guest rooms on the second floor.

To go to the staff room, you left the breakfast sun-room, went through our dining hall, then into the preparation room beyond.

At the far left of this room was a door to a small stockroom, which led to the stables and a stair down to Amelia's quarters. At the far right, sliding double doors opened on a stair wide enough for men carrying platters to pass each other.

A hallway just as wide lay at the bottom of the stair, running underneath the entire far end of the courtyard. Copper pipes ran along the ceiling. The first door to the right led to the kitchens.

To the left, portraits of the staff hung above white cabinets. Vents on the floor and ceiling allowed warm air to pass through. Wide openings above a counter to the right allowed platters to be handed to the waiters.

The staff room lay past the kitchens, also to the right. At the far end of the hall were quarters for our butler Pearson and his family, and a stair up to the parlor area.

The staff room was white, with two long black tables, one for the men and boys, the other for the women and girls. Two doors at the back of the room led to the unmarried men's and women's quarters. Another door to the far right led to a stair which went up to the courtyard. To the right, a large dumbwaiter transported crates or large items in need of repair. Windows high up along the wall to the right let in light and air.

To the left hung rows of bells and levers, marked for each room of the house. At present, the levers pointed down, but when we rung, they pointed up, showing what room the bell rang from.

Tony didn't attend the morning meeting that day. Writing his end-of-the-year accounts always took him much of the morning. So I stood in front of the staff to give their orders for the day's work, Pearson standing beside me to my right.

"As we will be calling on Mr. Polansky Kerr for luncheon," this produced murmurs and glances which made Pearson frown, "you may spend the holiday with your families."

Essential personnel — Amelia and Michaels — would remain on duty until we left. Pearson, as our butler, was always on duty. The rest of the staff would be free until time to prepare dinner.

"I — but not Mr. Spadros — will be 'at home' until noon should anyone call, and we should be back for tea. I shall message if we are delayed."

"Very good, mum," Pearson said.

John Pearson, an impeccably dressed man with thinning brown hair, came with the Manor when Tony and I married. A wedding gift, if you could consider a man and his family as such. I met Pearson the first day I entered Spadros Manor as a child, and his presence always made me feel more secure.

"Pearson is a most proper butler," Molly Spadros once said, "as was his father before him."

Meals were on time and well made, the Manor kept spotless, and not so much as a nickel was ever found missing. Pearson's wife Jane ran the kitchens, his daughter worked as a maid, and his sons waited table and did repairs.

Of course, the fear of your body being found in the river one morning should you trespass is a great motivator. But there was something steady and discreet about the man, making his post a natural position for him.

The clock struck half past ten. I went to my study through the stairs to my right, which led up to the parlor.

The small stack of items from the Ball lay in a basket on a white table by the window. I sat at my desk, the only item of furniture truly mine: dark cherry with brass handles.

I wanted to know more about the Red Dogs, and Jacqueline Spadros couldn't do that sort of inquiry. Thus letters to my contacts, short and coded, were often the way I worked.

To my contact in the Clubb desk at the *Bridges Daily*:

> Dear Mr. Blackberry —
>
> Your help with any news about a lost pup. Red-haired, goes by the name of "Card." Last seen in the shop area.
>
> Any information richly rewarded.
>
> Yours, Miss Pamela Cavendish

And another to my contact at the employment office:

Dear Mrs. Stake (whose name was actually Miss Stack, but there was no one else at the office with a similar name) —

Background information on a Mr. Reddington, deals in business stamps and cards. Claims multiple residences. Prior business selling exotic dogs. Known associates appreciated.

In Gratitude, Mr. Jack Split

And so on.

The clock struck eleven as I handed the letters to Pearson. "Would you bring in some bourbon?"

He had a slight hesitation before saying, "Of course, mum."

"And my cigarettes, please."

He returned in a few moments with both, and lit a cigarette for me.

I drank a couple glasses while I smoked and read the *Bridges Daily* editorial section once again. I thought I might like to talk with this reporter, Thrace Pike.

Why speak with this annoyance?

He interested me. I wanted to meet the man, to hear his thoughts. Did he truly want to overthrow the current regime, or was he unaware of the implications of his work? Did he pose a threat, or was he a rash young man destined to meet a shower of bullets in an alley? I wasn't sure, and I needed to learn if he was an ally or an enemy before whatever he planned affected my life.

The Visit

Dirty snow lay beside the road on the way to the Kerr residence. Mist drifted through the trees, even though the sun stood at high noon, a pale ball behind the clouds.

The Spadros quadrant was the southeast of the city. The Hart quadrant, where Mr. Kerr lived, was the northwest. So we rode through Spadros quadrant, across the bridge to Market Center, then over the bridge to Hart. Thorny hedges, wrought iron, and patrolling guards kept the reality of the Pot and slums from view.

The Kerr twins and I grew up together. I felt glad to see both of them again, for very different reasons. But they reminded me of my home and all I had lost. "I have never been to Mr. Kerr's home. Is it far?"

Tony said, "Just in the fair part of Hart … not too far."

"How fortunate for Mr. Kerr that he was moved to the Hart lands." Why Hart, when Mr. Kerr lived the majority of his life in the Spadros portion of the Pot? No one entered a Family's area from their Pot without paying a steep price. It was unheard of for one Family to take another's Pot rag. Was this the insult which caused Roy Spadros to hate Charles Hart so? That seemed excessive even for Roy. But I did wonder what great boon Mr. Kerr gave the Harts in exchange for such a release.

"Mr. Kerr has done well," Tony said. "An old man shouldn't have to languish in the Pot, especially one with such a distinguished heritage."

I stared at Tony. Did he mock the Kerrs? He seemed sincere.

Anthony Spadros: so different from his father at times, and at other times, very like. He could be ruthless, and also kind; vicious, yet also gentle. I often didn't understand Tony, or why he did what he did. Even his words the night before didn't fully explain his actions.

"Why did you marry me?"

Tony took my hand in his and kissed it. "Because I love you."

His answer, while on the surface, fine, bordered on madness. No one in Tony's position married for love.

Why did Roy Spadros agree to it, nay, encourage it? I was no grand lady; I was a nobody — worse, a Pot rag, an untouchable, raised in a brothel, trained as a whore.

Most people in the Pot grew up in a brothel. And yes, Ma taught me the work. But she never let me do any, even when men asked for me. At the time, it made me unhappy, because I felt different than the other girls. She said the Masked Man wouldn't like it.

Who was the Masked Man? Some whispered he was a quadrant money-man. I never learned his identity until much later, but even as a small girl I knew he was important.

I remembered the way I saw him as a child. Capable, larger than life, his dark cloak and clean scent billowed into the room ahead of him. His brown leather mask showed light skin around warm blue eyes. The way the Masked Man moved said don't test me, and no one ever did.

When I was young, I hoped the Masked Man was my daddy. He treated me kindly, and took an interest in me. I liked when he came to see us.

The whole situation puzzled me. I didn't understand why he hid his face, why he visited, why he took such interest in me. Yet many years later, here I sat, married to the second most powerful man in Bridges, riding in a carriage fit for a queen, pulled by the finest carriage-horses in the land. Perhaps this was what the Masked Man intended.

I felt Tony watching me. If anything, he was attentive. "You don't mind going out on a holiday?"

"Not at all. It gives the staff a day of rest."

He let go of my hand and turned to the window. "You are too kind to them, Jacqui ... you think too much of them. You must be careful, or they will take advantage. They are your servants, not your friends."

"Look, she fancy," Poignee said as I passed.

I felt appalled. "What did you say?"

"Don't put on them airs. You damn lucky but you a Pot rag, same as us."

Treysa and Ottilie snickered.

"I understand." I did understand. It didn't stop me from treating them as people. I don't think Tony saw them that way.

"I'm sure you're glad to see your playmates again after all these years," he said. "I was allowed very few."

I stared at him, mouth open, and grasped his hand. I had forgotten about his older brother, the true Spadros heir, poisoned when Tony was two. No one spoke of the child, and I had never even learned his name.

"Ten was the only one my father allowed near me." Tony smiled, as if thinking of pleasant times long ago.

"Ten?"

"Ten Hogan ... Sawbuck."

I stared at him until I remembered the imposing fellow at the ball, Tony's "right hand man." In truth, I saw the man very seldom. "Oh, yes, of course."

"Everyone called him Sawbuck ... we had another cousin Ten, and everyone confused them. He's my mother's sister's son." He paused, then laughed. "I suppose no one ever told you!"

"I knew you were related, of course, but not in what way." Sawbuck looked nothing like Molly; I wondered what his parents were like.

"From the first time Ten learned about my brother, oh, I was two or three so he must have been eight, or perhaps nine ... when he heard of it, he said he would watch over me, that he would never let anyone hurt me. He has kept his word." Tony leaned his arm on the window's edge, and leaned his face on his hand. "It's still strange that he calls me 'sir,' even now, but my father would have nothing else." He stared out of the window.

How odd the situation must feel. "It sounds lonely."

Tony smiled, and shook his head. "It is of no consequence." He squeezed my hand. "We are safe, and so shall our children be. I shall make sure of that."

I leaned back, glad for my morning tea, as dangerous as it might be if anyone learned of it. I would never bring children to a world where they might become targets for an assassin.

***

Hart quadrant's streets and sidewalks were made of closely laid red brick, with curbs painted white. Joseph and Josephine Kerr greeted our carriage. Josephine wore a pale blue morning dress and a gray shawl. Joe wore a gray blazer and vest, with navy blue pinstriped pants.

I think.

I couldn't tear myself away from his eyes.

But then Joe shook Tony's hand, and I remembered others were present.

Joe cleared his throat, color rising in his cheeks. "Would you like a tour? Our home isn't grand as yours, but it's sufficient."

The Kerr's row house sat on the corner, made of brown stone. It had white molding around the archway and polished wrought-iron railings. Wood paneling and tile graced the front hall. The housekeeper, a middle-aged lady, met us at the door: Marja, my kitchen maid Ottilie's mother. She nodded her head to me.

Joe asked, "Is Mr. Kerr ready for visitors?"

"Aye," the woman said, "he's in the parlor. I've set a fire for you. Luncheon will be ready in a bit."

"Thank you, Marja." Josie turned to me and Tony. "Grampa is a bit gruff, but he means well."

Tony and I smiled at each other, used to Roy and his rages.

I had never met the Kerrs' grandfather. He took the twins in after I went to Spadros Manor that final time: they called it "finishing." This was training on how to live where people wore clean clothes, took baths, and ate with something other than their fingers, when they ate at all.

I found my finishing painful and confusing. I can't imagine what it was like for them, having never set foot outside the Pot until then.

From Joe's description, I expected Polansky Kerr IV to be a gray, frail man wearing a robe and slippers. I felt pleasantly surprised to meet a ruddy, well-groomed gentleman. Mr. Kerr kissed my hand and chatted with us without so much as a cane to lean on. "My grandchildren speak of you often, Mrs. Spadros, so I feel as if I know you already."

I wondered where the gruffness Josie spoke of was. But then even Roy seldom raged in front of company when first met. I smiled at Mr. Kerr. "I hope to make actual acquaintance."

Marja came in. "Luncheon is served, sir."

"Come," Joe said, "we don't have a chef as you must, but Marja's cooking is quite good."

Mr. Kerr took my arm, Tony took Josie's, and we went into the dining room.

Joe was right; the food was quite good, the meal and wine, light and flavorful. But Joe spoke truth on another matter. The china, while antique, was mismatched and chipped. The house was small, old, and in need of a decorator's touch. Some of the silverware had been bent and imperfectly straightened. The table cloth was threadbare in spots. Not grand as ours, but sufficient.

Tony took a drink of wine, leaning back in his chair and spoke to the twins. "Congratulations on attending the Grand Ball." He turned to Mr. Kerr. "You must be very proud."

Mr. Kerr smiled. "Why, thank you. I'm much indebted to Mr. Charles Hart for his generous invitation." He paused. "I hope it's a sign of greater things to come." He became animated, moving his arms as he spoke. "My grandfather told me many times of when he was a boy, how beautiful the city used to be, how Benjamin Kerr raised the dome and sunk the pilings, lo these 500 years ago. The gardens, the bridges of gold, the buildings … a magnificent creation it was then." His lined face became that of a man transfixed with the wonder of his vision. "One day the Kerr family is going to —"

Josie spoke brightly. "Would anyone like another glass?"

That was interesting. I raised my empty cup.

Mr. Kerr chuckled, untroubled by Josie's interruption. "You were right, Joe: she's had four already and not a sign of it on her."

Joe leaned back in his chair. "And I'd wager she had quite a bit more before she arrived."

Tony's face darkened. "What are you insinuating…?"

Joe leaned forward, a brief look of panic on his face. "Nothing at all, I assure you! Please forgive me. I am truly sorry to have given offense."

Tony relaxed. "Her taste for strong drink has been commented on in the past, and not in a good way. I would have no stain on her honor."

Well, that was kind of him. I was sure I would hear about it on the way home, though.

Josephine laughed. "One time when we were small, a truck full of vodka tipped, and we stole several of the bottles…."

A loud screeching noise a few blocks away, then the shriek of grating metal and a crash of breaking glass. Us Lowballs hid, glancing around in case a rival gang got past the watchers and High Cards. A minute later, Joe dashed up laughing, brown hair dark with sweat, carrying a crate of liquor bottles filled with clear liquid. Josie followed behind, lugging her own crate.

"Full proof it was, and most of us couldn't drink more than a swallow. It burned so! But Jacqui drank half a bottle straight down, before the police came and we had to run. She didn't so much as stumble the rest of the night, and she couldn't have been more than nine!"

I was thirsty. I loved the warmth in my chest as I drank. I felt more alive.

Tony turned to me, mouth open, and I grinned at him. "I liked the taste. In any case, Josie exaggerates. I was twelve, and already large for my age."

I could hardly forget the night Air died.

Tony took my hand. "I have worried that she had some ailment or sorrow to cause her to drink so."

I felt bitter; he didn't understand anything. Trying not to snort in amusement, I put my hand on his and smiled.

Joe did not smile. "How admirable. And how happy you look. We must take a stroll among the roses. It's been so unseasonably warm that some are still in bloom. The snow dusted on them looks quite charming."

"Oh, yes!" Josie said. "Grampa, will you stroll with us?"

"Of course."

I took Tony's arm as we strolled in the small garden, bounded by a wall of brown stone topped with wrought iron. The sky was overcast and no snow fell; whatever snow might have been on the roses had melted. The roses were pretty, if wilted from the chill.

Strolling in the Kerr's garden seemed fine enough, but I couldn't avoid Joe's comment.

Was I happy?

I had no reason not to be. My husband was not harsh, or brutal, or even unkind. As far as I could tell — not that I cared one way or the other — he was even faithful. I had every comfort imaginable and time for diversion of my choosing, such as the people I helped as an investigator.

Most of the cases were petty: navigating the maze of bureaucracy at Market Center, following a man suspected of infidelity. Helping those in the Pot and the slums around it helped me feel less disloyal for leaving them to shiver in the cold while I slept in luxury.

But every move I made, even to drink a glass of wine, shouted my strangeness in this world. And to be so near to Joe again was utterly intoxicating.

He and Josie chatted arm in arm, and I felt a sharp twinge of jealousy, yearning to feel Joe's touch on me again. I recalled the last time we kissed, the way he smelled, the promises he made, the way he touched my body …

We completed our circuit and approached the back stair. I stumbled on the rough walkway, but Tony caught me.

"Your face is flushed," Joe said. "Are you warm enough?"

I felt embarrassed. "Quite."

"Perhaps we should go inside," Tony said.

Mr. Kerr said, "Would you like to visit my library?"

Books lined the walls to the ceiling, with a movable ladder to fetch the upper ones. The furniture was leather, or mahogany with brass handles on the drawers. The pieces looked worn, as did the reddish-brown carpeting. A well-worn mahogany and ivory-colored chess set stood on a small table in the corner, along with two chairs.

Mr. Kerr had come into some money, but long ago.

While Mr. Kerr showed off his books, Josie and I sat in the window seat, and she showed me her drawings, which she kept in a portfolio. "This portrait of your father is exceptional."

Josie smiled. "Thank you."

"Is your father well?"

Josie shrugged. "I assume he's drunk as usual."

Ely Kerr suffered serious bouts of melancholy. They say this worsened after his lover Josephine died giving birth to their twins.

A dim alley, the smell of alcohol, sitting next to a weeping blond man. "He hates me, Jacqui. My daddy hates me."

I felt surprised at the memory. How old was I? "Josie, may I ask a personal question?"

"Why, Jacqui, you may always ask, whatever you wish."

I glanced around and lowered my voice. "You are young and beautiful, and your grandfather is well. Why are you unmarried? Could he not arrange something to your liking?"

Josie shook her head. "He's forbidden me to marry. I'm being trained to take over his affairs, should he fall ill or pass on." She gazed out of the window. "It's of no consequence; I'm too busy with my own affairs as it is. Another man's household would just get in the way." She giggled. "A fine spinster I sound."

Why her? Joe could take over Mr. Kerr's business. "You're the prettiest spinster I've ever seen. Are you happy?"

She put her hands in her lap. "Completely. I have useful work, my family around me, and a bright future. I couldn't be happier!"

Moved by her joy, I grabbed her hands and kissed them, as I did when we were young. "I'm so grateful. I've worried about you. It's good to see you happy and well."

She smiled, blushing, and pulled her hands gently away, which made me feel she put a distance between us. "It's gratifying to hear you say so. I'm glad you never forgot me. I've missed you."

"I've missed you too." I would have spoken of how lonely the years had been, the hurt of hearing of her but never from her. But those words no longer seemed appropriate.

Joe, who sat across the room with his leg up on the arm of the overstuffed chair smoking a cigar, rose. "Would you like to see the rest of the house?"

So we toured the house, which was much like what we had seen already. And soon we were on our way outside.

We made our goodbyes and got in our carriage. As the carriage pulled away, I noticed a man across the street wearing brown. He moved out of view before I saw his face. Had he been watching us?

I leaned back and closed my eyes, feeling light-headed and weary, glad to be going home.

The visit seemed different than I thought. Joe was charming, but distant; he hadn't once smiled during our entire visit. Josie was a talented woman with her own life. And Mr. Kerr was a mystery. The noise of the horses and carriage cut the melancholy ache I felt.

"Did you enjoy your afternoon?"

I felt startled. "What? Oh, yes, it was lovely. It was good to see my friends after so many years. And their grandfather is an excellent host."

"Yes, he was. I'm surprised at the poor way he's spoken of. I don't understand it." Tony stared out of the window.

Bitterness rose within me. "I understand very well. People hate those who dare to rise from their 'place' and show they're as good as those born to wealth and power. Every slight shown to me the last six years has proved that well."

"Jacqui …" Tony said, as if saddened by my tone. "There is a long history of hate for the Kerr family. That I do understand."

People blamed the Kerrs for allowing the violence which destroyed much of the city, especially the areas which now formed the Pot, which they say used to be beautiful. The Kerr name became a byword, a proverb of what to avoid.

Yet his grandchildren attended a Grand Ball. Even after being sponsored into the quadrant by the Harts, for Mr. Kerr to climb from the slums to his current place in Bridges society was a monumental achievement. I wondered how he did it.

"Pity they petitioned Hart rather than Spadros," Tony said. "It would be grand if they lived closer."

To see Joe every day, to run into him at the shops?

It would be torture.

The Attack

When we returned to Spadros Manor, several of Tony's men waited on the steps, porch, and walkway. They straightened, focusing on us when we arrived. After we alighted from the carriage, Sawbuck spoke to Tony privately.

I did see some of Molly Spadros in Sawbuck, perhaps around the eyes.

Tony turned to me. "I'll tend to this and meet you inside, in perhaps an hour."

So I went to my study, read my mail — well wishes for the holiday — and after, I practiced my piano.

Roy and Molly Spadros gave us the grand piano on our wedding day. I was not good at playing, nor did I particularly like to. But apparently it would be a slight on the Family honor for Mrs. Jacqueline Spadros to be asked to perform yet unable. No one had ever asked me to play, so I wasn't sure how this all mattered so. But I practiced anyway. I did seem to be making progress, considering five years before I had never seen a piano.

While I played, I considered how my relationship with Tony had changed these past ten years.

Once Roy Spadros moved my father from the Pot to the slums, my life changed forever. I didn't go anywhere. But no matter how much I hid, a different set of men grabbed me at random times, dragging me to Spadros Manor as I screamed in terror.

Different scullery maids stripped, bathed, and dressed me each time. Then they locked me in a room with Tony as I wept in humiliation or raged at having to endure this strange, quiet boy.

There we sat until time for whatever torment, lesson, or amusement Roy planned for us.

Over the years, we went (on my part) from sullen resignation to our state of marriage.

I was not unhappy. I just ... existed. I realized I was no longer sullen: I had simply become resigned.

The thought made me sad.

Tea-time came and went. After tea, I dozed for a while on the sofa in my study, waking in darkness, disoriented and weary. The light from the street-lamp created a golden stripe on the far wall. Where was Tony?

I lit the lamp on the table and picked up the basket of items Amelia found in my pocket after the Grand Ball. An envelope from Jonathan with three pressed daffodils inside: "the sun shines when I am with you." That made me smile.

A few calling cards, with invitations to visit written on the back. Then a blank card. I turned it over: a stamp of a red dog, the same dog as on the wall outside David's home.

For heavens' sakes. That man of Tony's was quick, to have obtained a card before we even left the Ball. Perhaps one of the Associates thought to keep a card to show us. I felt pleased Tony had such intelligent men on his staff.

I put Jonathan's flowers on my desk and the stamped card in my drawer, meaning to give it to Tony when he got home.

A knock on the door. "Time to dress for dinner, mum."

Upstairs, Amelia helped me into my red crushed taffeta dress, which Tony liked very much but I hadn't worn for a while.

We did this every night, even though we had no guests. Roy and Molly insisted on it for so many years it became a habit. They reasoned if we acted as if we had guests, when they did arrive our actions would appear natural from constant use.

I was putting on my jewels when the front door closed downstairs. Where could they have been?

Voices argued as Amelia laced my dinner shoes. I stood and examined myself one last time, then went into the hall.

"I must insist, sir," Pearson said. "I can have the doctor summoned at once."

The doctor? I crossed to the staircase.

Tony was being supported by two of his men. Their clothing was dirty, disheveled, and spattered with blood. Sawbuck entered last, facing outside, holstering his revolver once he shut the door.

I descended the stairs. "Whatever has happened?" I grasped Tony's hand, which felt clammy. "Help him to a chair, and bring an ottoman for his feet." His men did so. "Amelia, bring a basin of water and a cloth. Pearson, summon the doctor."

We had stolen a new mechanism from the Clubbs, the Telephonic Telegraph. This machine transmitted sound through wires using electricity, so you could talk to others located far away. It was a marvelous creation; I couldn't believe the Clubbs had hoarded such a thing.

Though Roy scoffed at the device, Tony saw the value of it at once. It took months of installing wire under the cobblestones to our private surgeon Dr. Salmon's office. Now we could summon the doctor at once instead of waiting for a messenger boy.

We had finished the project just in time. The men were dirty and sweaty, but Tony was pale, his breath coming in short gasps.

"Where are you injured?" I turned to the men. "Was he shot?"

"No, mum." Pain crossed Sawbuck's face, and I imagined his distress. "But it was an ambush: they carried lead pipes, and he took a solid blow to the ribs."

I said to Sawbuck, "How did you come to be in an ambush?" I spoke to all the men. "Bring chairs and tell me the whole tale."

Tony's men turned towards him, and he nodded. They drew up chairs and sat.

"When you arrived," Sawbuck said, "we gave Mr. Spadros word of a Party Time shipment hijacked. He insisted on seeing the scene of the incident and the route taken.

"We went to the scene and tended to the injured men and horses. When we returned to the warehouse, the four guards scheduled to be on duty were missing. It was most suspicious.

"When we entered the building, six men ambushed us. We shot three and the rest fled. They focused the attack on Mr. Spadros in particular."

I witnessed worse beatings as a child. "Anyone else injured?"

"A few were," Sawbuck said, "but they were taken home to their families. The guards are still missing."

"See … that the doctor … visits the injured," Tony gasped, "at my expense. And not a word to my father."

"Yes, sir. I'll tell the men and their families again, in the strongest terms." Sawbuck glanced at me, concern in his face.

"Don't speak," I told Tony, "until the doctor has seen to you."

Tony closed his eyes, grimacing with each breath. I washed his face, loosened his cravat, undid his collar, and combed his hair.

Dr. Salmon arrived and pronounced Tony's rib broken. Tony's men carried him upstairs, then the doctor bathed his right side, which was badly bruised, and strapped his ribs. This seemed to ease the pain. The doctor dosed Tony and left a tincture of opium. "Keep him quiet for as long as possible. The less he moves around, the faster it will heal."

"Doctor, my husband would like his father not to know of this. What shall we say?"

Dr. Salmon thought a moment. "Your husband has had an attack of pleurisy. He will be ill for at least two weeks."

I handed him a silver dollar. "Thank you for your services."

Every time I touched a dollar, it reminded me of how I got here. When I was twelve, a Party Time addict named Peedro Sluff said if I washed my face, brushed my hair, and was at the corner of Shill and Snow by ten, I'd get a dollar.

Before this, I'd never seen a dollar; it was more money than anyone I knew had. So I said okay. Air tried to keep me from going there, truly he did. I should have listened.

When I stepped into the hall, Sawbuck said, "How is he?"

"He will be well. Tell anyone who asks that he has pleurisy."

Sawbuck gave a small smile. "I will. Thank you, mum."

After the men left, I checked on Tony, who slept, then washed my face and returned to my cold meal. "Pearson, please fetch Michaels and Amelia."

"They're at dinner, mum."

"Have them bring their dinners and sit here. I need your help. I don't want to upset the others by going downstairs."

The three came up, carrying their meals and drink, and after some hesitation, joined me at the table. Jacob Michaels was young, thin, and had dark hair. Tonight he looked nervous, but he sat, as did Amelia. Amelia's eyes and nose were red, her face fearful.

"Pearson, please sit, it's fatiguing to look up at you so." I smiled to soften my words.

"If you insist, mum."

I took a deep breath, and let it out. "If anyone asks, Mr. Spadros is stricken with pleurisy —"

Pearson raised an eyebrow. "Pleurisy?"

"Yes. Mr. Spadros doesn't wish his father to know of tonight's dealings until we have some idea as to who the perpetrators were."

"But," Amelia said, "the men ..."

"Sawbuck will see to the men and their families. Pearson, please see to the staff. I would hate to have any further losses due to this."

Pearson said, "You will have no troubles on that account."

I smiled, relieved. "I knew I could depend on you. In any case, Mr. Spadros may be unwell for several weeks. If anyone asks about injured men, they were ..."

"Dueling?" Michaels said.

"Brawling," Pearson said. "As rough men will."

"Brawling! Very good. The doctor says Mr. Spadros should keep as quiet as he can. So he'll need assistance and to have meals brought to him. I think we will need to not be at home to callers for at least the next week, but we can see how he fares."

"That does sound wise, mum," Pearson said. "I'll notify the bridge guards."

"Thank you." I took a bite of cold chicken, feeling exhausted. "Michaels, please set up a bell for his room."

"At once, mum," Michaels said.

"Please do so quietly."

Michaels smiled, his face regaining some of its color. "All that's needed is to let down the pull cord and place it within his reach; it's been there all along."

Ah. I had no idea of the mechanisms behind a Manor house bell system, even after all these years, only that they connected to the levers in the staff room. Were the cords threaded through the walls somehow?

"Thank you, Michaels. Please, eat. I'm not in the mood to sit alone, after such a day."

Amelia had been studying me. "So your visit with the Kerrs was acceptable?"

I had almost forgotten it, with all the trouble. But the way she spoke made me think she was more perceptive than I thought.

"Perfectly. But ... it was like returning home after being gone for many years. Things change."

All three nodded, their focus going inward. I felt pleased with myself; my statement would divert her questions for some time.

The Attempt

Every few hours Tony woke in pain. I dosed him with opium then held him as he gasped until the medication took effect.

It reminded me of Air, a month before he died. We sat on the cold ground by the fence, and I held him as he coughed up blood. Eleanora screamed, long hair flying, banging on the black iron bars with a piece of metal until the lady at the poorhouse called a doctor. I felt sorry for two-year-old David and six-year-old Herbert, who clutched her skirts and cried in terror.

I couldn't smoke around Tony: this made him cough. Even with Amelia and Michaels there to assist, I dared not leave him for long. It took several days before Tony was well enough to sit in a chair, so I wasn't able to venture out as I wished.

At times, I felt trapped, at other times, close to tears at his suffering. I thought once, gazing at Tony as he slept, perhaps this is what a mother feels for her child.

We were in a terrible situation, and so sudden.

A reporter writing an editorial against the Families. Someone forging a note from Madame. Air's little brother missing. A couple who knew of my business and told others about it. At least one man following me, watching me. The Red Dog stamps. A focused attack on Tony by a group of men. Our guards missing. A shipment hijacked.

I needed to do something. I often wept in frustration, not knowing what to do to help.

A fourth-page article in the *Golden Bridges* appeared: "unidentified bodies in the river, dead several days." Other than that, Tony's adventure went unnoticed, and we were grateful.

Roy and Molly Spadros visited shortly after. Since Tony slept, they took me to the far end of the garden for my shooting lesson while Roy questioned me as to how the house fared.

Roy insisted on holding lessons at least monthly, up until now when Tony was away. I couldn't see when I would ever need to shoot someone.

"We're in the Business, dammit," Roy said the one time I asked. "Someone pulls out a gun, you better defend yourself."

So I practiced in my morning dress on grass still damp with dew. I fired while lying flat, on both knees, on one knee, standing, one handed, two handed, with my right hand, with my left hand ... I seemed to have some talent for it.

Roy often shouted or struck the ground beside me, or kicked me, or forced Molly to stand next to the target. The only way I could bring myself to pull the trigger was to focus only on the target. The world became silent; Roy's curses and blows vanished, Molly disappeared. The target was all I saw.

I didn't always hit precisely at first, but I have never once missed a target.

Roy examined the paper target. "You're almost as good as Molly." I breathed a sigh of relief once his back turned.

Molly took my arm as we walked back to the house, while Roy followed several paces behind smoking a cigar. "I'm glad no harm has befallen you. Rumors of an attempt against you came before the Ball."

"Against me. Me in particular?"

Molly nodded.

This was startling. "From where? Why did you not say so before this?"

She glanced away. "I don't know the threat's exact nature. My husband didn't wish you to know."

Perhaps to see what would happen? Roy took a perverse pleasure in harm coming to anyone, but seemed to especially revel in harm coming to me. The protection we received was all for Tony's benefit.

"Well, other than Mr. Spadros being so ill, things have been peaceful." We strolled along, and a bird flew past.

"I heard you visited the Kerrs last week."

"Why yes." I wondered how she heard.

"How is Mr. Kerr?"

"Quite well. I didn't know you knew him."

Molly smiled. "I knew Mr. Kerr when he ran a speakeasy in the Spadros Pot. You're not the only one born there."

I stared at her, and she laughed as if my expression were the funniest thing in the world.

Molly, born in the Pot? Did Roy know? Surely he didn't know. How did she end up here?

But then Roy came up beside Molly, and she took his arm. "Darling, let's see if Jane has a treat for Katherine. She loves it so when you bring her something." Katherine was Tony's younger sister and very much Daddy's girl.

Roy seemed pleased with the idea, and never asked why Molly laughed.

Ma told me once if you did your job really well, a quadrant-man might make you his mistress. You and your children would never have to work the beds again. She told me she knew a woman who left the Pot that way, sponsored by her Family man and set up with her own shop.

Being sponsored by a Family and moved into one of the quadrants was the highest achievement for a Pot rag. "Real freedom," Ma called it.

Had Molly managed to do this? But how? With who? How did she end up married to Roy? For her, the dream seemed to have turned into a nightmare.

We later had tea in the parlor. "It's strange," Roy said, "Anthony was never ill as a child. Did the doctor say why he got pleurisy now?"

I shrugged. "I have no idea. The doctor was definite on the diagnosis, though."

Roy said, "He's a good one, Dr. Salmon, been in our family since I was a boy." He lit a cigar. "I hear some of the men have been brawling."

"Oh? Oh, yes, they … I don't know what they were doing. Mr. Spadros was quite stern with them."

"Heh." Roy blew a smoke ring into the air.

"Sir, I would like your advice on a matter." That tack seemed best to take with one so mercurial as he.

Roy leaned forward. "Go on."

"I read in the paper last week some were unhappy with the current state of affairs …"

Roy scowled.

"… and it occurred to me that a novel way to silence such talk would be to attack the issue head on. With your permission, I would like to invite this wayward reporter to discuss the benefits our house bestows upon the city."

Roy leaned back, one hand to his chin, and crossed one leg over the other. "It's risky. Depends on the reporter and what his ideas are. If he's a crusader, seeing how we live could make him even more set against us."

I smiled. "But of course, the editor of the *Bridges Daily* has been the recipient of much of our favor, has he not? A word and anything unpleasant would be sent to the trash can, and we would know this reporter was one we … couldn't work with."

Roy laughed. "Clever girl! Loosen the fangs, so to speak."

Molly looked at me sideways, as if she guessed what I had in mind, and gave a slight smile.

***

A few days later I had an awed Thrace Pike seated in my parlor. Mr. Pike was twenty, lean, and dressed in a threadbare dark brown suit which was out of fashion by close to ten years. He had a shock of straw-colored hair and eyes so dark as to appear black. When he appeared at the door, he looked like a crusader, and for a moment I reconsidered my plans.

I recalled my mother's skill at turning men to her favor without taking them into her bed. This gave me an idea as to how to gain this reporter's goodwill and information both. I wished I could see my mother for advice, but Roy's threats still frightened me. I dared not go to the Spadros section of the Pot to see her, and I didn't know if she could meet with me without harm befalling her. It seemed Roy's eyes and ears were everywhere.

From my contacts I learned Mr. Pike kept a locket with a small portrait of his wife and newborn child in his waist band, given to him by his grandmother. He wore no ring. A pale indentation in his finger suggested he either felt unhappy with his situation or his family had fallen on very hard times. During my tour of our home, rather than admiring the house, he hung on my every word. At the time, I thought, crusader or not, my scheme might still work.

Amelia remained in the corner with her needlework after bringing us both some tea. I placed my chair so Mr. Pike would be illuminated, yet I would be in shadow.

The sun broke through the clouds and lit the room, revealing Mr. Pike's eyes were not black, instead a very dark brown.

"I'm sorry Mr. Spadros is unable to meet with you. Business, you know." I smiled.

"I understand, ma'am. What sort of business does Mr. Spadros engage in?"

"Managing these estates is enough work for any gentleman, don't you think? Overseeing the staff, examining the books to make sure none of our holdings is mismanaged, directing repairs of our buildings ..."

Tony did all these. He also oversaw the casino and directed the Party Time shipments, but I didn't think Mr. Pike needed to know that.

"Yes, I see." Mr. Pike opened his notebook, then hesitated. "May I ask why you wanted to see me?"

"I read your editorial at New Year's, and I wanted to hear more of your thoughts."

"Really." He seemed more at ease. "What part of my editorial interested you so?"

"Well ..." I unwrapped my shawl, placing it aside.

Before meeting with Mr. Pike, I put on a new corset which matched my skin tone, with a neckline which cut straight across my bosom. I had Amelia lace my corset to enhance my decolletage — I dared not breathe **too** deeply, or I might show more than I wished — and wore a wispy, low-cut bodice covering made of veil material, also in my skin tone.

This bodice was normally worn over a darker colored corset or bodice at a ball or evening party, but worn straight over the skin-colored corset like this, sitting in relative shadow, it gave the appearance that I wore … very little. Only intent scrutiny would show the truth.

And scrutiny was what I desired. I have a sufficiently endowed body for almost any man.

This combination of clothing — while perhaps indiscreet — was perfectly legal wear, even in public. Yet I noticed, as I thought might be the case with a man so newly with child, his eyes were drawn to my body rather than to my actions.

When he didn't look away, I knew I had him.

"… Mr. Pike, you wrote that changes needed to be made — I believe the quote was, 'to the current state of … affairs.' What changes do you … propose?"

Silence does terrible things to a man. It makes him consider his words or makes them fly from his head.

Mr. Pike said nothing. His mouth hung open; his eyes rested somewhat below mine.

Very good.

I chose a necklace for this occasion with a long, thin pendant that dipped between my breasts. After a few moments of silence, I began to toy with my necklace, just to see the effect this produced.

Dip … dip … dip …

The color rose in his cheeks and his pupils widened. Very good. "Ah, well," he glanced at my necklace, "um, I have considered the recent, um, violence in the area … due to the, ah," another glance, "recent, um, gang activity."

"Oh, yes." I felt gratified to see him glance at my necklace again. "Their brazen appearance, out in the open …" I took as deep a breath as I dared and let it out. "… it's intriguing. Could you … tell me more about them?"

His face turned crimson, and he swallowed, shifting a bit in his seat. This would have the effect of making his trousers much more comfortable than they appeared. "Well, um, ma'am, um … there are always so many."

He then grimaced a bit. I didn't believe the man's face could turn any redder, but it did.

This was highly entertaining.

"Um," he said, "uh, the most recent ones … um, the police are calling Red Dogs, because of the stamps found on walls or on cards, um, such as you might use for calling."

I nodded, and began playing with my necklace again. "What do the police know of these scoundrels?"

"Well," he said, not looking at me, the color subsiding from his cheeks, and I realized he had found a topic he could focus on safely, "they are all young, some as young as 12 or 14, uh," he glanced briefly at my necklace, and his face reddened again, "mum, but, uh, apparently led by older boys who direct their actions. A lesser gang, to be sure, but they are causing a great deal of mischief at present."

"These older boys. What do the police know of them?"

"Very little." He stared at the wall behind me. "The smaller ones call them aces, that's all I know. Two chips and an ace is what the boys say, and the chips just do what the ace tells them."

"This is what I don't understand: what changes should we make to improve the situation? The Spadros Family provides employment, shelter, food, clothing, and safety for our whole quadrant. Would you take these benefits away merely because some children misbehave?"

Thrace Pike blinked, realizing he had been caught. "Perhaps I wrote hastily, madame. Of course I wouldn't want the city to suffer. But … surely you agree that the conditions in the poorer areas — when people see the opulence of the Families — could lead to a certain dissatisfaction and what you call 'misbehavior' in our younger citizens."

This wasn't going the way I wanted it to.

I had an idea.

I rose, re-wrapping my shawl to cover myself, and Amelia rose as well. "Then we must do something to help! I invite you to accompany me to our poorer areas so I may donate to the needs of our people. Would you be able to join me, say, next Tuesday at noon, by the charity house outside the Spadros Pot?"

Mr. Pike picked up his overcoat and held it in front of him. "Most certainly," he said, not meeting my eye. "Thank you for your invitation, and your gracious hospitality."

After he left, Amelia chuckled. "You are a wicked woman, mum. He dare not write anything specific about our meeting today, and there will be little of negativity to write about on Tuesday, unless he is more cynical than he seems."

I wasn't sure. He was supposed to leave in a warmer mood towards me … but he almost seemed angry.

I hoped I hadn't made matters worse.

The Card

Tony improved over the next few days and was able work in his study for short periods of time. I remained with him in case he needed anything; he seemed less short of breath when I stayed nearby. His men brought back reports frequently. To my surprise, Tony allowed me in the room while he heard them.

Jack Diamond, the obvious suspect for the attack, had been confined to his rooms after the fiasco at the Grand Ball. He remained there still, as confirmed by a rather large bribe to one of the maids who did his cleaning.

Mr. Julius Diamond, furious with his men for not preventing Jack's outburst at the Ball, shot several and banished the rest to their Party Time manufacturing plant on double shift duty. They were working the night of the attack.

The family of the man whose execution Tony ordered the night of the Grand Ball seemed as baffled by the attack as anyone. They held valid and confirmed alibis for that night. Even so, Tony sent men to "encourage" them to move from the city, to prevent any ideas of revenge.

My inquiries about the Red Dogs returned one by one. Most were of little use, but one described a "chip": a young man of about fourteen, blond, blue eyes, thin face, missing the small finger of his right hand. He was last seen in the Spadros quadrant outside the Pot placing a Red Dogs card at the scene of a crime, and the police wanted him.

***

The Spadros slums was a place for the desperately poor. But at least the slums had the protection of their Family. The Pot was on its own when the bullets flew.

On Tuesday, I went to the poorhouse to give out charity. I brought several of my maids, some Spadros ladies (mainly wives of Tony's upper level men), and a carriage-truck laden with food and drink.

The scene appeared quite different on this side of the fence.

Though the sun stood high, fog still lingered, and the air was chill. Forlorn-looking men loitered near a broken steam-pipe warming themselves. Others stared at us as we passed, hoping for a handout, or perhaps a third job. Women sat on the curb holding pale crying babies. Children a bit older with drawn, hungry eyes swept the cracked sidewalks in front of their ramshackle homes.

For all their suffering, they would have insisted they were better off than in the Pot. I remembered women across the fence calling us whores, as if providing for your children by the sweat of your brow was a foul thing, while their own children starved. They only offered us scorn, and I never gave them any of Ma's bread. After I was taken from the Pot, it haunted me, wondering if their children had survived.

Air's head came to my shoulder, and he panted, trying to keep up. "Jacqui, please, let's go home. I'll get you a dollar another way."

I stopped and faced him. "What's wrong with you? You coughed blood! With a dollar you could get medicine and get better."

Air stared at me. "Some sell little kids."

"So?" People bought little kids by the hour in Ma's place every night. Except me. I feared I wasn't good enough.

"Not for that." Air's lower lip quivered, and tears filled his eyes. "They take them away. To hurt bad. To kill." He coughed. "I don't want anything bad to happen to you, Jacqui. I would rather die."

"I'll be careful." I didn't want Air to think I was scared, so I didn't stop. But I walked slower.

Air scanned the ground until he found a broken bottle. He held the bottle in his small fist as if planning to use it.

The carriages stopped and we all alighted. A crowd gathered, quiet but eager to see what we had brought them.

To my surprise, instead of Thrace Pike, Mr. Durak, the editor of the *Bridges Daily,* arrived with several camera-men.

Mr. Acol Durak was a man of middle years, brown of hair and skin, with some white at the temples, wearing a dark brown suit. Solid, all business, and did his job — to make sure the Spadros Family was never put in an unacceptable light — for which he was well paid.

Although his appearance at this event was puzzling, he was a pleasant enough man, and I was not unhappy to see him. "What brings you here?"

"Had no choice," Mr. Durak said. "Pike told me about this, seemed ready to cover the story. Found his resignation letter on my desk this morning."

"How very odd. Did the letter explain why?"

"I quote: he 'couldn't do his proper duty under the current circumstances.' It seemed a most vague and unsatisfactory letter. He will be getting no recommendation from me, wherever he chooses to go."

I smiled at him, but the whole situation felt unsettling. "Well, Mr. Durak, I'm glad you're here." I turned to my ladies. "Let's get to work."

The charity day went very well. While my maids packed the empty baskets, the ladies took photos with the poor children for the paper. I used the time to stroll through the crowds with the last of the sandwiches in my pocket.

I noticed a young man off to the side who fit the description of the Red Dogs member. I walked over, and he hid.

"I'd like to give you a sandwich. No one will harm you." A blond head peeked around the corner, and I gestured him over. "I won't hurt you. What's your name?"

"Stephen."

Stephen had lost the baby fat around his face that David still had, and gained height. Yet he didn't have the strong build and heavy beard of a man. I handed him the sandwich, and he immediately began chewing.

"How did you lose that finger?"

"Caught in machinery at the mill," he said with his mouth full, and shrugged. "Don't hurt no more."

"Do you know someone who wants a half dollar?"

Stephen's face brightened. "Me, miss."

"Meet me at the train station at eleven tomorrow. I'll be near the bag area, dressed all in black with a veil, and a purple handkerchief on my parasol. Understand?"

"Yes, miss. All in black, purple kerchief."

I smiled. "See you tomorrow."

***

Tony felt well enough to join me during luncheon, which encouraged me no end. Perhaps now I could get some work done.

I sat in my study after luncheon, drinking a few glasses of bourbon while planning our quarterly dinner party for Queen's Day, a month hence. A party which fell on a holiday required early notice if we wanted our guests to attend.

Pearson knocked on the door; Master Joseph Kerr and Miss Josephine Kerr had come to call.

"Splendid," I said, not feeling at all so. Joe's name stirred up a mix of emotions I felt unready to handle. "Please inform Mr. Spadros and ask where he would like to greet them."

"Yes, mum," Pearson said.

I poured another glass of bourbon and drank it.

A few moments later Pearson returned, saying that the pair awaited us in the parlor. Tony stood in the hall behind Pearson, his face pale, and I went to him.

"Make no mention of my condition," Tony whispered.

Surely we could trust the Kerrs? "But —"

"Not a word, or I'll have Pearson send them away. Understand?"

I didn't understand, but something in his face and tone said he would have no argument. So I nodded, and we went to the parlor together.

"Welcome," Tony said. The twins stood to greet us, both wearing navy blue and white. They had removed their coats, and Joe his hat, but Josie still wore her bonnet.

Tony shook Joe's hand, wincing so slightly perhaps only I noticed it, and kissed Josephine's hand, while Joe glanced at Tony then kissed my hand in a perfunctory manner.

We all sat, Tony holding firmly to my arm. Joe appeared perfectly relaxed. Josie sat in a stiff manner, as if sensing something wrong and not understanding it.

"To what do we owe the honor of your visit?" Tony said.

"We wished to return the great favor you bestowed on us when you visited our home," Josie said. "We have not had callers in some time."

Tony smiled. "Friends of Mrs. Spadros are friends of mine. I hope we'll see more of each other in the future."

"Why, thank you," Joe said.

A housemaid came in with tea, set the tray down, and carefully poured four cups of tea. We watched her in silence. She then began to hand the cups to us, beginning with Josie.

"I owe you a debt for your handling of the situation at the Grand Ball," Tony said.

Joe accepted a cup from the maid. "It was nothing." He took a sip of his tea. "Master Diamond is easily distracted. I merely told him there were ladies who wished to make his acquaintance."

I laughed, sure Joe said no such thing.

First of all, Black Jack had never shown the slightest interest in women, either in my sight or from any rumor. From the way Jack reacted, it was clear Joe said some other thing entirely.

I felt bitter. "You are most skilled with words."

Everyone stared at me, including the maid.

Tony said, "He certainly is."

What was wrong with me? I acted like a love-addled girl. Joe came calling on a duty visit, nothing more. He had not spoken to me in six years, and then only when forced to; certainly his silence made his feelings plain.

"I'm sure Mr. and Mrs. Spadros are quite busy." Josephine rose, and so we all rose as well, Tony leaning heavily on my arm. "It has been good to see you."

"I'm so sorry you can't stay longer," I said.

"Yes," Tony said, "please come again."

We helped them with their coats, saw them to the front door and to their carriage, and away they went. The smell of rain lay in the air.

Tony said. "What were you thinking? That was quite rude."

I glanced away, feeling embarrassed at myself.

"How much have you had to drink?"

Not enough. "I'm fine. I'm sorry I was rude. I'll write and tell them so."

"No. If they were offended, it'll only remind them of the offense. If they were not, it makes us look weak, and they'll have a record of the offense to use against us. Say nothing. If they treat you coldly, apologize in person."

I nodded, grateful that he had prevented me from making a mistake in this regard.

The day was overcast and cool, and the street, wet, as if it had rained recently, although I had not heard it. Even though it wasn't yet tea-time, on this winter's day, lamps were lit down the street.

It still seemed strange, this theater, even after seeing it for so many years. But for a "first return visit after a great personage visits you," their part was done perfectly. "Linger no longer than fifteen minutes," said the book. Although their visit was closer to ten minutes, even with their time waiting, than fifteen.

I hoped they weren't offended.

As we turned to go inside, my eye fell on something farther down the stair.

"What is that?" I went down the steps, and stooped to pick it up. A card, stamped with a red dog. The sight made me uneasy.

Tony frowned. "What is what?"

I peered up and down the street, but saw no one. "Nothing. Some child's litter."

"We have servants for that."

I closed my hand over the card and pretended to throw it away when we got inside. "I should finish planning the dinner party before tea time, if I hurry."

"Make sure you invite the Kerrs," Tony said.

"All three?"

"If we have room, yes, all three."

It was clear he felt snappish. I didn't blame him; I'd embarrassed us both. "See you at tea then."

He returned to his study, closing the door with a sharp click. I went into my study, shutting the door, and took out the card.

Like the others, it resembled a business card, stamped with the red dog symbol instead of print. The other side was blank.

The card felt barely damp. No raindrops lay upon it. The color on the stamp had not bled.

Someone left the card right before we came outside.

The Kerr coachmen would have frightened off slum boys who dared to come here, much less leave something on our front steps.

I studied the card. Why would someone put a Red Dog card on my doorstep? Who would dare to put *anything* on the doorstep of Spadros Manor?

Then fear gripped me. I recalled the man outside Madame Biltcliffe's shop on New Year's Eve, the one who I felt watched me. I also remembered the man I thought watched us outside Mr. Kerr's home. Were they the same man?

But something disturbed me more. Did David's kidnapper think I took the case? That I searched for him even now? Had someone followed me, the trail leading them here? I went to the window and peered around the drapery, but could see no one.

What could I do? If I told Tony I was being followed, I would find myself confined to the house, or followed by Tony's men everywhere "to keep me safe."

But if I told no one, and this man caught me …

I stared at the card, fear and anger colliding. Then I opened my desk drawer to lock it away … and saw the other one.

Tony never asked about the other one. His man had been here twice and never mentioned it. Was the kidnapper at the Ball?

I threw the card in and slammed the drawer shut.

I would go to the fires of hell before I threw away the morsel of freedom I had gained because of some scoundrel.

The Lie

The next morning, I pored over the newspaper, searching for clues as to the nature of the Red Dogs.

Little had happened overnight. There were no ads denouncing us, no editorials seeking new ideals …

"Anything of interest in the paper today?" Amelia said.

"Nothing noteworthy. Perhaps the villains took the day off."

Amelia laughed.

But I would not be deterred. The Red Dog cards were either taunts or attempts at intimidation, and the thought of either infuriated me. I meant to get to the bottom of this.

At first, the idea of the kidnapper being at the Ball left me bewildered. But I realized there were many men at the Ball besides those announced on the list. Waiters, retainers, cooks, Men's Room attendants, even the coat-man himself.

"I read the piece on your charity adventure in the newspaper," Tony said at breakfast. "Father will be pleased." This was the longest speech Tony had given since the Kerrs' visit the day before.

"It was most productive."

"What about the interview? When will it print?"

I shook my head and shrugged. "Never, so far as I know. The man resigned."

Tony frowned. "For what reason?"

"I don't know. Even his editor Mr. Durak couldn't say. His resignation was sudden and unexpected."

"Jacqui, what happened? In the interview."

I glanced at the maid. Tony waved her out of the room. "Come sit with me."

What should I tell him?

I moved to sit to his right. "Nothing happened. Amelia sat with us and we had tea. I asked Mr. Pike what he meant by his editorial. We had a short conversation. He mentioned the poor, so I invited him to come with me to dispense charity. He agreed to come but never arrived. Mr. Durak came instead."

"How odd." After a few moments, Tony resumed eating. "I can only hope the man resigned for reasons that have nothing to do with our family."

"I apologize for yesterday. You're right; I drank too much. I didn't expect them to call … and I wasn't myself."

Tony shook his head and shrugged, telling me not to think of it further.

I felt relieved. "I thought if they are upset, we should know before the Queen's Day dinner, to avoid controversy with so many guests present. Might I invite the younger Kerrs to luncheon before then, to make sure all is well?"

Tony nodded. "That's a good idea."

***

After the morning meeting, I told Pearson I was going to the dressmaker's and would be home for luncheon.

Madame Biltcliffe's storefront had beveled glass and polished cedar under wide eaves. Perfectly dressed and coiffed mannequins stood in the window around an empty chair made of oak trimmed in brass.

A large placard on the chair read:

Currently Engaged By
Mrs. Anthony Spadros
For Her Spring Gown

If anything, Madame Biltcliffe excelled at salesmanship.

My day footman Honor took my hand to help me out of the carriage, and yes, I thanked him. Society etiquette be damned. I detested the notion that I must ignore a man's assistance.

Honor nodded without expression and closed the door.

Madame Biltcliffe made the dress I was visiting her for weeks ago, a green silk shantung gown and jacket with black cording, quite intricate. All it needed was hemming, but fussing with the dress seemed as good an excuse as any to get away. Tony had no idea what making dresses entailed or how long one should take.

Being the dressmaker to Mrs. Anthony Spadros brought Madame Biltcliffe a good deal of business. So our arrangement was most satisfactory.

As a "shop maid," I could go many places "Mrs. Spadros" could not. Besides, it wouldn't do to have someone peek behind the curtain where I supposedly posed for dress-fitting and find an empty room.

I changed into Madame Biltcliffe's deep mourning (with veil) and left through her back door, arriving at the train station at the stroke of eleven.

The train station was like most — a concrete slab floor with concrete pillars holding a wooden roof. Large clocks adorned the top of every fourth post, while benches of dark wood with black wrought-iron armrests completed the scene. The sky was gray and misty, the sun failing to shine upon the tracks.

Stephen arrived twenty minutes late, out of breath. I followed him around the corner and we sat at a bench.

"A man was … after me," Stephen panted, "had to lose him."

Fear gripped me, and I took a deep breath, trying to calm myself. "What did he look like?"

"Didn't get … a good look … at his face. He was dressed … like a gentleman … all in brown —"

Could it have been the same man?

"Didn't know he was following until … I went round several corners and he was … still back behind. Scared me, he did."

Why would he follow Stephen? Was he there on charity day?

I peered around me. Several men in brown hurried to their trains, fussed with their luggage, talked with their wives, or entertained their children.

Surely a gentleman would have been conspicuous down by the Spadros poorhouse? Wouldn't Mr. Durak, the editor, have noticed a man who didn't belong in their group?

I glanced at the clock; I had a short time before I must leave. I took out the half-dollar, and Stephen stared at it. "I'm looking for a boy of twelve that's gone missing."

Stephen grabbed the top of his hair with his left hand and stared at the ceiling while his breathing slowed. Then he dropped his arm and faced me. "I don't know of anyone gone missing. Did he run off?"

I shook my head. "I don't know. All I know is there was a stamp on the wall of a Red Dog —"

The young man stood. "Wasn't me, miss, I swear!"

"I'm not blaming you. Here, sit down."

He didn't move. A train came into the station and stopped, passengers coming and going around us.

"Come on, please. Sit. I'm not with the police. I just want to find the boy for his mother."

"Okay." Stephen sat. "What do you want me to do?"

"I know you're with the Red Dogs, okay? I don't care. Do they talk about the boy?"

He shook his head. "Nobody never tells me nothing. Just do this or do that. The ace, he gets word what to do and then he tells us, and we do it. He gives us sweets and a penny each time. The penny helps my Ma a lot. Usually all I do is put the card down, but I just started."

"What's the ace's name?"

Stephen shrugged. "They call him Clover. He's older, like eighteen, and he has a patch on his eye."

"Who tells Clover what to tell you?"

Stephen shrugged. "I dunno. I never seen him, or heard a name. That's all I know, miss, I swear."

The chime struck half past eleven.

I handed him the half-dollar, and he stuffed it in his pocket. "There's another one if you learn more about the boy. He's twelve but looks ten, with dark hair and eyes. Name's David Bryce."

Stephen nodded gravely. "It's bad to take little boys." His face twisted in disgust. "Not what we do at all. I'll help find him."

"Don't take chances. Meet back here in one week, same time. If someone follows you again, go to Madame Biltcliffe's dress shop on 42nd street. Leave a message for Eunice Ogier with Madame Biltcliffe's girl Tenni. She looks like me from the back."

"Okay, Miss Ogier." He smiled. "Thanks."

I sat a few more minutes then made my way back to Madame's shop, changed clothes, and went home. I got back with time to spare.

***

After luncheon, I went to my study to plan out my calling schedule. I couldn't pretend to go places indefinitely: sooner or later I had to actually call on someone, or people would talk. I opened my calendar and began a list. Who visited and when, who left a card when Tony was hurt, those who had left invitations in my pocket at the Ball …

A knock at the door. "Come in."

Inventor Maxim Call entered. I had never seen the man above ground since I came here, nor had he ever addressed me. I curtsied. "To what do I owe the honor of this visit?"

"Come here, girl, I have something to show you."

Maxim Call was a grizzled old man, wiry and brown, with piercing blue eyes. He was a Spadros cousin, a distant one, but cared little about Family intrigue. Or social niceties, it seemed.

I followed him into the hall, mystified. Pearson hurried to ring the bell which warned the staff that I came downstairs. The Inventor went through the parlor and down the stairs, then through the kitchens to a door in the far wall. The maids curtsied as we passed.

The Inventor descended a winding flight of metal steps around a copper pole which felt hot to the touch. At the bottom of the steps was a white hallway, lit with electric bulbs from above. We entered a round room large enough to encompass the entire Spadros Manor, including its front porch, gardens, and stables.

The high-ceilinged room was warm, smelling of sulfur and sweat. In the center lay an 8-foot tall cylindrical cage which reminded me of lace. A box almost as large sat inside. Pulleys and chains emerged from this, going through the ceiling into tunnels above. Many pipes lined the walls. Vents in the ceiling matched those I remembered seeing on the floors above us.

The decor was old. The quadrant-folk called it Art Deco-dent, a reminder of the Old Days with its greedy, wicked men. I recalled the damaged grandeur of Ma's cathedral, the smooth lines of steam automobiles. The mobs called the horseless carriage an offense against nature, and burned the factories that made them.

But this room teemed with mechanism: copper pipes, brass gears and pistons whirring. Liquids bubbled in glass tubes, and several Apprentices moved about the room.

"Quit your gawking and come here."

I blinked, embarrassed. I had indeed been gawking. I went to the Inventor's side.

"You know why we're down here?"

"You … tend the Magma Steam Generator?"

"Pish, the Generator is two miles below us. Yes, we tend it. But we do much more here." He gestured to include the room, and I turned to look. A man wearing dark goggles used a bright torch on metal, another tinkered underneath a huge weapon.

I turned back to him. "How may I help you?"

He grinned. "You're a quick one. I did want to see you about the Generator. Tell me what you know of it."

Very little, actually. "I know it's inside the city piling, here, under the house. It seems odd, though. Why did they put the piling here?"

He laughed. "You have it wrong way round." He gestured to an Apprentice, who brought two breathing masks, and we put them on. The mask felt quite confining, and the air close, but the sulfur smell vanished after a few breaths. "Want to see it?"

I nodded, excited at the opportunity. The list could wait.

Going to the box in the room's center, the Inventor opened a door in the side of it. It was an automatic hoisting device, large enough to carry people, lit by an electric light above. Once inside, I realized this was another cage, only with a finer mesh.

The Inventor pressed a button, and we began to move. It felt strange and marvelous to descend into the earth, to see the rock move around us. The temperature rose every minute, oven-like, and I began to sweat.

"Many pilings anchor the city." His voice came muffled from inside the mask, and it reminded me of the Masked Man. "The one here happened to have a scientific building over it to study the magma. The first Acevedo Spadros captured this building and refurbished it as his home."

I nodded. It did explain the odd shape.

"It's good for you: this building can withstand a bomb blast. Of course, there is a danger, having molten rock in your basement." The cage came to a halt, and he opened the door. A walkway through a large, dark, empty room with an orange glow to our left. Steam curled in the air. "This is as close as we can go."

We hurried to a door, which he opened, and we entered a small, well-lit room. After he closed the door behind us, he opened another one just ahead. This little room let us view the curling orange steam through thick windows.

The hole the steam exited seemed vast, many hundreds of feet across. The view was breathtaking.

The Inventor took off his mask. "The air's good here." Once I took off my mask, he pointed at the orange steam. "The magma is many hundreds of feet below us. We wear special suits to venture further. Water drops to our generator beneath us; the magma's heat turns the water to steam, which powers the mechanism."

"So what is the problem?"

"Magma steam is corrosive. The combination of intense heat and corroding effect is destroying the drill tubes and pilings."

I stared at him in shock. "What can be done?"

"There lies the problem. We don't know. Eventually, the whole thing will decay until the tubes collapse. The magma will cool and harden, and all will be well. Except that we will have insufficient steam for the Generators, and lose electricity and heat for the city."

He folded his arms. "Four hundred years our city thrived. The Coup did us in." His voice was wistful. "Thirty years of warfare, without tending the tubes … and many of those who knew how were lost." He shook his head. "I suppose we must all live in this world our parents made, playing the wretched cards they've dealt us. My life has been spent trying to learn how to slow the decay of our tubes, but I fear I will end in failure."

"Why are you telling me this?"

"If the Spadros drill tubes are failing, the rest of the city's are as well. We Inventors must be allowed to work together if we have any chance of learning how to stop the process."

I had a revelation: perhaps this explained the Clubb's invitation at the Grand Ball. Were they trying to cultivate us as partners? "I still don't understand. Why tell **me** this?"

"Roy Spadros will not listen. Your husband doesn't understand what this will do to our quadrant. You have seen cold and darkness and famine."

That I had.

A beautiful fat rat ran by, dark against the fallen pillars, but the snow made the stones too slippery to give chase. Shivering, I felt disappointed at missing the chance to catch it. My stomach rumbled at the thought of finally having meat for dinner.

"What can I do?"

"Talk with your husband. Beg him to listen. Tell him what it was like for you."

I could do the first. I wasn't sure the second would help much, and … I wasn't ready for the third. "I will try."

***

I wasn't sure how to broach the subject of the Magma Steam Generator. So I said nothing. Tony didn't speak for most of dinner. "I hear the Inventor brought you downstairs."

I felt glad he brought it up, but he almost sounded angry. What was wrong? "He did."

"Horrible place. I won't have you down there again."

His words stung. "I enjoyed it there." I loved watching the orange steam as it curled.

Tony gave a short, bitter laugh. "Did you now. Did he tell you the world was ending, too?"

I felt hurt by Tony's sarcasm, angry at his disrespect. It wasn't like him. For all his gruffness, Maxim Call had spoken to me like a person, someone to be respected.

He looked up. "What's wrong now?"

"You shouldn't take the words of an Inventor lightly."

Tony glanced at the servants. "Out."

They curtsied or bowed, and left.

"Why would you speak to me that way in front of the staff?"

"I might say the same to you. What I don't understand is why you would ignore such a threat to the city?"

Tony put down his fork. "What do you want me to do?"

"He wants to be allowed to speak with the other Inventors—"

"These Inventors always want to work together. This. Will. Not. Happen. I will not have other Families stealing our work. "

"He said he might learn how to fix it if —"

"We have the finest computers in the world. His Apprentice plans a machine to perform the computations of a hundred men. That is what Maxim Call should focus on, not —"

He missed the point entirely! "And how would it work without power?"

Tony brought both fists down so hard his plate and silverware bounced and his water goblet overturned. He sat for a moment, not breathing, his knuckles white, his face down-turned. "I can't ... take anything more, Jacqui! Please."

What happened? I had never seen him like this before. Filled with compassion, I ran to him, kneeling beside his chair. "I'm so sorry. Please forgive me." I rose, and Tony leaned on me as I smoothed his hair. "I don't mean to burden you."

He put his arm around my hips. "Why did you go down there without an escort?" Tony sounded wounded, afraid.

What did the servants **say**? "It never occurred to me. Maxim Call is old enough to be my grandfather."

Tony sighed, closing his eyes. "But the rest are not." Water from his glass soaked the tablecloth, began to drip to the floor. "If you must go down there again, you must go with your maid."

Amelia would never go down there; she hated small spaces.

He held my hand against his cheek, staring at the table. "I … I just want to keep you safe. I won't have your reputation smeared. I won't have…."

Won't have people call me a Pot rag whore.

Someone inside me wept behind bars of glass. "I understand."

Later, he lay beside me, fingers interlaced in mine, his shirt off, the covers back. His left side was still horribly bruised, and the look in his eyes seemed to match somehow.

***

Tony asked me to run the morning meeting without him. When I returned, Tony and his men were in his study, with orders not to be disturbed until tea.

So I asked Pearson to arrange kitchen inventory. When I saw the three new kitchen maids, I was filled with horror.

"Hey, you need be giving us more money." Poignee stood in front of me in my study, hands on her hips. Ottilie and Treysa stood beside her. "You wouldn't want us telling Mr. Spadros about your romp with Joseph Kerr, now, would you?

I laughed, but I felt uncomfortable. Pearson was right; I should never have hired Pot rags, even if they were my friends once. "A romance at sixteen, with a man I won't see again? I'll tell him myself."

The one girl who wasn't new said, "I'm sorry about your friends, mum." Her voice held compassion, and remorse.

"We were friends, until they came here." Then it all changed. Why couldn't they be content with the bounty they were given? Why did they have to grasp for more?

I wondered where their bodies lay. And how I would explain Ottilie's death to Joe's housekeeper Marja, Ottilie's mother.

***

The maids and I were in the middle of the work when Pearson appeared: Mr. Roy Spadros was here to see me.

"Me?"

"Yes, mum," Pearson said. "He was most insistent."

The old monster sounded in a foul mood already. I took off my apron, washed my hands, and hurried upstairs.

When Pearson opened the door to my study, Roy stood by my writing desk rifling through my mail.

My mind went to the letters I received from my sources, which weren't often so well coded as mine. Did I destroy them all?

"May I help you, Mr. Spadros?"

Roy stalked over and glared at Pearson. "Get out."

The door closed with a click that startled me.

In his thick hand Roy held a pamphlet, and he shook it at me. "What the hell do you think you're doing?"

I grasped my hands together to stop their trembling. "Mr. Spadros, if you would tell me what has upset you, I would know how to answer."

"This." He flung the pamphlet at me, which hit my arm and fell to the floor. He began pacing the room, leaving me to pick the offending paper from the floor.

Slaves To Debauchery And Fear No Longer!

Written by Thrace Pike

I felt stunned. "Pike?"

> Inside the vaunted Family Manors, those opulent dens of thieves, lie bags of rottenness that need lancing and soon.
>
> Men who feed off the suffering of others with their lust for gold while their people starve in the streets, placating their cries for bread with shows of charity to gain the approval of their peers — which the corrupted editors of this foul city's

> newspaper are eager to encourage for a fee, and the assurance that they will not be targeted for assassination — these men should be supported no longer.
>
> Women who flaunt their bodies to inflame righteous men, to distract them from their duties as the keepers of morality in this city, simply for their own perverse amusement…

I put the pamphlet down, shocked and embarrassed. "This man is mad."

Roy stalked over to me. "The whole thing stinks of your whorish ineptitude."

I moved around the chair towards him, appalled. "Surely you don't think I did anything improper! Our meeting lasted no more than ten minutes. My maid sat in the room the entire time."

Roy backhanded me across the face with such force that I fell against the chair. My dress ripped at the waist when I hit the chair's wing. "Shut up, bitch. Your maid told me everything. You're lucky I don't kill the both of you." Roy turned and began pacing as I rose, clutching my face. "That man is a Bridger. This is going to get them marching again for sure."

I leaned against the chair, shocked.

The Grand Order of Rational Respectability In Bridges: fanatical religious folk. So fanatical that the Grand Order ejected the Bridgers from their organization eighty years ago. Bridgers believed Party Time was the gateway to hell, and used violence to prevent its production or distribution.

Bridgers weren't afraid of the Families: killing a Bridger just made the rest angrier. They didn't take bribes, and wouldn't respond to blackmail. Once they began, they didn't stop. We could kill them all, but that gave the Feds just the excuse they needed to come after us.

"They haven't realized how much we profit from Party Time," Roy said, "that's the only thing keeping them from tearing this town apart."

I had set one of them against the Spadros Family.

Roy came from across the room and faced me. "All the things I taught you, and you go to the Pot whores for your ideas?"

My mother was a Pot whore. Who else would I look to but my mother? As a child, I watched my mother use the same technique many a time.

But I failed; my eyes stung with the shame of it. "What do you suggest I do?"

"Fix your face, get your maid settled. I'll think of something."

Amelia. I made a quick exit before he changed his mind, taking the pamphlet with me to cover the tear in my dress.

What had he done?

I searched the entire upstairs and main floor, except Tony's study, where the men still met, to no avail. I found Amelia downstairs in her rooms, her hair in disarray, crying in her husband Peter's arms.

Chairs and tables were overturned; broken pottery and blood lay on the stone floor. Blood stained the lap of her apron; her brown eyes were red from weeping.

When she saw me, she began to shake. "He made me tell, mum, I wasn't going to, I swear, but then," she sobbed, "he cut me ..." She began to wail, putting her face in Peter's chest, and he smoothed her hair.

Their three children, two girls and a boy, peered around the corner with frightened eyes. The oldest and youngest had eyes of brown; the boy's eyes were light blue.

Peter said, "If we could leave, we would, but Mr. Roy would follow us, no matter where we went. We thought it'd be better here, that Mr. Anthony could protect us. But ..." He shook his head and turned Amelia away, then looked over his shoulder, anger in his brown eyes. "She's your maid and under your care; you're supposed to shield her, not put her into harm."

"I'm sorry," I said, but it felt hollow. I turned to leave.

Peter said, "Don't come here uninvited again."

I took luncheon in my rooms. My hands shook. I tasted blood. My teeth hurt. By the time I ate and put on enough powder to hide the large darkening bruise on my cheek, Roy was gone.

He cut Amelia.

I felt caged; I had to go somewhere, anywhere, or else I feared I would go mad. I hid the torn dress and pamphlet in the back of my closets, changed clothes, and found a hat with a pale pink veil which matched well enough to be passable. I told Pearson I was going for a stroll and would be back by tea time.

The overcast sky matched the gray cobblestones. The remaining bits of dirty snow and horse dung left by the sweepers were melting to gray puddles, just as my life seemed to be melting around me.

When Roy's father Acevedo Spadros was murdered by his own men 20 years ago, Roy began a rampage which ended with most of his father's men and their families tortured to death, down to the smallest child.

Roy left one alive from each family: tongues torn out, maimed beyond recognition, and dumped in the Pot. As a child, I saw one of those men; Amelia and I had indeed fared well. Rumor had it Roy built a room in his new home where he tortured those who crossed him.

I resolved not to tell Tony of Roy's attack. It would only upset Tony, and what could he do in any case?

I needed Roy Spadros to deter Jack Diamond. But when he outlived his usefulness, I would kill Roy myself.

By the time I returned, a soft rain had begun. Pearson shook my coat out in the hallway before hanging it. "I'll have the girls dry it properly."

As if I hadn't cut the kitchen inventory short mid-morning. As if my maid wasn't tortured in her own quarters. What hold did Roy have on Pearson? "Thank you."

"I had your maids' rooms cleared to return their effects to their families. They had a number of items from your study, including some letters. I have placed them on your desk."

Why would they steal letters? "I'm sorry I put you through such trouble. You were right: I should never have brought them."

"No trouble at all. But it's my missus you might speak to."

Poor Jane. She probably never thought she'd have to train Pot rags when she became mistress of the kitchens.

"Mr. Anthony awaits you in the parlor."

The room smelled of hot biscuits and honey. Tony smiled when he saw me. "There you are! You must be chilled after your stroll." He paused. "Why do you still wear your hat?"

"Oh. I forgot." What else could I do? I took it off, placed it on the sofa, then turned towards him to sit.

"By the Shuffler! What happened to your face?"

"Does it look bad?"

Tony sat stunned for a moment. "I can see you've powdered it, but your cheek is swollen and red."

I smiled. "After your father came calling —"

"My father was here?"

"Oh, yes, did Pearson not tell you? I told your father you were in a meeting and he left straight away. But after I saw him to the door, and he got in his carriage and left, an insect lighted on my cheek and I was stung cruelly! It swelled, and for a while I felt ill, so I took luncheon in my room."

Tony took my hand. "I'm glad you feel better now." He paused. "How odd. A stinging insect in this cold weather."

"It is odd, almost unbelievable. It was a horrible sharp sting."

"I'll call for the doctor and have the eaves inspected for nests. I won't let this happen again."

I went to the looking-glass. "The swelling has subsided somewhat; I think the cold air did it some good."

Tony's reflection nodded, his face distorted by the bevel at the edge of the mirror.

A ridiculous story, but the best I could manage. Yet Tony seemed to want to believe me. He went to the door, told Pearson to call for the doctor, and resumed his seat.

"How was your meeting?"

He shrugged.

"Were the guards ever found?"

"No. I fear they're dead. They were good men, with families …. We'll find the villains who attacked us, sooner or later."

Tony stepped outside of the room while Dr. Salmon examined my face. "What shall I say happened?"

I told him of Roy's assault, and the story I had given Tony. He chuckled at that, and said he would corroborate my tale when he next spoke with my husband.

"Doctor, can anything be done for Mrs. Molly Spadros?"

Dr. Salmon's face became solemn, and he shook his head. "Only if she wishes to divorce him."

I shook my head, filled with melancholy. Roy wouldn't tolerate it; he would kill her before he allowed her to live free.

He patted my hand. "Don't fret yourself on her account. She is a much stronger woman than she appears."

The Note

I made the mistake of reading the rest of the pamphlet. It went on for many pages, Thrace Pike describing me so well he all but printed my name. I felt humiliated. I told Tony I felt unwell and spent much of two days in deep melancholy.

I brought trouble on my Family, offended two of my friends, and three others were dead. A scoundrel followed me, my husband was hurt, Air's brother was missing, my maid had been tortured. And I could do nothing about any of it.

A house maid drew my bath while Amelia was "indisposed." I was careful not to let the maid see my midsection. The corset's boning pushed into me when I fell against the chair after Roy's attack, leaving a purple mark.

It would be difficult to blame that on a wasp.

During this time, a copy of the *Golden Bridges* arrived, and I almost threw it in the fire. A whole day I feared those men's biting scorn. But I realized I needed to know what people said, so one day, after Tony left, I opened it.

As it turned out, there was very little there. The *Golden Bridges* had a column called, "Hog Scrapple," and halfway down the column, it read:

> GB: Item three: The pamphlet.
>
> IR: Methinks our young Bridger protests too much.
>
> GB: My thoughts exactly. Any ideas as to

> who he's talking about?
>
> IR: Well, Goldie, my boy, I'm always up for a bit of fun, but a night in a torture room isn't my idea of a good time.

Perhaps I had done better than I imagined.

I wondered how Mr. Pike learned about our bribes to his editor. The fact that Mr. Pike's editorial was published at all seemed surprising, when I considered it.

The third day, Amelia stormed in and threw open the drapes.

I squinted at the sudden light. "What's this?"

Amelia began beating the chair cushions with a vengeance. "I worked too hard and suffered too much to have you take some other maid."

I sat up. "I didn't know you were ready to return."

She faced me. "I will never be ready. But life would be no better somewhere else, and Mr. Roy hurt you as well." She began to cry. "I should've let him kill me."

"Oh, Amelia." I got up, put on my robe, and went to her, taking her into my arms. "Come, sit here with me." I brought her over and we sat on the side of the bed, although she sat gingerly. "I was wrong to do what I did. I put our whole Family in danger, and I put you at terrible risk." I took her hands. "But I must ask: what exactly did you tell him?"

"I told him about your instructions for the corset, and the events with Mr. Pike." Her eyes widened. "But nothing more, I swear! Only what was asked about that day."

I sat for a moment, wondering if I could believe her, then nodded. "What time is it?"

"Half past six."

I chuckled. She must have been brooding about this for hours already. "I must tell you about my dress ..."

I lay in bed waiting for my morning tea and listened to Amelia fuss and fume over the great rip in the waist of my dress.

Amelia would probably never talk to Roy again. But sooner or later, she would talk to someone, given the right incentive. I had to be more discreet.

When Amelia finished pinning my dress, she said, "Oh! I must fetch your tray!" She made a second trip for the newspaper, a package, and my mail.

Amelia reached in her pocket. "I think this is also yours." Amelia handed me a note addressed to her, but addressed *from* Madame Biltcliffe's shop.

Inside were two notes:

The first was in Madame Biltcliffe's hand:

> My dear lady, I found this in my post box and thought it might be for you. If not, I apologize. —MB

The second was scrawled on a wrinkled paper:

> To Amelia: I must speak with your mistress on a matter of much urgency.

I turned the paper over, but there was no indication as to who it might be from. "Perhaps it would be a good day for me to visit the shop. Kindly send a message to Madame Biltcliffe as to which time would be best for me to arrive."

I opened the *Bridges Daily* with dread, but there was still no news article about the pamphlet. I wondered if Roy had something to do with that.

In with my package, which contained a new copy of the *Golden Bridges*, there was a flyer:

To-Night!

Learn The Truth About Party Time!

Tent Meeting, 9:30 pm

Market Center Plaza

All Welcome

I sighed. So it had begun, just like in the stories. First the tent meetings, then the protests, then the marching, then the storming of buildings thought to house places where Party Time was made or sold, armed with axes.

Could the attacks on Tony's men be Bridger work?

Tony had never considered the Bridgers as suspects, but sent a message to his men when I raised the subject at breakfast. "It's nice to be back in the Business. I was beginning to feel caged."

I chuckled. "I can picture you pacing like one of those fabled East Indian tigers, growling." I curled my fingers like claws.

Tony smiled.

Pearson, standing by the sideboard, raised an eyebrow.

"I heard an interesting tale yesterday," Tony said. He had been most attentive to me during my melancholy, often telling me amusing tales. I think he felt unhappy with himself for his part in our argument the other day.

"Oh?"

"Mr. Julius Diamond was displeased with the performance of Master Jack Diamond at the Grand Ball, and threatened to cut off his funds if he causes further trouble."

I laughed.

"The truly amusing part: when my father heard about Master Jack's outburst, he told Mr. Julius Diamond at the Grand Ball that a further insult to any member of our family — or yours — from a member of the Diamond Family would be taken as a personal attack on him."

Roy threatened Julius? "Oh, to be present at **that** meeting …!"

Tony chuckled, wincing at the end, and the maid giggled. Even Pearson had trouble keeping himself from a small smile, which felt most gratifying.

After breakfast and the morning meeting (which Tony did attend), I finished my kitchen inventory with the maids and sat with Amelia in the parlor as she mended my torn dress. I pretended to do needlework, but in truth, I pondered the situation at hand.

The letter was likely from Mrs. Eleanora Bryce. I wondered what calamity had struck for Eleanora to contact me in such a disjointed manner.

Could this man who followed me and Stephen have frightened her? I should have warned Eleanora when the man in brown began following me. I didn't think she was in much danger with her son there; Herbert was only sixteen, but tall as a grown man. Surely his presence would deter an attack. Wouldn't it?

***

Clouds covered the sky, and the wind blew chill. When I arrived at Madame Biltcliffe's dress shop, Mrs. Bryce stood outside wearing mourning garb.

Mrs. Bryce didn't acknowledge me until I changed into Tenni's uniform and met her in the back alley. Then she clutched my hand and began to weep. "I'm so grateful you came. I didn't know who else to call." She moved away and I hurried to keep up. Tenni wore a half size shoe smaller than I did; my feet soon began to hurt at the rapid pace.

We went through an unfamiliar maze of half-lit alleyways, stopping in front of the Spadros quadrant morgue. The building, a sad shade of gray, stood apart, a few mourners holding each other in the street outside.

Since I played Mrs. Bryce's maid, I opened the door for her and curtsied as she went in. The room was the same gray, and the attendants wore bone white. The smell of death lay in the air.

Mrs. Bryce would have told me if David were dead, so I felt puzzled. Not knowing what happened or who died, I waited as she gave her name and information. In a few moments we stood in another room, cold and gray, at the side of a body.

The attendant lifted the sheet: Herbert Bryce lay on the slab.

I felt astonished. Not three weeks ago, the young man sat in his mother's shop, very much alive.

Mrs. Bryce burst into tears.

I glanced at the attendant, who left. "What happened?"

"After your visit," she sobbed, "he wondered if he raised money, you would change your mind and find David. He went to our neighbors, but no one would help us. After we saw the story of you feeding the poor in the paper, he said it seemed you had no time for us. The next morning he was gone. The constable contacted me yesterday: they found him in the Diamond slums, dead. Strangled." She stared at his unmoving face, tears streaming down her cheeks.

Diamond. What was he doing **there**?

Then I saw the blue finger-marks on the young man's neck.

More people lingered in the intersection than seemed normal for that time of night. A large crowd waited in the alleyways, doorways, and driveways, behind rusted clockwork machinery and broken-out windows, but quiet, hoping to see something happen.

Roy Spadros and Peedro Sluff stood in that intersection, separated by several yards, facing each other.

Peedro was a foul-smelling drunken addict, with a temper to match. The wisps of black hair on his balding head were as thin as the rags on his filthy thin body. His glazed eyes told me he had taken a lot of Party Time already.

Roy Spadros said, "I trust you have what we agreed on."

"Yeah, I do," Peedro Sluff said, in his whiny voice.

"And where is she?"

"She'll be here. If not, I can show you where she lives." If anything, though, Peedro's body tensed even more, as if preparing to act, but afraid to try. He took a deep breath, and his right hand twitched.

A brown-haired man dashed towards us from the right, several blocks away. Another money-man, but not so old as Roy Spadros, maybe eighteen or so. I liked him at once. A block away, he shouted urgently, but I couldn't make out the words.

Peedro Sluff froze uncertainly as the younger man raced towards them. Then Peedro whipped out a revolver from behind his belt and fired, the motion smoother than I could ever have imagined. People shrieked, scurrying behind fallen beams and broken hulks of steam automobiles.

Something drew me from the alley like a magnet. I should have been frightened, but at the time it felt like a dream. I had seen men shot before. This made no sense; the younger man shouted a warning, not a threat.

Where did Peedro Sluff get a gun? Where did he learn to shoot?

Roy's men dashed up from the street behind him, guns out, but Roy waved them off.

Peedro Sluff dropped his arm to his side and spoke to Roy Spadros, his breath steaming. "He meant to kill you."

It didn't seem that way at all. The man tried to warn someone, yet got shot for it. It seemed so unfair.

Roy Spadros gave a slight smile, as if he found the whole thing funny. "Then you have my gratitude."

What a world we lived in. Young men murdered attempting to save a life, their valor used to further a villain's scheme! Why did Herbert, or that friend of Jack Diamond's ... why did they have to die? A poor decision, a few minutes haste, a wrong turn down a street, and life disappeared.

My eyes fell on a card lying on the table near Herbert's slab, the sort used for business. But instead of a name and location, it had a stamp of a dog on it, all in red, with a note next to it: "Found on the body."

Would taking the case have prevented this?

I made the right choice not to take this case. I helped people pay their rent and find their cats. I had no experience in solving a kidnapping. It was a police matter.

Why would Herbert leave his mother alone? How — and why — did he go to Diamond?

Finding Herbert in the Diamond quadrant did explain why Stephen hadn't heard of a boy being held. Even if his "ace" was as tight-lipped as Stephen said, there should have been some rumor or indication of a young boy held against his will in Spadros.

Across the river, though, anything might be happening and no one in Spadros would know. Foot traffic wasn't allowed over the bridges. The river was too cold and fast this time of year to swim. Few uppers had reason to cross into another Family's territory unless invited. To a lower like Stephen or his ace, Diamond quadrant might as well be another city.

"I'm sorry about Herbert. He seemed like a good boy."

"He just wanted to find his brother. Now they're both gone."

I shook my head. "I'm sure the police will find David."

Her eyes never left her son's body, but her face screamed that she had lost all hope.

The Surprise

When I returned home, Tony, his mother Molly, and his sister Katherine played croquet in the garden. His father Roy sat under a lawn canopy smoking a cigar.

Why was Roy here? What did he tell Tony?

A maid stood behind Roy, waiting for orders. Roy's men watched our surroundings; I imagined they scanned for marksmen. Not that I expected any to appear on the Spadros Manor grounds. But when you had as many enemies as Roy, paranoia became prudent.

Katherine Spadros was almost thirteen and in that gangling awkward age of intensity and drama. She dropped her mallet and charged, auburn hair flying, to envelop me in a crushing embrace. "Oh, Jacqui, I'm so happy to see you!"

"I'm happy to see you as well." When she let go, I took a breath. "Who's winning?"

"Mama, but I'm second."

I lowered my voice. "You should let your brother win, since he's not feeling well."

Tony winced. "I heard that. I am neither incapacitated nor infirm."

"Would you like to play?" Molly said.

"She can't come in the middle!" Katherine said. "It's not fair!"

I chuckled. "I'm content to watch." I took a chair across from Roy, who ignored me, as I did him.

I was not happy to see Roy. If he had spoken to me right then I might have stabbed him with my boot-knife.

I asked the maid for brandy, sipping it, trying to forget the throbbing of my face and abdomen. I lit a cigarette and took a drag. When he glanced my way, I blew smoke in his direction, daring him to say anything. He disappointed me. I would have liked an excuse to put my knife in his cold dead eye.

Tony watched me without expression. I smiled at him.

As we walked back to the Manor later (Katherine did win after all), Roy spent a moment whispering with one of his men, then walked along grinning.

"You look pleased." I hoped the villain choked to death on whatever torment he planned.

Roy chuckled. "You just read the papers tomorrow, Missy ... I'm planning a surprise."

I recalled the third time I was taken to Spadros Manor, a few months after my father shot Jack's friend. After bathing, scrubbing, stuffing me into a dress, and this time, a "training corset," which I detested, the maids led me to Roy's study.

Roy said, "I'm planning a surprise," which at the time meant sending Tony on an errand with his mother and taking me in his carriage on a tour of his holdings.

"How do you like Anthony?"

I shrugged. At twelve, I rarely thought about boys one way or the other.

"When you are grown, you and he will marry. Then you will own all this."

Oh, I thought at the time, it would be good to own all this. I had no idea what being married meant. No one who lived in the Pot had money to get married.

Roy seemed in a particularly introspective mood that day. "I fear Anthony doesn't have it in him to do what it takes to run this Family. But I think you do." He turned to me. "I'll teach you how to do what I do. If my son needs help, will you help him?"

"Yes, sir." After many beatings, I learned to say this in reply to anything Roy Spadros asked.

After that, I received two sets of lessons when I went to the Manor, which increased to two or three times a month. One set of lessons took place with Molly and Pearson: reading, writing, painting, needlework, managing a household, doing accounts.

The other set of lessons was with Roy. Roy taught me to shoot, to kill without a gun, the structure and purposes of the Family Business, strategy, tactics.

Many times, Tony joined us for the lessons, but not always: Tony had never seen me beaten after the first time, which sent him into hysterics. As far as I know, he had no idea I knew anything about violence. I don't know what he thought, but Tony never showed any jealousy about his parents teaching me.

As time went on, I began to feel in two worlds. I returned to the Pot clean and fed, with fine clothes, new knowledge, and new connections. In Spadros Manor, I felt dirty, unwanted, and misunderstood. "Are you going to kill the man?"

Roy laughed. "Don't even try, Jacq — you're out of your depth. Just watch and learn."

I seethed at his cold, mocking tone.

Pearson met us at the back door and addressed Tony. "Will your family be staying for dinner, sir?"

Before Tony could answer, Roy said, "No. I have things to do."

Thank the Floorman. Dinner with Roy was torture in itself.

Once they left, Tony sighed. "I'm glad they didn't stay. I exerted myself too much, and Katie hugs much too vigorously." He looked pale. "Would you tell Pearson we'll be dining in our rooms tonight?"

I took Tony's arm. "Only my corset saved me a fractured rib from Katherine's pincer-like embrace."

"Pincer-like." Tony began to laugh, then winced. "Don't make me laugh," he said, but a laugh burst from him, "it hurts."

"Perhaps you need a corset."

"Ow." Tony laughed again. "Stop."

"Poor dear." I put on a sober demeanor, "I will be completely grave henceforth."

He began laughing. "You are utterly wicked." He went from laughing to complaining and back again all the way up the stair.

I accompanied Tony to his room and got him seated with a book, then returned to tell Pearson of the changes. "And I will need to speak with Amelia after dinner."

When I returned to our rooms, Tony stood by his dresser, putting the opium bottle away.

I felt chagrined. "I had no idea you were in such pain."

"I only took a bit more." He returned to his seat. "I wanted to sit with you up here, instead of going through such fuss as to dress for dinner. We have no one to entertain or impress tonight."

"I'm glad!" Since he was left-handed, I sat to his right.

Honor came in with the tray, set out our dinner, uncovered our plates, and poured our wine. "If it please you, sir, Michaels will be available for the next hour should you need anything. I'll be going to my mother's for her birthday." Our night footman would be on duty after that.

"Send her our blessings," Tony said.

"Thank you, sir." Honor bowed and left.

After the door closed, Tony took a drink of his wine as I began to eat, then picked at his food. I was halfway through my meal when he said, "You dislike my father."

"Dislike is not the word I would use."

Tony said nothing.

Rage boiled up. "He is your father, not mine. Nor my husband, nor my kin. Am I required to love him? He stole me from my home …" I stopped, coming too close to revealing his attack on me.

"You hate him." Tony put his fork down. "I hated him once … long ago.…" He sighed. "Hate ties you to the one you hate as tightly as love. Far better, if you can't love, to do neither."

His words cut me to my heart. I kissed his hand, grieved at the thought of Tony having Roy for a father.

Tony turned my face to his. "Don't cry." Pain lay in his voice. "Not for me." He kissed my forehead and smoothed my hair. "I'm well, and we're safe here. Please. Be happy."

I blinked my tears away and tried to smile.

"Forget my father. Let's enjoy our dinner."

For a few moments, I forgot everything but the peace of companionship, holding hands with Tony while we ate.

But then I remembered my evening was far from over.

Should I go to the tent meeting?

I needed to. In truth, it shocked me that Mr. Pike published the pamphlet. He must've done it before leaving the newspaper, unless the Bridgers owned a printing press themselves.

The publication was madness, especially for a man with a wife and child depending on his salary. What good did Mr. Pike think publishing the pamphlet would do, other than fixing the eyes of the four Families upon him?

Knowing what little I did of Mr. Pike, he probably felt publishing his pamphlet was the right thing to do, no matter what the cost to himself or his family. He was more than likely to end up dead.

Thrace Pike was too much the crusader, but I wished no harm on him. If Roy planned some hurt to come to the man because of me, I needed to warn him. If not, I had to learn his plans, if only to protect myself.

When dinner was cleared away, I poured Tony some red wine from the sideboard, putting a drop of opium in his cup. Since his back was to me, he never noticed.

I handed him his glass. "To your health." He clinked glasses with mine, smiling, then drank. I leaned over and kissed him. He set the empty cup down and took me into his lap, whereupon we made pleasant use of the time.

Twenty minutes later, he snored in his chair.

I had never heard him snore before. At the time, I thought he must be very tired from his difficult day.

About then, Amelia arrived, and we got Tony into bed.

"I need to go out tonight."

Amelia gave me a questioning glance but said nothing.

I replaced my wedding ring with a plain band from a poorhouse sale. Several carats of jewels seemed too much for one finger, but Tony insisted I have the best. Amelia helped me out of my corset, and I changed into an outfit which buttoned up the front. I only used this outfit when on cases, so no one would recognize me.

This dress was high necked, of plain cloth and dark brown. I wore a dark brown hat with a thick veil. With the veil, even I couldn't tell who I was when I looked in the mirror. I used a scarf to cover my hair, and added various bits of padding to change my shape from time to time.

Leaving off my corset made me appear heavier, shorter, older. It also meant Amelia didn't have to wait there to help me undress when I returned. I had a pair of shoes that I only used on cases, so even my shoe print wouldn't give away my identity.

"If someone asks, you left me sitting with Mr. Spadros, and he left orders not to be disturbed."

"Yes, mum." Amelia peeked into the hall. "No one out there."

I turned off the lamps, went into the hall and closed the door.

We went through the upstairs storage room, then down the stair by the preparation room. Amelia peered out, then gestured to me. I slipped through the door and into the stables. Dodging the stable boys, I made it to the front of the house.

The streets were wet and deserted. Soon I found a public taxi-carriage and was on my way to Market Center Plaza.

***

A large crowd milled about on the island, surrounding men and women hawking their wares. Butchers stood in their booths, cutting meat to sell the next day. Children sold sweets and hot chestnuts from trays round their necks. Cigar smoke and perfume wafted through the air.

A large white canvas tent stood on the damp grass, the base of the canvas open to the air at about mid-thigh level. Rows of wooden folding chairs faced a dark wooden stage. There some already sat, some stood, but most milled about. A tired baby cried, and his mother comforted him. Thrace Pike and his compatriots spoke together near the front of the stage.

A bell sounded and people began filling the seats. I took a seat near the back at the end of a row, clutching my dark brown handbag like any other lower-class widow.

Air and I raced down the grimy, trash-strewn alleyways until we got a couple of blocks away from the cops, then leaned against a wall, laughing. We escaped them again.

Snow glittered on the ruins of old Bridges: the bombed-out 'scrapers and mansions, the fallen statues, the broken fountains.

Air surveyed the scene, his face full of wonder. "'Tis near pretty, here at night."

I nodded. It would have been prettier if the quadrant-folk hadn't destroyed it all. "Why they bomb it?"

"Ma said people got mad," Air said. "Rich men ate, they couldn't."

I shook my head. People were so stupid. "What's different between then and now?"

Two to three hundred lower-class people almost filled the tent. A stout young woman wearing a gray dress which made her look like a man in a skirt went to the stage and began speaking about Mr. Pike.

Mr. Pike's father and grandfather were in law, but after his father died, he became a reporter. The woman left out the part where he was no longer employed.

Mr. Pike appeared, to a smattering of applause. "Ladies and gentlemen, thank you for coming out tonight to hear me speak. I hope to enlighten and inform you of the facts about the illegal drug called Party Time …"

A man up front spoke, and laughter flowed around him.

"I understand," Mr. Pike continued, a bit louder, "that this drug has been used in Bridges for many generations and in the past was a part of normal social life. However, with the harmful effects that can occur —"

A man a few rows down from me yelled, "— there ain't no harm in it! You crazy do-gooders do more harm!"

"… seizures, hallucinations, even death from overdose …"

An old woman across the room threw her hands in the air. "Garn! You'd have to drink a whole bottle to have all that happen!" Laughter broke out in several places in the tent.

"… myself and others can't stand by and watch our town brought to destruction by those who lord over us with one hand and drag us down with the other."

Voices began speaking out from all over:

"Now, wait just a minute —" a man said.

"You took away our socializing, now you're going to take our Families too?" another man asked.

"What will we eat when they're gone?" A woman said. "You gonna give us jobs?"

"My kids are alive now because we have work from the Clubbs," another man said.

Several people nodded.

"You're too young to remember when this city was tore apart by the gangs," an old man said. "The Families beat them back and brought the city peace."

Several cries of "Yeah!" came forth from the crowd.

A middle-aged man rose. "I know who you are. You're Bridgers! You and your axes destroyed my Grampa's saloon when I was a boy, about near killed him. I'll listen to no more of this!" He spat and walked out, to applause. I recognized him; it was the man Roy whispered to at the house this afternoon.

So that was why Roy felt so pleased with himself.

Mr. Pike said, "Please … please just sit and listen to what I have to say …"

But the roar of the crowd made him impossible to hear. An apple knocked his hat off, and Mr. Pike retreated.

Most people walked out. Some went up front to talk with him (or at him). The woman in the gray dress handed out pamphlets … which looked suspiciously like the one Roy threw at me.

I watched the scene for some time. If enough people left, would Mr. Pike speak to the crowd which remained?

The tent creaked in the wind.

More people went to the stage than I expected, which was somewhat concerning. Roy was right: I was beyond my understanding in this matter. Killing Mr. Pike, while it would have been easier, would have not only proved his point, but made him a martyr to his cause.

A fight broke out near the stage and a whistle sounded in the distance. I moved to the side of the tent, not wanting to spend the evening questioned by the police. A constable entered the tent and I ducked underneath the canopy. Whistles and scuffling continued behind me as I stepped around the tent posts.

Stars shone that winter's night. My breath left in clouds matching those passing high above the city near the full moon. The landscape resembled a photograph in grays and blacks: dark, yet lovely. The lights of Clubb quadrant twinkled in the distance across the river. A zeppelin passed by, farther still, and I watched its journey. Then I walked further from the tent to lean against an unlit lamp post, taking a cigarette from my handbag.

A voice, from behind. "Light that for you?"

It was Mr. Pike, of all people. I let him light my cigarette, trying my best not to laugh.

I pitched my voice lower; I was a middle-aged widow. "Thank you, sir."

"Don't pretend." Something in his eyes and voice made me think rather than seeing me, veiled and high-necked, he saw me as I looked at our previous meeting. "When you went under the canopy rather than through the tent door as any usual woman would, I recognized you."

I stared at him, afraid. "Why are you here?" Had he approached to unmask me? To humiliate me further?

"I could ask the same. Did you want to see how well your little trick worked?"

I felt relieved. "Mr. Pike, I knew nothing of the 'trick,' as you call it; I wanted to hear what you had to say. You may not believe it, but I agree with many of your points." I took a drag of my cigarette through my veil and blew smoke at the uncaring stars. "Unfortunately, we're not always free to do as we wish."

Thrace Pike's face, half-lit by the moon, seemed both resolute and sad. "We're always free to do what we wish. Either way, there are consequences we can't escape."

I could say nothing to that.

The wind gusted, and my veil blew up, exposing my face. I pulled it down again, securing it better this time.

"You're hurt," he said, raising his hand.

I shrank from his touch. "You were free to publish your pamphlet, as you wished. Either way, there were consequences I couldn't escape."

Mr. Pike stood still for a long moment, staring past me, his jaw tight. Then the set of his face changed: he had come to some definite decision. He took hold of my upper arms, which shocked and surprised me so much I did nothing.

"I will not surrender. If your husband, or your father-in-law, or whoever sent that mob wants war, then war I will give them."

I stared at him, stunned. "By yourself?"

"If that's what it takes. I will see this city restored to one where law, not crime families, rule. Where people can move about their city safely, not limited by checkpoints and retribution. Where everyone has an equal say and a man can advance in life with honesty, not crawl in servitude to some trumped-up self-appointed monarchy."

Could he really mean this? I saw no subterfuge in the man's eyes. He could publicly humiliate me one day and lay hands on me another, speaking lofty words as he did so, without any guile.

He gazed into my eyes for a long moment, and he seemed then to realize where he stood and what he did. He let go.

I turned towards the river, relieved. "Noble, even admirable." The man seemed determined to get himself killed. "But the Families will never allow changes in the way matters stand." I faced him. "You don't realize how dangerous these men are. If you oppose them, they will destroy you."

"We shall see." Mr. Pike tipped his hat. "Good night, madam," he said, and walked away.

***

I made my way home, slipped in the back door by the breakfast room, and up the winding back stairs. I cracked open the door at the top of the stair. To my relief, our night footman wasn't there. A glow came from around the corner, and I realized the man patrolled the hallway.

I crept into the darkened hall, opened Tony's door, and went in. Tony snored in his bed, slowly and loudly, with slight hitches in his breathing, as if something was stuck in his throat. It frightened me: he had never sounded like this before.

I hurried into my closets, taking off my dress, hat, and shoes in the darkness, listening as Tony snored. I found myself holding my breath, waiting ... waiting ... waiting ...

He wasn't breathing.

I ran to the bed in my drawers and chemise, stockings still on. "Tony! Wake up!" I shook him, but he didn't breathe. "Help!" I grabbed the bell-cord and pulled it.

The night footman rushed in. "What's wrong?"

"He's not breathing!"

He stood, stunned, then turned to the maids behind him. "Call the doctor!" Feet ran down the hall as I continued to shake Tony's shoulder. "Lift him up," the footman said, so I did so.

"Tony! Tony!" His head sagged forward, his lips dark and bluish. I shook him. "Wake up!"

Maids rushed into the room, screaming and crying. "Get out of here," the footman said. "Give him air."

Give him air? I leaned over, took a breath, and put my mouth on his, blowing as hard as I could. His chest rose sharply.

"Uhh." Tony grimaced. "Ohh."

My vision blurred. "Oh, please, Tony, wake up."

His head slumped forward again, and the footman helped me sit him up better. "Do that again, breathe to him," the footman said, so I did so, harder.

"Aaaah!" Tony's chest rose. "Ow!" His eyes were closed, and his head lolled, but he took a breath on his own.

I never felt so grateful to see someone breathe before.

We held him upright for some time, and I breathed into him when he needed it. "Oh, Tony, please wake up." I didn't know how much longer I could do this, and it frightened me.

Shoes came stomping up the stairs, along the hall, as the footman and I held Tony up straighter. He hadn't breathed again, so I blew in his mouth as hard as I could.

At the same time, I heard the door open behind me. "What are you doing?" Dr. Salmon said.

"He's not breathing, Mrs. Spadros is breathing to him. It seems to help," the footman said.

"Uhh, ah," Tony said.

"He looks better," I said. His lips were pinker.

"Dealer preserve us," Dr. Salmon said, shocked. "How much opium did he take?"

Did I do this? I shrugged, mouth open, shaking my head, feeling close to tears.

The footman said. "Do that breathing again."

I breathed in until my chest felt ready to burst, grabbed Tony's face, and blew with all my might.

"Aaaah! Stop!" Tony yelled, and opened his eyes: his pupils were tiny, his eyes full of tears. Their unnatural form terrified me.

"You weren't breathing, sir," Dr. Salmon said. I glanced at the doctor; his shirt tails were loose around him, his jacket and vest open, his hair wild, as if he galloped straight here without a hat.

Tony focused on him. "What?" Then his head slumped to the left as his eyes closed.

"Did he have any alcohol?" Dr. Salmon appeared more concerned than I had ever seen him.

I nodded. "Two glasses of wine that I saw."

The doctor shook his head. "We need to get him up walking."

By this time, Pearson had entered the room, dressed, but barefoot, with his hair uncombed. So the footman and Pearson got Tony up, walking him around the room as he snored.

Pearson glanced at me. "Where is Amelia?"

Now I knew how he kept order. She had been crying in the hall but dashed in.

"Tend to your mistress at once," Pearson said.

Amelia stared at me blankly, then grabbed my robe and covered me with it. It was then I realized my state of undress.

I sat on the side of the bed, my face in my hands. If I had returned five minutes later, Tony would be dead.

"How long ago did he take the opium?" Dr. Salmon said.

I stared up at him. "Right before dinner." What time was it now? "An hour and a half, maybe two?"

"Dinner was at eight, mum," Pearson said, as he lugged Tony along, who still snored. "It's well past ten."

Dr. Salmon shook his head. "Too long ago for an emetic." He went to his bag and took out a device, listening to Tony's chest for several seconds, then let out a sigh of relief. "His heart is sound. It just needs to work through him." He moved some of the vials around in his bag, then came up with a tiny bottle containing yellow powder.

I watched as the doctor moved to Tony's tea table and took out a small set of brass scales. He measured a tiny amount of the yellow powder. He peered at me over his shoulder. "Was his appetite good? What did he eat?"

I stared at Dr. Salmon, not remembering what we ate.

"We had pork roast," Pearson said. "With winter peas and fatback."

Dr. Salmon nodded. "The heavy meal saved him."

The Threat

Dr. Salmon dosed Tony with a purgative, yet it was many hours before he felt safe to leave us.

I couldn't sleep. I might have killed Tony, and it haunted me.

The doctor stayed in a guest room, returning every few hours to listen to Tony's heart. Tony woke with a terrible headache, dreadfully ill, and little memory of the night before.

"You must never drink alcohol when you take opium," Dr. Salmon said. "I told you this before. And no extra doses. Do you hear me? If your wife hadn't been awake, you'd be dead now."

We sat in Tony's room. Tony, bent over his tea table, leaned on one elbow. He nodded, his face pale and sweaty. But his breathing was normal, as were his eyes. I never wanted to see them look that way again.

Dr. Salmon got up and paced around the room, stretching his arms over his head. I held a damp washcloth, wiping Tony's brow.

A soft knock came at the door, and Dr. Salmon opened it. Michaels came in with a tea tray, and Tony gestured for him to put it on the table.

Dr. Salmon put his hand on Tony's shoulder. "The liquids will help, sir. As much as you can drink for the next day or two." He glanced at Michaels. "Get him a pitcher of water."

"Yes, sir." Michaels poured a cup of tea for each of us then left, while Dr. Salmon went out into the hallway.

Tony leaned back and sighed. "The last thing I remember is holding your hand at dinner." He gave me a weak smile. "I'm sorry I frightened you."

I brushed his hair back from his face. "I'm just glad you're better," I sobbed.

"Ah, now," he took my hand and kissed it, "all will be well." He took his cup of tea with his other hand and drank it down. "See? I'm obeying orders. Being ill is thirsty work." He smiled. "Let's see the mail."

I wiped my face, then took up the stack of Tony's mail and sorted through them. "Here's one from your father."

Tony opened the letter and read through it, scratching his arm from time to time.

"Hmm. Your wayward reporter, what was his name … Peak?"

"Thrace Pike."

"Oh, yes, Pike … well, Mr. Pike has been outed as a Bridger."

"Dreadful!" Tony expected some reaction, so I gave it. I hoped the mob chased Mr. Pike home.

"We won't be having trouble from him for a while."

"Why is that?" I felt grateful that Tony said "a while." Rivers are such a final place to end up.

"This morning, Mr. Pike asked to be taken on as a law apprentice at his grandfather's firm and was accepted."

"Really?" Mr. Pike was more resourceful than I thought. But if his grandfather wished to apprentice him, why did Mr. Pike become a reporter in the first place?

Tony began to sweat and looked pained; his stomach was hurting him again. Michaels and I helped him to his feet. "In any case, learning law should keep him out of our hair for a while."

I wasn't so sure that this was a hopeful development. Mr. Pike the reporter had to submit his work to an editor, who could quash the story. Mr. Pike the lawyer could become a major threat, and lawyers tended to be more difficult to get rid of.

***

Stephen never arrived at our next meeting. Although I strolled along the train station bag area for over an hour without seeing anything unusual, I had the feeling I was being watched. So I did what I always did when followed: I went to a bar.

The Pocket Pair, while disreputable, had an excellent staff, very good food and drink, and an owner more than willing to help a lady in distress, especially if the lady happened to be me.

Vígharður "Vig" Vikenti was a burly fellow, a bouncer until Roy's men shot the original owner for being late on his protection money. Vig took over the bar, changed its name, got some "working girls" in the back rooms, and became an upright, paying member of Spadros society.

Even twenty years later, a look of displeasure from Vig sent the toughest men backing off in fear. So while it appeared to be the sort of place to avoid, I enjoyed visiting.

Vig liked me, and not in a fatherly way. But he'd never been crass about it. He kept several girls in my size working the back rooms who were happy to trade dresses for a day or two and discreet enough not to blab.

I was sixteen and on my first case when Vig saved me from violation and assault, beating the man senseless with his bare fists. Since then, we had been "buddy friends," and he always knew who I was no matter what I wore.

So when I came in the door, he yelled from behind the bar, "My buddy friend! Come let me give you a drink!" The man playing ragtime on the piano didn't miss a beat. Then I realized our night footman sat playing!

I felt astonished. But I couldn't stare at the man or he would surely wonder why, or look my way and perhaps recognize me. So I ignored the people eyeing me curiously — I was veiled and wearing mourning, after all — and walked through the smoke-filled oak-paneled room to the bar.

"You're in trouble again," Vig said, in a tone at least 100 deci-Bels decreased in volume. I nodded.

He gestured to another man to take over the bar, then escorted me to a back room and closed the door. The delicious smells of his mother's cooking wafted through the air. "Tell me what troubles you."

I raised my veil. "I think someone is following me."

He walked out, closed the door behind him, and came back several minutes later. "Man in brown across the street, standing with a smoke. Keeps watching the front. Looks like a cop. I'll take care of it." He examined me. "I got a new gypsy gal, just your size. She's got some nice dresses. I'll send her in."

"Thank you, Vig." I stood on tiptoe to kiss his cheek. "One day we'll sit and drink together, I promise."

"You always promise." He winked. "You go home to your Manor. Vig will keep you safe."

He left, and I mused about good friends and promises. A woman came in, a bit older, but with brown hair and a similar form, carrying a basket. Perhaps a bit shorter and heavier, but I could slouch. I switched dresses with her without learning her name. She grinned when she saw my boot-knife on the left and my revolver in its calf holster on my right, and smiled in earnest when I gave her the half-dollar.

"Your face." She handed me a small looking-glass. "Use rouge or lip paint on it, then powder it, and it will look better." She patted the lip paint over the marks of Roy's hand, which were turning green, then applied another coat of powder.

It did look better.

"I'll have your dress sent in a few days. Thank you."

She nodded. "You were never here."

I went out the back as a fight broke out near the front, spilling into the street. I chuckled as I strolled back to Madame Biltcliffe's.

She in turn laughed when I entered her back door. "Today you're a gypsy?"

"Vig will send your dress."

"Ah. Then you had trouble. You are safe?"

I smiled. "Yes, I am safe. And grateful for your concern."

But I rushed home, fearful.

Neither Madame nor Tenni spoke of a message from Stephen, and someone followed me to Vig's bar. I didn't want to have anything to do with the police, nor to have the young man fall into their hands. I didn't relax until I stepped inside my home and Pearson closed the door.

"Mum," Pearson said, "a constable is here to see you."

***

Constable Paix Hanger: a tired-looking man in a rumpled uniform, navy blue with brass buttons. He stood in my parlor as if he'd rather be anywhere but Spadros Manor. He seemed familiar.

I neither removed my hat nor lifted my veil. I had decided to wear a veil until my face healed, to keep unwanted questions at bay. "May I help you?"

"Yes, mum." He stood with his hands behind his back, feet apart. "I am investigating a case of a missing child, and would like to ask some questions."

I realized he was the constable at the tent meeting, who I went under the canopy to avoid. Part of me felt glad someone investigated David's disappearance, yet another part felt afraid. Why was he here to see me? Did he recognize me that night?

"I am at a loss." I sat, and gestured for him to sit. "Anything I can do to help, I am glad to."

The constable perched on the edge of the sofa. He smelled like the fresh winter breeze. "Are you familiar with a woman by the name of Eunice Ogier?"

"Should I be?"

The man's face never changed; in that, he reminded me of Tony. "I have in custody a boy who says this woman Eunice Ogier asked him about the missing boy by name. He also says this woman was there at the same time … 'a rich woman,' he says … gave food to the poor. The only group there on the day he mentioned was yours.

"He stated she gave him food as well. I thought she might have been one of your ladies. We would like to learn what she knows of the matter."

I shook my head. "I know of no living woman by that name. I'm sorry." I paused, then said, "Could she be a relative?"

The constable shook his head. "The boy's mother is his only living family." He rose. "I'm sorry to have bothered you, mum."

I rose as well. "I wish you the best of success."

"Thank you, mum."

After he left, I removed my hat, went to my study, and sat at my desk. Why send someone here? To see how I would react? Was it a threat? Or were they stupid, to think I would have a kidnapper's accomplice in with my maids?

It was their protocol, I finally decided. They knew I would tell them nothing. But they could now show that someone asked.

No one from the Pot would talk to a policeman, but Mrs. Spadros had to at least pretend to. Hopefully this would be the end of it.

I wrote a letter to an old friend, sure it would divert Constable Hanger for a good long while.

When I went up to dress for dinner, Amelia said, "Mr. Roy was here today."

My stomach twisted in fear. "Did he hurt you?"

"No, mum. He asked to see Mr. Anthony, and they were in his study for a short time. Mr. Roy sounded quite displeased. When the girl went in later to clean, a table was upset and one of the vases lay broken."

Roy must have learned of the attack. I took a deep breath: horrible scenarios of torture appeared in my mind. "Is Mr. Anthony well?"

"He seemed well," Amelia said, "but he left shortly after Mr. Roy did."

The front door opened and closed downstairs, and I breathed a sigh of relief. Tony was at dinner, and didn't appear further injured, yet said little. After dinner, he said he felt tired and went to his room.

Tony hadn't done this in some time. I went to my room and after Amelia helped me undress, lay in bed.

So much had happened to him; I wasn't surprised that he felt disturbed. I felt glad to sleep alone for once. But I caused a good deal of his troubles, and I wanted to help.

Ma told me once, "When a man is most in turmoil, then he needs a woman."

So I rose, turned out the lights, and took a deep breath. I had never gone to his room before; he had always come to mine. Gathering my courage, I went through our shared closets, carefully opening the door.

Tony lay in bed, eyes open.

I made a slight noise, and Tony peered in my direction. "Who's there?"

I knelt by the side of his bed, brushing his hair back from his face. "I missed you."

He shook his head, just a little. "Not now, Jacqui, I'm tired. Please … no, just go to bed."

"Why? What's wrong?"

He wouldn't look at me.

Feeling humiliated, I hurried away before he saw my tears.

***

Peedro Sluff grabbed my left arm with his left hand and yanked me in front of him. I shrieked at his touch: at his smell, I came close to retching. "This is my daughter," he said, and shoved me forward.

I stared back at Peedro. **This** *was my father?*

Roy Spadros let out a cold, cruel laugh, as if claiming utter victory over someone he hated more than anything in the world. "You're sure about that, are you?"

I felt frightened, confused. Fear flashed through Peedro's brown eyes, which turned into determination. "If she goes, I go with her."

I woke in darkness, heart pounding. The room was quiet and empty; I felt relieved that I hadn't screamed.

I put on my robe and peeked out of my room. Our night footman, who played the piano in Vig's bar, paced towards Tony's door with a candle in his hand. He listened at the door, then walked back, a golden glow beside him. He smiled when he saw me. "May I help you, mum?"

I stepped into the hallway. "I wanted to thank you for your help when Mr. Spadros was so ill."

"Of course, mum, it's why I'm here."

"I don't even know your name."

"Blitz Spadros, mum. Mr. Anthony and I are cousins." While he didn't resemble Tony in any other way, they shared the same smile. "Glad to help. I don't need much sleep, so I might as well do something useful." He chuckled, then gestured with his head. "I better go check on him. Have a good evening."

He had a holstered pistol on his right hip. I watched as he walked back to Tony's door and listened to him breathe.

As I drifted to sleep, I felt grateful we had such loyal men.

***

The news that morning had a column on a missing boy, with mention of a "woman of interest." The description only said this woman had brown hair.

That trail was cold; Stephen spoke to the police. I had no intention of contacting the young man again.

Someone followed me from the train station. That meant they had a better description than what they published. I wore a veil, true. But they had the policeman's description. Plus a whole room of people saw the proprietor greet me. Which meant the police questioned — or tried to question — Vig and the girls.

I laughed. Vig probably threw them out with his own hands.

Amelia gave me a curious glance but said nothing.

At breakfast, Tony said nothing about his encounter with his father or his words to me the night before. He left for a short time after morning meeting.

So I wrote the dinner party invitations. After I gave the invitations to Pearson, I sat at my desk, thinking.

Air's little brother dead, his youngest brother missing.

Grief threatened to crush me every time I let myself think of this. But if I were to have any chance of helping David, I knew I must force myself to.

A false note on Madame Biltcliffe's stationery. A Red Dog card in my pocket at the Ball. The card on my doorstep.

The card on my doorstep was the true mystery. Who could step onto our street in front of the Kerr coachmen, without being challenged? Not a slum boy or a hired waiter.

But then I remembered: the constables found Herbert Bryce in the Diamond quadrant.

I clasped my hands to my face in horror.

Jack Diamond.

If that madman had harmed those boys, he would regret the day I proved it.

But then I felt afraid for my safety. A low-class scoundrel would be unlikely to touch me, even on a case. But if Jack Diamond thought I was doing my own investigation and gained the presence of mind to take advantage of it, I was in terrible danger. One word to Tony, or worse yet, Roy, and …

I wasn't sure I would survive. Jack could wreak his vengeance on me without ever being a suspect.

That was the card's meaning: not a taunt, but a threat. Jack showed he could reach me anywhere, even Spadros Manor.

How dare he threaten me?

I pounded my fist on the desk. *To the Shredder with you, Jack Diamond! Burn in the Fire!*

Jonathan's pressed flowers fell, wafting to the floor.

This had gone on long enough. I would find David Bryce and free him, or die trying.

But how?

My only real clues were the Red Dogs and the Diamond quadrant. I didn't know how to contact one, and going to the other left me open to Jack's men, who would have orders to apprehend me should I appear.

There seemed little choice in the matter. I would have to go to the person I least wanted to see and ask for help.

The Conflict

A run-down liquor shop in the Spadros slums: the door, warped; the floor tiles, cracked. The room smelled of mold; the lamps were dusty and streaked with soot. No one stood behind the counter, so I wandered among aisles of bottom shelf swill for several minutes before someone appeared.

"Who's there? What do you want?" From his speech, he had taken quite a bit of Party Time already.

I emerged into view. "Your door-bell is broken."

"Oh," my father said, "it's you."

Peedro Sluff was still a dissolute wretch, who would sell his soul – assuming he had one – to supply his lusts, especially if the transaction involved Party Time.

"So this is what you traded me for? So you can snort Party Time all day?"

"Aww, Jacqui, you're not happy wearing silks and eating pheasant? Give me the cash you're throwing around, then."

"Mr. Roy Spadros gives you money every month. Should I tell him you want more?"

My father gave me a sullen glare, a sour smell wafting through the room. "What do you want?"

"A man named Clover, with an eye-patch."

"What do you want him for?" He gave me a leering grin. "A little fun?"

"He has information I need."

"Why should I do anything for you?"

"Because you don't want me as an enemy."

His eyes widened. "You're a bitch, you know that? I try to help you all the time and you don't appreciate any of it."

Peedro hadn't done a thing to help me in his entire life, assuming he was even present at my conception.

He squirmed at my silence. "Okay, yeah, I know him."

I kept staring at him.

"He comes here every day after work, buys a six-pack of beer. Half past six, every night, except Sundays. Now get out of here."

"Thank you."

"Where's my money? I should get something for helping you upper sluts."

"When I talk to Clover, you'll get some."

My father growled. "Get outta here, you filthy whore, before someone sees you."

I love you too, I thought bitterly, and left.

***

I got home for tea, and sat with Tony in silence. Every time I had anything to do with my father, it left me feeling melancholy.

Did my mother love Peedro? She never spoke of him except with scorn, never showed warmth towards him, avoided my questions about him. The night Air died, she warned me away from him. She must have loved Peedro once; she could have had a child with anyone.

Peedro must have been a very different man twenty-two, twenty-three years ago. I wondered what happened to make her hate him, to make him sink so low.

"Jacqui?"

Something in Tony's voice made me feel uneasy. I forced myself to smile. "Yes?"

"Would you tell me again what happened to your face?"

Did Tony not believe me? What could I tell him?

He couldn't learn that Roy attacked me. If he knew what happened, he would confront Roy about it. That terrified me almost as much as Roy did. I regarded him warily. "What would you like to know?"

He sat staring at me for a moment, not moving, not breathing, then shook his head. "I'm sorry. You've told me everything."

Not showing the relief I felt in that moment was the most difficult thing I had done in my life. But his life depended on it.

Tony leaned across the table. With great precision, he placed his hand on mine, yet his voice was stern. "I have asked my father not to come here again uninvited. He is not pleased with me, but he will do as I ask."

I felt stunned, my heart pounding. The table turned, the vase broken … he seemed fine last night, yet I surveyed him for signs of injury with a sense of dread. "Did he hurt you?"

A small sad smile crossed Tony's face. "My body is no more hurt than it has been."

"Thank the Dealer." I let the wave of relief which washed over me show; tears came to me unbidden. "What happened?"

"That is between he and I," Tony said, but his voice was gentle. I felt he learned something terribly painful in the encounter with his father, something he wished he hadn't. So I didn't ask anything more.

But he came to my bed that night, just to hold me and take rest together. For the first time, I felt glad he wished to be there.

***

Two days later, a horse truck drove past Peedro Sluff's liquor store and parked down the street. When a young man wearing a patch on his left eye came past, he found himself deposited in the back of said truck by a rather large man. The doors slammed.

I sat on a crate near the driver's compartment. My face, hooded, lay mostly in shadow. An oil lamp stood on the floor, turned low.

Clover scrambled to crouch in the low-ceilinged truck. "What the hell?" He was gangling, disheveled, and smelled of smoke, with light brown hair and the beginnings of a beard. "Who the fuck are you?"

"Tell me about the Red Dogs."

Clover laughed. "Who says I know about them?"

"I do. Who do you get orders from?"

"Why should I tell you anything?"

"Because if you don't, the man who plucked you from the street could set you down somewhere worse. For example, the morgue. He watches you now."

Clover glanced around and gulped. "O … okay, miss, no offense. Yeah, I know the Dogs … they give orders through their man. Don't know his real name; he said call him Morton. I only seen him once; he sends a message when he wants something done. He gets his orders from the Big Man Himself, he says, but he never said what the Big Man's name was."

Morton. An odd name. "What does Morton look like?"

Clover shrugged. "Like us, I guess, only older. Brown hair."

I wondered how this man survived to adulthood with such poor observational skills. "Who else is in the Dogs?"

"Don't know, and that's the truth," Clover said. "They said there's other treys, but we don't never hear nothing about them, so if one of us gets caught we can't tell nothing."

Smart. "Treys?"

"Yeah, an ace and two chips. I guess Morton must give them all orders." He paused. "Unless there are other ones like Morton who give orders. That I don't know."

Since this depended on secrecy, but had to be expandable, there were at least a few Mortons in Spadros. In each quadrant. Although I didn't recall seeing reports from the Hart quadrant.

"Do you know about boys being taken? They found a Red Dog stamp at a kidnapping, and found a boy dead with a Red Dog card on him."

At this, Clover's eye widened in fear. "I swear, I don't know nothing about that. Garn, they start blaming things like that on us and we're done for."

"So you think someone is trying to discredit you?" At his blank stare, I added, "Blame you for things you never did?"

"Yes, miss, I do. The worst I ever told my chips was put a rock through a window. Morton said it would get rid of the Families, so honest folk could walk without being scared a'them."

The words sounded an echo of Thrace Pike's words, that night after the tent meeting. But Mr. Pike's style seemed completely different.

"I'm done here." I banged twice on the truck wall and raised my voice. "Give the man something for his trouble."

Vig leaned in, grabbed Clover by his jacket, hauled him out, gave him a coin, and sent him on his way. We drove a few blocks, then the truck stopped. A moment later Vig opened the back door. "We gotta talk."

I climbed out of the back and stood at the end of the truck. "What's wrong?"

Vig put his fist on his hip and stared away. "I like you. I help you when you have trouble. I ride you anywhere. But I'll not be no Spadros enforcer."

I frowned. "What do you mean?"

"You **used** me to scare the boy. You don't even ask. You say, ride me there, get the boy. Nothing else."

"Vig ..." How else would I get the man to talk?

"No. I live in Spadros, but I'll not work for them."

I had no idea he felt this way. "I didn't think you'd mind."

Vig looked outraged. "What do you think I am? A brute?"

"Vig, that's not how I see you. We're buddy friends, right?"

"Are we?" He shook his head. "I'll not be no enforcer ... not even for you."

"I'm sorry, Vig ... I didn't know. I was wrong to scare him. I'll never do it again." I looked in his eyes. Had I lost his friendship? "Can you forgive me?"

His face softened. "Get in the truck." So I did.

A few moments later, the truck lurched forward again and soon I was around the corner from my own back door. Vig did not tarry; once I was out of the truck, he left without saying good-bye.

***

"Did you have a pleasant walk?"

Tony and I sat in the parlor, across a small table from each other, sipping port and eating cherries covered in dark chocolate.

It was a lonely walk from Vig's truck. His reaction shook my confidence. Was I someone who used people? "Yes, it was lovely."

"Two of our guards have been found."

"That's wonderful!"

"Well, perhaps. They were dumped outside the warehouse, bound, gagged, and hooded. They didn't know where they were held. They were not treated well." Tony looked disturbed, and I dared not ask what he witnessed.

"Did they say anything else?"

"One other person was held. A young boy." Tony shuddered. "The child was being treated worst of all."

I felt stunned at the revelation. Could this be David Bryce? What link lay between the men and the boy? "Did the men know who took them?"

Tony shook his head. "They said the man wore all black, his face covered with a black cloth, or veil like what you ladies wear perhaps, but thicker, so they couldn't see what he looked like. Not even a small part of his skin showed, nor the color of it, nor even his eyes, but they did say that he was a huge man, monstrously tall. He kept them blindfolded most of the time, or in the dark, and tied."

"Well, that sounds pleasant. Did he say why he took them?"

"No," Tony said, "that's the true mystery. He didn't seem to want anything with the men, or even the boy, except to torment them. Tormenting the boy seemed to amuse him more than anything else, especially when the boy would cry for his mother."

A wave of grief washed over me, picturing Air treated so. I covered my face with my handkerchief to hide my tears.

"Oh, my love, forgive me! I never meant to distress you." Tony turned towards me, a slight grimace revealing the pain it cost him, and took my hands. "Please forget my words. From the descriptions the guards gave us, we should find the boy."

I tried to smile, wanting to keep his mind off the subject of the boy, who could only be David Bryce. "What of the other guards?"

Tony shook his head. "The guards know nothing of them. They speculate the men were killed, but we never found their bodies." He took a deep breath and let it out. "It's clear a scoundrel is on the loose, of greater depravity than any we have seen in quite a while."

I had no idea who this person could be. Jack Diamond, while tall, was not excessively so; there were few men in the city who fit this description.

Tony said, "I spoke with your friend Joseph Kerr at the Gentleman's Club today …"

My heart fluttered at Joe's name. I missed him so much. Did he ever think of me?

"… and in passing I mentioned our troubles with that street gang, the ones with the red stamps …"

"The Red Dogs?"

"Yes, that was the one. In any case, Master Kerr said he heard rumors … he called it the Red Dog Gang … that it started in the Diamond quadrant. He speculated Master Jack Diamond might be behind the mischief. It sounds like the sort of random violence that would appeal to him."

This dovetailed too closely with my thoughts to be anything but disturbing. "Has anyone seen Jack Diamond of late?"

Tony shrugged and took out his pocket-watch, winding it. "Who knows what the man does? I suppose his family must keep track of him. It surprises me that he's allowed to roam freely, when he might be better suited to a ward."

This discussion unsettled me. While Jack Diamond was unwell, he owned property. If Fortune frowned on his older brothers, Jack might one day inherit the Diamond Family Business. To be known for speaking ill of him could be an unhappy habit should he come into his own.

I would have to warn Joe about his loose speech. Jack Diamond made a formidable enemy. "I don't like speaking of others who aren't present, especially to speak of them poorly."

"Forgive me. You are much kinder than I to concern yourself with the reputation of a man who has threatened you in public."

"But that's it exactly. Master Diamond has spoken his mind and vented his rage. We know of his malice, and unless he were to go completely mad, he dares not carry out his threats. If you, or I, or my father were to disappear or be harmed, suspicion would immediately fall upon him."

Unless, of course, he got someone else to do his dirty work. A forged note on Madame Biltcliffe's stationery to the wrong person could ruin me. "What concerns me more are those whose malice towards our Family is silent and hidden."

"I hadn't considered this aspect of it," Tony said.

The fire crackled as a log shifted.

What did David have to do with this?

Tony said, "Who holds men and boys just to torment them? And why target me with violence? I've received no threats, no demands, no word as to motive. And this hidden motive is more puzzling when I look at who might want to cause me trouble." He paused. "Even Bridgers wouldn't torment innocent children."

Then he shook himself. "Let us forget this villain." He smiled. "It's been too long since we took comfort from each other."

So he finally felt well enough. I remembered the situation a few nights before with sadness. But I forced myself to smile, perfectly willing to think of Joe for an evening, even though nothing would come of it.

Why did I do this, when Joe seemed to have no interest in me? It was how I endured the marriage-bed of a man I didn't love. I suppose it was fortunate I never became a whore; I was most unsuited to the task.

***

I smelled gun oil and lavender. I stood at the door to the church wearing my bride-gown, searching for some way to escape this nightmare. Something cold and hard pressed against the back of my neck. A gun-hammer cocked, close behind my right ear.

Roy's voice came from behind. "You'll walk that aisle, and say the words, and make no fuss. Make us believe it, now and for all time, or you'll be dead."

I woke sobbing with terror, Amelia beside me in the gray morning light.

"There, there, dear," Amelia said, smoothing my hair, until I was able to catch my breath. Then she said, "You just had a dream. All is well."

I never dreamed this scene before, or even recalled it; I must have put it from my mind. But now the whole memory of that horrible day fell on me in full. I wept in earnest, unable to catch my breath.

"Do you want me to call Mr. Anthony?"

Fear gripped me; I stopped crying at once. "No."

He must never know: Roy made that quite clear. I wiped my face, forcing myself to appear calm. "No. It's all right. I'll be fine."

Amelia put rosewater in my pitcher, remarking that it might lift my spirits. After I washed my hands and face, the room did smell lovely.

My mail brought bad news: while Joe and Josephine Kerr would attend the dinner party, Mr. Polansky Kerr had a prior engagement.

Damn. That left me with an extra seat.

Molly stood before an easel, which held a diagram. "It is vital that the number of men and women at a dinner party be equal. No one should feel slighted or uncomfortable by being the odd number."

Even at twelve years old, Tony and I listened attentively. Roy impressed upon us that being good hosts was as important as anything else we did. So here I was, ten years later, with a dilemma: who to invite that would not take offense at being invited to fill a seat? The answer to this must wait; I had more important items to consider.

Unless I found this man Morton (perhaps even if I did), I would have to search for David Bryce. The major problem in doing so, other than the danger from Jack Diamond's men, was entering the Diamond quadrant itself.

Public taxi-carriages wouldn't drive to another quadrant without a definite address, and I had no contacts there. Entering the Diamond quadrant in a Spadros carriage without an invitation would attract all sorts of attention, none good.

I felt like one of Air's automatons, running into one wall or another until I found my way.

The Man

Tony left after breakfast to attend to the Business. When Pearson was out of sight, I went into Tony's library, closing the door behind me. While larger and finer than Mr. Kerr's library, it continued the gray, pastel blue, and white theme which covered most of our home. So I preferred the library at the Kerr's.

But I didn't come here to admire the decor.

"Holy Writ," I murmured, "Casino Management ... Fall of the Western Empire ... Business Communication ... Here it is!"

A street atlas of the city of Bridges, a slim volume, but important in my case. I opened the book onto Tony's desk, being careful not to disturb anything. After studying several maps of the Diamond quadrant, I decided to visit Mrs. Bryce.

Mrs. Bryce appeared in better spirits, and although thinner and paler than I remembered, glad to see me. She invited me in her back room and offered me luncheon, but her plate seemed so bare I told her I had already supped. She didn't argue, eating my tiny portion as well as hers.

She peered at me. "Do you have any news?"

I nodded. "I have evidence that David may be alive."

Mrs. Bryce sobbed while I sat silently, recalling how unhelpful Amelia's words were earlier. At last she said, "I'm sorry," and wiped her eyes.

"A group of men was recently kidnapped. They described a young boy held alongside them. The description of the boy matches David's."

Mrs. Bryce stared at me in shock. "This is horrendous!"

"It is, yet the men couldn't tell us where they were being held. I have reason to believe your son is in the Diamond quadrant."

Mrs. Bryce nodded, tears filling her eyes. "Yes, where my poor Herbert was found."

"I must ask — do you have any contacts, or friends, or associates in Diamond? A person I might make a delivery to, or you might visit?"

"There's a fabric shop, much like mine; the owner imports his material from Europe. I've been there once before, but the prices were too high for me to order anything. I have his card here somewhere." She began to search the room.

Several people came in, milled about, and left without purchasing anything. I attended the counter, dressed in Tenni's shop maid uniform, yet no one paid me any mind.

Finally, she said, "I have it!"

"Very good. When can we visit? I can return on —"

"I will wait no longer." She got her keys and hung the "closed" sign on the door. I followed her outside; she locked the door and went down the street.

Her decisiveness seemed such a departure from her usual manner that I felt completely surprised. After a moment's hesitation, I followed. Perhaps I would have the same reaction if my child were missing. I couldn't imagine bearing a child in the first place, so the point seemed moot.

I found a public taxi-carriage that would take us to the Diamond quadrant, and soon we were off to the address on her card, the taxi-carriage's wheels rattling over the cobblestones. "How did you come to be in Bridges?"

What I wanted to ask was "How did you come to leave Bridges?" But I couldn't ask, not yet, or she would realize who I really was.

Mrs. Bryce sighed. "My husband was an importer, but not a competent one. He died suddenly, leaving a large amount of debt which I was unable to pay. First, the better part of my inventory was seized, then my customer lists were taken, then I was threatened with eviction.

"I saw a notice in the paper advertising shops for rent in Bridges, so when the creditors informed me they were taking our home, I gathered what inventory was left and brought my sons here." She stared out of the window. "At times I feel it might have been better to stay and face the debtor's prison."

Debtor's prison? Her city sounded harsher than Bridges, if such a thing were possible.

The carriage came to a halt, and we alighted to the silver-gray cobbles. The temperature had dropped, and I wished I'd brought Tenni's overcoat.

The shop was in the better part of the Diamond quadrant, and I could see why the prices might be too high for Mrs. Bryce.

I felt eyes on me, and a light-skinned man in brown turned away before I could see his face. A shiver of fear went down my back. "Let's get out of here."

A few streets over, we found a taxi-carriage which would take us to the slums "to see our aunt." For an extra penny, he brought us to a rundown street a few blocks outside the Pot, just west of the main roadway. "It might be hard to find a taxi-carriage here," he said.

Clever man. "Would you wait for us?"

He thought for a moment. "I suppose I can .... If you have another penny...?"

I glanced at Mrs. Bryce, who nodded.

"When we return, I promise."

He nodded, then pulled his goggles down around his neck, tipping his hat over his eyes and leaning back.

We cut between two buildings and down an alley.

From the description the men gave Tony, it seemed they were held in a larger building, such as a warehouse. Few such buildings lay in Diamond, which wasn't known for its manufacturing. Most of the warehouses were in the western part of the Diamond section of the Pot. For this reason, I planned to limit the search to the west Diamond Pot, which was all we had time for.

The only good thing about each section of the Pot is that it is narrower than the rest of the quadrant it belongs to, being at the "point," if you will, closest to Market Center. I decided to begin at the south end and work my way north.

I felt glad the warehouses were concentrated in the western Diamond Pot. I didn't want to have to travel the tunnels under the roadway dressed as I was. All sorts of scoundrels and ruffians loitered in such places.

Even though the Diamond Pot was fenced with wrought iron, as was the Spadros Pot, this fence also had openings, either melted away by ray blasts or by the many bombings. It didn't take long to find one and slip through.

Someone whistled from high up and to our right, and it reminded me of my days in the High-Low Split. Our watchers whistled if they saw someone: one for quadrant-folk, to beg or steal from; two for another gang attacking; three for the cops.

We dodged packs of dogs and men, wove around sleeping forms, piles of trash, and the occasional curious onlooker. An old woman with dark brown skin leaned on a battered broom at her door. Dirty, ragged children just out of infancy spun a broken bottle. A man with pale skin roused from sleep peered at us then covered his head with a piece of cardboard.

Strangely enough, we were never challenged. Also, the streets were too clean. The piles of trash were well-stacked, no smell of filth or urine permeated the air, and no corpses covered with carrion lay about. It seemed strange.

Perhaps they conducted their affairs differently here.

This area must have survived the wars better than Spadros quadrant; more of the buildings stood undamaged. Several of the buildings were locked (and more to the point, bolted) on all sides. As we could hear nothing and had no way to force entry, we left those. Others were unsafe to enter, and after hearing no reply to our shouts, we left those as well.

"This is so frustrating!" Mrs. Bryce said. "My poor child could be in any of these and we wouldn't know it."

No bolts secured the next building, a one-story brick warehouse. So I retrieved my picks (which I had secreted in my bodice) and began to work on the lock.

Steps came from behind. "Ah, now look here," a man's voice came, also from behind, along with a pair of hands traveling around my midsection.

At his touch, I slumped down, backwards, and to the side. Moving forward and likely taken off guard, he fell to the other side, being thrown over my shoulder and against the door by his own actions.

I'm not sure how to explain it better: I never learned the technique's proper name. It was one of the first lessons Roy taught me, and he claimed knowing the name would interfere. "You brood too much as it is." I practiced the maneuver many times, but never used it in reality before.

I pulled my dagger from my left boot-sheath and put it to the man's neck.

Pale skin, a crooked nose, and light brown hair. A dirty laborer's shirt with orange-brown pants and a coat twenty years or more out of fashion. The clothes looked as if they came from the items the poorhouse threw out, too threadbare and torn to sell. His face was smeared with dirt, and he smelled as if he hadn't bathed in a week.

"Hey, now." He glanced down with surprise and fear in his eyes. "I was just having a bit a fun with you. No need for knifing." His speech was slurred, as if he had an impediment.

I stepped back. "Fun's over, move on."

He picked up his cap and put it back on, but not soon enough to hide a look of deep chagrin. "You smell too good for any maid a hers," the man gestured at Mrs. Bryce. "And not many maids know they way round a knife, either."

And I did; I learned knife-fighting as a child, from Josephine Kerr herself.

"Tis none your concern." I fell back to Pot-speak, I suppose, without meaning to.

"No dummy, me. Pot rag dressed a slum maid, smelling like a lady. And armed." He took off his cap and bowed. "Please to meet you, Mum Spadros."

No dummy indeed. "Hush, you fool. Black Jack would see me dead."

"He would. And you too pretty for that rascal, so I keep my trap shut." He smiled, and his swollen gums lacked several teeth.

"You gotta name to give?"

"Eh," he said, disappointed, "knew you would get round to asking. You can call me Morton."

"Morton!?"

"So twas **you** napped Clover!" He laughed and shook his head. "You think my treys don't talk? When Clover told me a men blaming us for napping lads, I had to set things right."

I thought this was fairly admirable for a man who taught boys to vandalize. "You hear a lad taken?"

The man scrutinized us. "Aye, just ta other side ta fence, or so they say. Jack's old barn, not used much now. One a ta whores sneaking out heard ta boy a-crying."

I nodded, and fished out a penny, but the man waved me off. "You forget so soon. Help you own, aye?"

"Aye," I said, abashed. "Thank ye."

"Stay warm," he said.

"Stay warm," I turned to leave, but then thought of Stephen. He didn't sound like an outsider, but who else would talk to the police? "Wait." Morton turned back. "Red Dogs take outsiders?"

He spat. "Never." Then he went round the corner.

Mrs. Bryce frowned, as if puzzling out something. "So do we go there?"

It could be a trap. Pot rags don't steal from each other, cheat each other, or betray each other — usually — but they will anyone else. Since I wasn't a Pot rag anymore, I wasn't sure how I qualified in his eyes.

He didn't look like a Diamond, which made me suspicious. I had no proof he was even from the Pot, other than an accent.

But we might not get a better chance. "We go."

Someone whistled, close by. We hurried through the maze of alleys, around broken fences, and down streets piled with the rubble of war after war. It began to snow as we went.

For once, Mrs. Bryce said nothing. I heard her panting as we went round corner after corner, across streets, through alleys, then through another melted hole in the wrought iron, until we got a couple of blocks from the building Morton mentioned.

Two gentlemen carried a struggling package, boy-sized, which they placed into a carriage. One had light brown skin and wore brown, the other had dark skin and wore white.

"David!" Mrs. Bryce said.

The men climbed in and the carriage moved away.

I ran after them, Mrs. Bryce behind. Then I slid to a stop. "Follow me!" I ran for our carriage. A dozen blocks away, the carriage still stood there. "Go to the end of the street, then follow the tracks." After I helped Mrs. Bryce in and shut the door, the driver did so.

"That was him."

"Who?"

"That man in white … it was him. He came to the shop … a few weeks … before David went missing." She paused, panting. "He was the only one … who came by … the week we moved here. All three of us came out to the store front to meet him."

I leaned back, horrified.

"I thought he was a neighbor." Mrs. Bryce stared at her hands. "Why would he take David?"

We sped down the lane, following the tracks, as the snow fell with more intensity.

I jerked away from a motion out of the corner of my eye, so Mrs. Bryce's slap barely grazed me. "What the hell are you doing?"

"You got my Nicholas killed!" She unleashed a flurry of slaps and punches, which I deflected as the carriage barreled along. I knew this was coming, but the timing of it surprised me.

Finally she stopped, weeping. "You got him killed! He would have done anything for you, and you got him killed. He was just a little boy."

We were born the same day.

After Peedro finished his negotiations with Roy, he let me go. The crowd began muttering about him killing a child, picking up bricks and iron rods as they moved towards him.

Jack Diamond glared up from where he knelt by his friend, shaking with rage, dark eyes full of tears. Even Roy Spadros didn't frighten me as much as the look in this man's face, which promised terrible vengeance.

The memory frightened me still.

I ran to Air, sobbing, but he lay dead. My vision blurred as I half dragged, half carried Air through the foul-smelling streets all that long walk home.

I didn't want the rats to get him.

My mother woke when, exhausted, I dropped Air's body with a thud on the wooden floor of our quarters. Once she deciphered what had happened, she sent her girls with messages and put me to bed.

The minute she left the room, I crouched next to the door until Air's mother came for his body. I listened to her screams, her sobs, her curses.

Eleanora said the same thing that night ten years ago: I got him killed.

I did get him killed. I thought about it every day; his death filled my dreams every night. There was nothing I could say.

After about a half hour, the driver pulled over and came round to our window. "Begging your pardon, miss, but I lost them for the snow," he said. "Can you tell me who you're following?"

I leaned out of the window. "It was a carriage like yours, almost exactly."

The driver shook his head. "The way that left back wheel was wobbling, he won't be driving it long. And the other had a divot outta the right back; when he made the turn back there you saw snow clear as day. That's got to be stole from the carriage-house on Market Center. It's on the repair list or I'm an old maid."

"Can you take us back to Spadros? I'll pay extra."

"Gladly." The man smiled. "Most fun I've had all day."

Mrs. Bryce didn't like abandoning our pursuit.

"What would you have me do? It's snowing. There are no tracks to follow." I paused for a moment, thinking. "Let me look into this further."

She wept. "My little boy … why are they holding him? He's done nothing wrong!"

We didn't know that, but it wouldn't help to say it. "I think I know where to look from here."

"So you'll find David?"

"Now you want me to help you. After all that?"

She glanced away. "Yes."

The whole world became silent.

Toss the deck — Jack Diamond thought I took the case already. "Yes, I'll find him."

"Thank you," she sobbed. "Thank you."

"But I must tell you true. I'm not the police. I'm just a woman. All I can do is find David, not catch the ones who have him, not bring them to justice. We might not even learn why they did it. If I get him home, you both may be in danger. These scoundrels may try to take him again. But I will find him. Will that be enough?"

"Yes." She wiped her tears with her handkerchief. "All I want is my boy back, even if for just one day."

I patted her hand. "I always find who I look for."

I neglected — for her sake — to mention that sometimes I found them dead.

The Motive

Tony hadn't returned by tea time, so I sat in my study alone and took my tea there.

A man in brown followed me to Vig's place.

A man in brown took the boy to the carriage.

At least one man in brown watched me. I almost caught a glimpse of his face several times. He always seemed familiar.

Could this be the same man in brown who followed Stephen and frightened him so?

At first I passed off Stephen's fear as a child's paranoia, but Stephen was more than a child.

This explained something which bothered me earlier. Perhaps the man in brown followed Stephen the day I was to meet him, frightening him so much he felt the police were his only hope.

And this scoundrel was allied with Jack Diamond.

I drank my tea with a sense of foreboding.

One reason I hadn't wanted to tell Mrs. Bryce I would find David was I wasn't sure I could.

There was more than pride at stake. Being a woman investigator meant most people didn't trust I would do more than take their money and apologize when I failed. Even most women would rather pay more and have a man take the job, feeling only a man would give a proper day's work.

My only leverage so far was I never failed to complete a case. All my contacts were given permission to say so.

For me to take the case then not find David Bryce — whether dead or alive — could mean the end of my career.

Not having had luncheon, I ate everything the maid brought me, not realizing it until I saw her surprise when she returned. "Will you be having anything else, mum?"

"Another pot of tea, please." I almost asked for rum, but I needed a clear head.

"Yes, mum." The maid turned to go.

"You're Jane's girl, aren't you?"

"Yes, mum, Mary Pearson." She curtsied low.

"Thank your Ma for the sandwiches, they were very good." Fortunately, they were good; we ended up having them for the next several weeks, until Tony tired of them and asked for something else.

"Thank you, mum." She curtsied and left with the dishes, coming back a few minutes later with a pot of tea and a fresh cup and saucer.

I pulled over an ottoman and put my feet up. There were so many questions. What puzzled me most about this case was the motive. Why did they take David?

The kidnappers never asked for ransom: neither gold, nor items, nor information. Instead of taking a rich child, they took a widow's son. They didn't sell the child to men who preferred such toys, but simply kept the boy, as they kept the guards.

These men gained nothing from the kidnappings other than a brief time of torment, which perhaps gave them a perverse sort of pleasure. In a way, this reminded me of Roy, but Roy seldom released his victims. That raised another question: why let the men go and not the boy?

Something in this felt personal.

Perhaps they meant to strike a blow at our Family by capturing Spadros guards and attacking Tony. I understood Jack Diamond's hate, if it were he I saw, two blocks away. If someone murdered Joe, I might want to strike back at them, especially if I were mad.

But what was the man in brown's motive? Why partner with Jack, of all people? Or was this man just a lackey?

Many of our servants weren't descended from the first Acevedo Spadros, as it turned out. But I never heard of the Diamonds using retainers from outside their Family.

After the murder of Jack's friend, the Diamond and Spadros Families were at war for almost a year. During that time, the Diamonds expelled anyone from the quadrant who couldn't prove ties to the Diamond Family. Many of those foolish enough to flee to the Spadros quadrant ended up in Roy's torture room.

For a while after, you had to be related to the Diamonds to even live in their quadrant. Even now, people said: Diamonds only protect their own. This man in brown didn't look like a Diamond to me.

So where did he come from? The man in brown must be a man of means or influence, to move so easily between quadrants. Even Jack Diamond would have trouble doing so.

Did he leave the card on my doorstep? I had seen no one skulking outside our home. With the attack, our men had been coming and going too much for strangers to get close without being seen. I wished I could get a better look at the man, or determine a way to identify him....

His clothing choice made a formidable disguise. Every fashionable young gentleman of means dressed in brown that season; there might be several thousand in the city.

The door opened and Tony came in. He still wore his overcoat, as if he came in straight past Pearson.

I rose to greet him, but he waved me to sit. "I can't stay; my father wants to take the route the guards remember and see what we find."

"But you're not completely well."

He raised his hand. "I won't be in danger. We have fifty men to search, and six will stay with the car. There will be no second ambush, unless this scoundrel has more men than we imagine."

If he did, it could be all-out war. "Be careful. I would have nothing harm you."

Tony smiled, and came over to kiss me. "I hope to be home before dinner. It should be quick, whatever we find."

And then he left me sitting with cold tea and fear.

Tony did return long before dinner, but sat quiet and pensive. After dinner, we sat in Tony's library by the fire, sipping brandy.

Finally, I ventured, "How did your expedition fare?"

"Poorly," Tony said. "We had the men describe the path, each blindfolded, each in a separate car, but neither destination showed sign of their captivity."

Two men, two destinations? This seemed odd. "Where did you end up?"

"Two warehouses in Spadros. Both guards were definite in that they did not cross a river."

They didn't cross a river. Why did these men move the boy?

Tony shook his head. "Where could this gang be hiding?"

"You think it's a gang?"

"What else could it be? No matter how large or strong, no man could overpower four armed guards, bind them, transport them, and hold them for weeks by himself. And six attacked me and my men."

This made sense. "And then there's the little boy...."

Tony clapped his hand to his forehead. "I completely forgot the child. I saw no sign of him. I don't know where to look for him. I'm sorry."

Even though I would rather find David myself, I felt a sense of loss at Tony's failure to find him. Someone needed to find him; by now, he must be in a terrible state, not even having other captors to comfort him.

What sort of monster would do this to a child? "This situation enrages me."

"I feel distressed as well. If the other Families hear our guards can be treated so, we could find ourselves under attack as they seek advantage."

I hadn't considered this. Should I tell Tony what I saw?

How could I? I wasn't supposed to even be in the Diamond quadrant, much less chasing child-murderers around the city.

The only proof of Jack Diamond's involvement? A glimpse of a dark-skinned man two blocks away wearing white and the word of a widow from the Spadros slums.

Against a Diamond heir, whose family owned the prison and had enormous power over the courts, it was no evidence at all. For the Spadros Family to make such a dire accusation without proof could plunge the city into war.

But I remembered what Josephine Kerr told us as children in the Pot: *never let anyone get the upper hand, or they will kill you.*

Josie ran our gang, the High-Low Split, with Joe as her backup. Even the High Cards listened to her. By the time I was taken to be betrothed, the other gang members in the Spadros section of the Pot were either part of the High-Low Split, or they were dead. "You're right in this. You must punish these men, and soon. No one respects those who can't protect and care for their own. This is why those in the Pot are so despised."

"I don't despise you, or your family. Never think that."

I put my hand on his. "I have never thought so. You have only offered comfort and support." No matter what Roy had done to me, this at any rate was true.

The Visitors

The next day, this article appeared in the *Bridges Daily*:

Saloon Raided, Owner Fined

> Last night, the Spadros quadrant saloon The Pocket Pair was raided by the police, who suspected the owner of selling Party Time. None of the substance was found on the premises, but several of the 'working girls' were jailed for being in the quadrant illegally. The owner, one Vig Vikenti, a native of Spadros, was fined $50.00 for hiring without letters of recommendation and released on his own recognizance.

Those ladies would regret not securing their papers. Whether they did a poor job at their last post, were on the run from a lover, or whatever circumstance led to this disaster. Wherever they were from, they were members of the Pot now.

I sighed, and Amelia, who was making the bed, glanced over but said nothing.

I felt as if this might have been my fault for bringing the shop under the notice of the police, but in my mail was a note:

> Vig is fine, no worries. Gypsy gal fine too. Was too rough with cops that day, they found a way to pay back. They don't like me. — V.

I could only imagine.

Immediately after luncheon, Constable Hanger returned, a bit less rumpled this time. Tony was off doing his monthly casino inspection, so I had Pearson show the man to the parlor.

"Yes, Constable, how may I help you?" I gestured for him to sit across from me. "Would you like some tea?"

"No, mum." He continued to stand with his feet apart and his hands behind his back. I thought it a nice touch: men liked to make a show of superiority, particularly when powerless. "Were you aware, mum, that letters were being sent from Eunice Ogier to the Spadros Country House?"

I frowned. "Eunice … Ogier …. Is that the woman you came here about last time?"

"Yes, mum. Apparently she was known by a member of your kitchen staff at the Country House."

"I shall speak to the staff about this at once."

"Yes, well, the woman said Miss Ogier left the city." He seemed disappointed. "I thought you should know."

"Thank you for telling me. Is anything else required?"

The constable hesitated. "Do you have mourning garb?"

"Why, no, I have never needed to purchase any. I have been most fortunate in that regard."

The constable nodded. "Yes. That is most fortunate." He paused. "Well, I'm sure you're quite busy. Good day, mum."

Interesting. He clearly suspected me. But it would be a brave judge indeed who signed the warrant to search Spadros Manor.

***

Later that day, Jonathan Diamond and his younger sister Gardena came to call. Gardena was two years older than I yet still unmarried.

I couldn't understand why. She had no elderly grandfather to forbid her marriage, and was attractive, poised, and intelligent. Perhaps too much so; some men disliked women who spoke their minds, and she had no qualms about doing so. Her unmarried state didn't bother her, though; she enjoyed life, and happily spent her father's money.

"I'm sorry that Mr. Spadros isn't here to greet you." It was strange: Tony had never once been here when Jonathan or Gardena came calling.

"When do you think he'll return?" Jonathan said.

I sighed. "Not until time to dress for dinner. Alas, today he must work."

"We must have an adventure, then!" Gardena said.

Jonathan looked pained. "Nothing too strenuous, I hope."

"Oh, I forgot, my poor dear brother still has the cold in his joints." Gardena flopped down on the sofa, royal blue dress and raven curls flying.

Jonathan sat with difficulty, leaning heavily on his cane. "Don't mock me. It's most unpleasant not to be able to run and frolic as you continually want to."

"Jon is old already, while I will be young forever."

I laughed. "I'll remind you of that when you're eighty."

Gardena stuck her tongue at me, and I laughed harder.

"So what shall we do?" she said.

I glanced at Jon. "Do you feel well enough for the garden?"

"I think so."

So we moved to the veranda, which sat off the dining room, with a fine view of the gardens. The day felt warm for this time of year, but Jonathan put his overcoat on before venturing outdoors.

I checked on my little bird, white with blue-gray markings. It hopped about a large white cage, which hung from a white metal stand. Tony asked me what I wanted for a wedding gift shortly before we married, and I chose this, so I would never forget.

I never named the bird. It had its own name which it knew itself by, and I felt it would be wrong to give it another.

Jon didn't look well, and I wondered why they had gone out. "Are you warm enough?"

He nodded. "Thank you for your invitation, by the way."

"I'm sorry it's taken so long to have you over." I smiled at Gardena. "I know there's someone who will be happy to see you."

Jon and Gardena gave each other a glance which seemed part puzzlement and part hope. "Let us speak with our father."

"I understand." I hoped Julius would relent and let them accept the invitation. What could Tony possibly have done or said to make Julius Diamond hate him so?

We sat silently for several minutes, then Gardena insisted I walk with her, leaving Jonathan bundled up, sitting with a cup of tea at the table.

"Never mind Jon," she said. "He's in a mood. I thought bringing him here would make him feel better."

"It's such a shame Jon's not feeling well. Does Jack have similar troubles with his health?"

"Him?" Gardena laughed. "His troubles have nothing to do with his body. He will likely outlive us all, unless he does something drastic."

I stared at her, appalled. "Has he ever talked of doing such a thing?"

She shrugged. "He talks on every subject, in every permutation. He has days where he doesn't sleep, days where he appears and acts quite normally, and days where he only sleeps. On his sleepless days, he talks incessantly.

"My mother bans him from the house when he is like that; his chatter keeps the whole house awake. So he roams the streets, talking with everyone in the quadrant. My father's men accompany him to make sure he keeps out of trouble."

Jack sounded much more disturbed than I thought. "Has he talked of …" I was going to say "me," but I didn't want her to get the wrong idea, "… us?"

Gardena looked at me sideways. "He speaks of you, the elder Mr. Spadros, your father … Sluff, is it? … and his departed friend Daniel. Daniel's death is an obsession with him. Jack's men were supposed to keep him away from you the night of the Ball, but they were distracted. My father was quite displeased."

Gardena put her arm through mine. "It's a comfort to be able to speak of this with you. I'm not supposed to, but you are discreet and sympathetic."

I smiled at her. "Thank you for your trust."

"Besides, you're not a Spadros, not really. You don't think like them, you don't act like them. You don't even look like them." She let go of my arm and twirled around. "My father would have kittens if he knew I shared such information, but I don't care what he thinks." She skipped around, then came up to me, speaking in a conspiratorial tone. "One day, we must have a sleep-over party, and do each other's hair, and tell our deepest secrets."

I laughed. "You are delightful! Should we invite Katherine?"

"Certainly." She no longer smiled. "And Calcutta Clubb, and even dull little Ferti Hart."

"I didn't mean to offend you. I thought it a nice way to spend time with you both. We can have our party alone, if you prefer."

"Yes, I do prefer. Katherine is bothersome, and too much wanting to please her father. He doesn't need to have any of *my* secrets, thank you."

I chuckled. "No, he doesn't." Jonathan leaned forward with his chin on his hand, staring into the air, and I felt uneasy at leaving him alone. "I think Jon despairs of seeing us again."

"We shall bring him flowers!" Gardena began collecting them from my garden, without so much as a by-your-leave. I watched her go here and there pulling them like a young girl, and wondered if she intended to remain such forever, or if she had some deeper intent for being here.

A maid came out as we approached the veranda and took the flowers from Gardena, returning with them trimmed and neatly arranged in a vase.

Jonathan smiled when he first saw the flowers but returned to looking morose.

"Whatever is the matter, Jon?" I said.

He leaned back, smiling brightly. "Oh, too much thinking, that's all."

I chuckled. "I'm not often accused of that. You can be my balance."

He immediately seemed happier. "I accept your challenge."

Gardena took a few quick steps off, turning to frame us as if a photographer. "Lovely! A picture of perfection."

I laughed.

Pearson came outside. "Mrs. Spadros, will your guests be staying for tea?"

I turned to them. "Will you?"

"Of course!" Gardena said.

Jonathan said nothing to dissuade her, so we went inside.

Whatever Jonathan's troubles were, he spoke of them no further, and we had a merry time talking and laughing.

At the stroke of five, Pearson came in, holding a glass. "Your water, sir."

Jonathan's face held deep gratitude. "Thank you, Pearson! How kind of you to remember." Jon took the water from Pearson, then opened his small velvet bag, removing several small clear vials filled with liquid of various colors, which he lined up.

Each had a number engraved on the side, and Jonathan put the three bearing the number "5" directly in front of him, the light from the setting sun shining through them as it peeked through the clouds.

He then took a small thin glass eye-dropper from the bag. He took two drops from each of the number 5 vials, placing the drops into the glass of water. He drank the water and put the vials away.

He had done this "for his health" for as long as I had known him, and I simply thought it an affectation. But up until now he had never seemed ill.

"Jon, what's wrong? Why do you take these?"

"For my health," he said, as he always did. "Oh, you mean today? It's nothing." He smiled. "I feel much better. The hot tea was invigorating."

Relief washed over me. "I'm glad to hear it."

About half past six, Tony returned, surprise on his face. "Good to see you." He shook Jonathan's hand, then he came and kissed my cheek. Gardena glanced at Tony, a question in her eyes. When I glanced at Tony, his face held no emotion.

"Good to see you too." Jonathan smiled. "Unfortunately, we must go; we have another engagement to dress for."

I felt confused; a few minutes before, they seemed ready to stay all day. "Thank you so much for coming." I walked them to the front door. "I was really glad to see you."

Pearson opened the door. "Until next time," Gardena said. Then they left, and Pearson closed the door.

I stood in the hall puzzled. "That was odd." I turned, and Tony was gone.

Tony seemed distracted at dinner, and went into his study soon after, closing the door. So I went in my study to finish setting up the dinner party.

I had been planning the menu, decorations, entertainment, and seating for at least an hour. I was wondering who I could invite to complete the table when Pearson knocked on the door. "A Master Blaze Rainbow to speak with you."

Pearson handed over a card.

Blaze Rainbow, Esq.
No. 5 Eighty-Fourth Street
Hart, Bridges

"At this hour?"

"He seemed most insistent to speak with you, alone. Shall I call your maid?"

I studied the card, front and back. It appeared a perfectly presentable calling card. I shook my head. "No need."

Who might this man be? What might he have to tell me which required such urgency?

"Very well, mum." Pearson didn't approve.

"Dear Pearson." I took his hand. "You may stand ready in case I should scream. But I doubt anyone who passed your scrutiny would attack me in my own study."

"Yes, mum." He seemed both relieved at standing guard and gratified by the compliment.

I prepared myself for the man's entry, curious as to the nature of his visit.

The door opened. The gentleman wore the latest fashion, with a tan outer coat and a dark brown top hat. He took the hat off as he entered the room, which shielded his face from my view until the door closed. He put the hat in his other hand, which held a polished oak-stained brown walking stick tipped in gold, and turned, straightening to look at me.

I felt astonished. "Morton!"

He walked into the room, finger over his lips. "Now, Mrs. Spadros," he said, his speech impeccable, "would any creature named Morton be in your study?"

I laughed, delighted. "How wonderful! However did you —? No, I won't ask, not now. How may I help you?"

Morton had a beautiful smile; his teeth were perfect. That was his best feature. I wouldn't have called the man particularly handsome. He was at least thirty, yet not much taller than I. His face was too angular, his nose too large, and his skin had not survived adolescence well. But today, he appeared quite the gentleman, wearing a brown suit and polished brown wingtips. "Any news on your missing lad's whereabouts?"

"I have hardly had time to do an investigation."

"I can be of assistance, if you are willing," Morton — or, I should say, Master Rainbow — said.

I felt suspicious. "What is your interest in this?"

"I believe someone is attempting to subvert the original goals of the Red Dogs, discrediting the group to further his own agenda. I intend to stop him."

"But why? What are the goals of this Red Dog Gang?"

He gave me a sudden, surprised glance.

"And why would you be involved with such a group in the first place?"

"Ah, my dear, I don't give up my secrets so easily. I will say only that many people are not particularly fond of your Family's rule over this city."

"But you're willing to help me."

Morton smiled. It was Morton of the Diamond Pot, yet it was not. The transformation was remarkable.

"I'm sorry you've come all this way. I have no information."

"Madame, if you do come across any, I beg you to allow me to accompany you. I could be an asset."

The man seemed quite motivated. "I have your card. If I should need assistance I'll contact you at once." The door to Tony's study opened. Tony and Pearson spoke in the hall, but I couldn't hear what they said. "I must now concoct a reason for your visit. My butler will certainly tell my husband of your arrival."

"Be at ease, madame. I have prepared for just such an eventuality. This may assist in your investigations."

Just then, the door opened, and in came Tony, who had a somewhat wary look to him, not sure what to make of all this. "I have not had the privilege of making your acquaintance, Mr. …"

"Rainbow." Morton handed over another calling card. "Master Blaze Rainbow, currently of Hart quadrant."

Morton and Tony shook hands. I stood there, amazed.

"And to what do my wife and I owe the honor of your visit?"

"I'm sorry to call at such a late hour, but Mrs. Hart was most insistent."

Tony frowned. "Mrs. Hart …?"

"The younger Mrs. Hart, Mrs. Helen Hart, put together a luncheon for tomorrow. The invitation for Mrs. Spadros fell behind her sofa cushions. She found the invitation this evening and was distraught at the idea that Mrs. Spadros wouldn't be able to attend." He produced an invitation. "But fortunately Mrs. Spadros has assured me her schedule is open." He paused, turning to Tony. "I hope this is still the case?"

"I … well, of course! Thank you for your kind efforts."

Morton bowed. "I won't keep you any longer." He handed me the invitation, which seemed thicker than normal, and left.

I put the invitation in my pocket, and we sat by the fire. Tony rang for Pearson to bring us drinks.

Blaze Rainbow's calling card sat between us.

After Pearson returned with the drinks and went on his way, Tony said, "I hadn't heard that the Harts were engaging gentlemen as their Associates. They must be either doing very well, or they have some very bored gentlemen."

I laughed. "Perhaps some gentlemen such as this Master Rainbow see a way to move up in the world."

Tony tilted his head, and his eyes widened. "I hadn't considered this." He smiled. "You're most perceptive."

I shrugged. It was the way the world worked. I felt grateful for the compliment, but I was no more perceptive than my husband. He lacked only the experience in moving from the depths, having been born to luxury and privilege.

Being a gentleman meant privilege of its own. But in a city where one Family owned a fourth of the city, having seized most of its buildings, country-houses, and lands, even the titled were lesser to those in the Business, whose privilege was unrivaled.

This privilege meant much more than just financial affluence. At Tony's word, men died, families were torn apart, whole neighborhoods were devastated. How could you not be shaped by being born to such power?

"Such energy in bettering oneself should be encouraged. And I like the idea of gentlemen rising in the Business. Hart is a genius." Tony leaned back, sipping his drink as the fire crackled and snapped.

Perhaps this Master Rainbow really was a gentleman. He seemed quite confident and prepared. But why pretend to be a Pot rag? Why run a Red Dogs trey?

Tony would never speak with the Harts, asking about Morton and his relationship with them. The Families considered such information secret.

Gardena Diamond's revelations about her brother Jack, for example, could be seen as treasonous. Her father might feel justified in beating or even killing her for betraying a member of her Family, should harm befall them because of her prattle.

These thoughts made me re-evaluate that entire conversation. Gardena either lied outrageously, or she trusted me much more than she should, to the point of utter foolishness, nay, insanity. But which was it? Could she have a touch of the madness which afflicted her brother Jack?

This concerned me quite a bit. I liked Gardena. I didn't want any sort of illness to befall her.

But there was an underlying motive for their visit which was not clear to me. Jonathan — who, if anyone was sane, it was he — seemed deeply troubled. His younger sister Gardena desired some response from her stories which I failed to give, and …

I shook my head. It made no sense.

"Is anything wrong?"

I frowned. "I had a conversation this afternoon which I'm not sure how to interpret."

"Ah, Miss Gardena Diamond."

I laughed.

"She often speaks in riddles. I often wonder if she has motives other than she states, so I guard my tongue when around her."

I considered the matter. "That's probably wise. She *is* a Diamond, after all, no matter how pleasant."

Tony smiled. "She *is* attractive," he said, the sudden huskiness of his voice showing the truth, "but … a man would despair were he to become attached to her. She is too changeable, too … too much the actress, and not enough the reality of life. I don't know how else to say it."

I nodded. It was a good description, actually.

The alternative was that she was a tremendously good spy. No one would ever suspect a woman who acted as she did of being a spy.

I leaned back, drained my glass, and poured another. This was a puzzle, and I always enjoyed them.

But Tony put his hand over the glass. "No more. We have sat talking for long enough. I would like to go to our bed-chambers."

I chuckled, noting the irony. Thinking of Gardena Diamond evidently stirred some passion in him.

The Finesse

In the morning, I opened the invitation Morton had given me the night before.

Inside the invitation was a note:

> Mrs. Spadros,
>
> I presume you are alone while reading this. If not, do not show any level of surprise or alarm.
>
> Mrs. Helen Hart did invite you to a luncheon, but it is next week, and you have declined because of a prior engagement. She is neither alarmed nor unhappy by your decline; the invitation was a formality urged on her by her father-in-law.
>
> Since I don't know the outcome of our meeting tonight, I can't advise you further. If you require assistance tomorrow, travel to the Hart quadrant at the appropriate time and go to the Ladies' Club. Enter, but do not sign in. Ask directions to the boathouse and visit the gate to dock 36. A maid of your size will be there. She is deaf and mute, but reads lips, and will bring you to a place where you can exchange clothing.

Interesting. He knew I changed clothes to perform my cases. Was he the man who followed me? No, I decided; the man I saw was much taller, more slender. Master Rainbow might be an excellent disguise artist, but no one could change their body to that degree.

The invitation will allow you to cross the bridge into Hart quadrant. I trust you understand what should be done with this note.

Your servant, BR

I smiled at the last line; I was female, not stupid. I threw the note in the fire. Try deciphering that!

Even without the note, and without having seen Helen Hart's writing before, I should know the handwriting was not hers. A bit heavy for a woman's. An excellent imitation, though: Morton was to be commended.

Amelia came in with my tray, paper, and mail, and I had her pick out a luncheon dress for me. I asked her to choose a color many ladies were wearing, suitable for visiting another quadrant, that had a hat with a veil.

She was very good at fashion; at first, I had chosen poorly and been reprimanded or embarrassed. Then Roy picked Amelia for my lady's maid, and her understanding of such niceties came in handy at times.

"Will you be needing me to accompany you?"

"No, spend time with your family. I may be delayed past tea — I'm not sure what Mrs. Hart has in mind for us!"

Amelia smiled. "It must be grand, going to luncheon parties and such."

I understood her feelings perfectly. "It must seem that way, but these are not friends. The invitation was a way to show off their wealth and status, and I must take care with every move I make. One wrong word could cause a great deal of trouble." I paused. "It will be a tiring day." Every word true, just not the way she took it to mean.

"I'm sorry, mum. Of course, I don't understand your life the way you do."

"I took no offense. I remember feeling as you do, until I saw the reality. There are trials with every form of life, they only differ in kind and severity."

"Yes, mum. I'll go draw your bath now."

Of course, she didn't understand. Who wouldn't prefer jewels, lavish meals, your own carriage, and a maid to care for your every whim? What could possibly be wrong with that?

I gazed out of the window at the overcast sky. Sometimes I wished I were back in the Pot. Even though survival hung on the edge, life was less complicated. How people felt about you was plain; their words, while harsh, were straightforward; and there was honor among those thieves.

***

The *Bridges Daily* held a surprising tale. A regulation was introduced to the city council overnight making it a crime for citizens to refuse to speak to the police, subject to a fine. If proof came later that they had knowledge of a crime, they could be jailed. The backer of the bill was Pike and Associates; it was introduced by an apprentice law clerk, Mr. Thrace Pike.

I laughed. Mr. Pike's regulation would not make him popular, but the Diamonds would be quite pleased. More prison inmates meant more money for them.

The *Golden Bridges* had as its top story:

YOUNG MAN FOUND DEAD

> A body in the Diamond section of the under-tunnels on Market Center was identified as Stephen Rivers, age 15, of the Spadros quadrant. Master Rivers died of strangulation, says the coroner.
>
> The young man, involved with the Red Dogs street gang, was questioned earlier as part of an investigation into the disappearance of David Bryce, age 12. Master Bryce's brother, Herbert, age 16, was recently found strangled in the Diamond slums. Could the three crimes be related?

I stared numbly at the portrait of the young man who so happily took my half-dollar. Did I send him to his death? I wondered if the man in brown who frightened him so caught up with him in the end.

Stephen and Herbert. Both searched for David Bryce, and both strangled.

Had they found David, and died for it? Did they discover some secret deemed important enough to kill in order to hide? Or did they run afoul of the scoundrel Tony's men described as loving nothing more than torment?

Cold dread crept along my spine. What was I involved with?

***

Honor helped me out of my carriage in front of the Hart Ladies' Club, and stubborn woman that I am, I thanked him for it. "Mrs. Hart will arrange my return, so you may enjoy the hospitality if you wish before returning home."

Each club had facilities for the coachmen while they waited for their personages to complete their business. I heard that the Hart quadrant amenities were quite good.

He smiled. "Thank you, mum." Then he glanced at the sky, which as usual, was overcast. "Wishing you good weather."

The Hart Ladies' Club had red doors edged with silver, and silver railings lined the brick steps. A man in red Hart livery with silver buttons and piping opened the door for me.

I entered the expansive red-carpeted lobby. Another man in Hart livery stood behind a podium of red-painted wood. Behind him lay many tables set for luncheon, some with ladies dining. "May I help you?"

"Would you direct me to the boathouse?"

"Certainly, mum. To your right, down the hall, then through the doors out to the docks. The boathouse is a brief walk, but straight on. Shall I call an escort?"

"No need. Thank you." I gave him a big smile.

He tipped his hat, cheeks reddening, and studied the papers he held.

The walnut-paneled hall was inlaid with the Hart Family symbol — red, edged in silver. The glass doors at the end of the hall held the same symbol on them. A man in livery opened a door for me at the end of the hall.

The walkway was smooth-cut, closely placed red brick, wide enough for groups of four to pass each other with room to spare, and lined with budding red roses on both sides. Silver-toned fencing stood to the right, far enough away so I saw just the tops of carriages passing by.

We were well protected: the only goal or dream high-class women were allowed to have.

The stories of women going on adventures seemed a myth of the far past, like the stories of travel to stars. Some said women even journeyed into the high aether.

But they also spoke of other cities and other ways.

One day, I would take the zeppelin, travel to other cities, experience these other ways of life.

I glanced at a movement outside the fencing to my right. Had someone been watching me?

I began walking faster, feeling uneasy.

Docks appeared to my left, the roses parting at each silvered and numbered gate, with walnut-stained benches trimmed in silver across from them. I approached the boathouse and passed it, continuing on until I reached gate 36.

A red-haired maid sat on the bench doing needlework; she smiled when she saw me.

I followed her out onto the white wooden dock, which had white railings topped with silver at each support. At the end of the dock sat a white yacht with white sails.

Morton, or I should say, Blaze Rainbow, wearing a light brown yachting jacket and tan trousers, appeared on the deck. "Welcome to the *Finesse*."

***

I hesitated to step aboard a stranger's yacht without an escort, especially — and the thought chilled me — the yacht of a man who only wore brown. But the well-turned boat and the presence of the maid, Zia, won me over.

He invited me indoors, offering me a seat in the oak-paneled cabin, which I accepted, and a drink, which I declined.

I recalled my mother's instruction: "Never take nothing, food nor drink, unless you trust the hand who gives it." Those words probably saved me more than once. Even if I did trust Morton, a man who wore disguises and tried to grab me in an alley, I had neither the time nor the inclination to dally over drinks.

"Master Rainbow —"

"Please, call me Blaze."

"Master Rainbow, I would like to express my condolences."

Morton blinked, as if surprised. "I don't understand."

I glanced behind me, but Zia gazed forward placidly. "Stephen. I read about him in the paper."

Morton frowned and shook his head. "How … Where did you come to meet him?"

"I fear I sent him to his doom. I asked him to look for the boy, and now he's dead."

Morton stared at the table for a moment, then shook his head. "It's not your fault."

The boat creaked as we sat in silence.

"If you knew the boy was being held in that warehouse, why didn't you retrieve him?"

Morton avoided my eye. "The building was guarded; I was alone. I sent messages for help, but you were the first to arrive."

He obviously felt ashamed of his inability to rescue the boy. "Master Rainbow, I appreciate your generous offer. If that offer still stands, I need transport to Market Center in such a way to neither attract notice of the Hart Family nor the attention of my servants, who are still on the premises."

He nodded, rose, stood pondering this for a moment, then exchanged gestures with the maid Zia.

Morton planned to travel directly across the river to the Clubb Men's Boathouse, then hire a carriage to Market Center.

"If you could bring me around to the Clubb Women's Center instead, I can make my way to Market Center from there without your help. If that is acceptable, we can proceed," I said.

The two spoke in their hand language again. Morton said, "I don't have a berth at the Clubb Women's Center, but I can leave you at the pier."

"That would be quite satisfactory."

After Zia and Morton cast off, Morton took the wheel, moving the boat into the river. He turned the boat to the left, to sail around the Clubb Pot. Then we passed the stubs of ancient bridges which used to connect the old downtown areas of the Pot.

The Opposition dynamited all four of those bridges at the start of the Alcatraz Coup 100 years ago. They say the destruction kept the Kerr loyalists from reinforcing, but it seemed a pity.

We rode to the Women's Center in silence, and I bade Morton and Zia farewell at the pier. Morton's eyes seemed haunted, as if Stephen's death hadn't felt real until then.

The Clubb Women's Center's pier, railings, and benches were beautiful polished oak, the wood trimmed in brass. Yellow roses lined the walkways, and the glass doors bore the Clubb Family symbol. I walked down an oak-paneled hall carpeted in gold to a podium like the one in the Hart Ladies' Club, painted yellow.

I descended the gold-carpeted, polished oak steps. To my surprise, Mrs. Regina Clubb came up the other side, followed by two of Regina's many granddaughters.

"Why, Mrs. Spadros!" Regina Clubb said. "How did you — I mean, how are you?"

Ah, so she kept notes on me. "I'm quite well, and you?"

"We're well, thank you. I was bringing the girls here for luncheon, and we were delayed."

"I won't keep you then." I curtsied smoothly, feeling glad to have an excuse not to chat. "Have a wonderful time." I continued down the steps, passing by her oak carriage trimmed in brass and its beautiful gold champagne horses.

Mrs. Clubb called, "You too!"

A full stagecoach passed, with "Casino Tours" marked on its side, and I smiled.

Around the corner, I found a taxi-carriage to bring me to the Plaza at Market Center. Clubb quadrant's lamp-posts were tipped with brass, as were their public banisters and street signs. The storefronts were all polished oak; the cobbles and walkways, made of sandstone.

As I rode along, I imagined Regina Clubb was wringing her brains like an old dishcloth trying to deduce how I got past her checkpoints.

***

When I alighted from the taxi-carriage, I saw two people I never expected to see. "Good afternoon."

"Why, Mrs. Spadros," Thrace Pike said, color rising in his cheeks. He wore the same threadbare brown suit, and did not meet my eye. "A pleasure to see you. Let me introduce you to my wife Gertie."

The stout woman who spoke at the tent meeting wore the same gray dress, but she looked better in the light of day, especially when she smiled. "Nice to meet you, mum."

This dress surfaced every few years due to the Cultural Correctness Committee's insistence that women actually wore the thing. No matter how often the CCC brought out historical documents and exhorted the populace, the dresses languished on racks and ended up at poorhouse sales.

Gertie Pike had a wide face and lank blonde hair. Her teeth, uneven, her eyes, too close together. But she moved like a woman in love, and seemed quite taken with her child.

I came round to look in their pram. Fortunately, the child took after its father. "You have a lovely baby."

"Thank you," Gertie said, blushing.

"Congratulations on your new position, Mr. Pike."

Thrace Pike looked startled. "Thank you."

Gertie said, "It's so wonderful; the rooms for law clerks with family are much nicer than ours before."

Her finger missed its ring too. Hard times indeed, if those dank sunless servant quarters seemed so much better than their previous ones. "How lovely for you."

Thrace Pike didn't meet my eye.

I smiled. "It was nice seeing you. Have a fine afternoon."

The poor lambs. So the stories ran true.

The Bridgers had many odd practices; the oddest, the way they arranged their marriages. Rumor had it that each chose the person they found the least attractive physically, so their relationship grew free from the distractions of lust.

It seemed a disaster waiting to happen, but I never once heard of a divorce amongst the Bridgers.

I was almost to the carriage-house when I heard feet running up from behind. A girl appeared beside me, hat in hand, auburn hair flying.

"It **is** you!" Katherine said. "I **knew** it was you!"

I had a most unladylike expression in mind. "Whatever are you doing here?"

"Mama and I were shopping, well, she is shopping and I was bored, so I asked if I could promenade the plaza, and Mama said yes, and then I saw you! So I had to come see you. What are you doing here? Tony said you were to luncheon with the Harts."

Hmm.

I began walking again, and Katherine followed, putting her hat back on as she went.

"I was going to luncheon with the Harts, but I don't like them very much. They act as if I am not there." I leaned over to speak in her ear, "So I gave Honor the slip and came here instead."

Katherine clapped her hands. "Splendid! We can have secret fun together."

"Indeed, it must be secret, for Tony would be vexed if I didn't keep an invitation."

"Tony needs a kick in his pants. He's much too far above himself. But I don't want you to be in trouble. I won't tell."

"How long do we have before your Mama worries for you?"

Katherine shrugged. "I told her I was to promenade, but I go much faster than the rest. Probably another half-hour at least."

"Very good. I want to see the carriages."

"Hurray! I love horses. Daddy won't let me have my own."

"The sooner we get there, the more we can see."

Katherine squealed with delight at seeing the stabled Hackneys. Soon the stable-man arrived, a middle aged fellow wearing a white shirt and brown cotton overalls, probably wondering at the noise. "Can I help you, mum?"

"Yes. My friend and I rode in one of your carriages yesterday and she lost her mother's locket. Her mother just passed, so she is distraught. I told her I would look for it."

"Do you remember the carriage-number?"

"Why no." I felt dismayed. "But the left wheel seemed unbalanced. In fact, I asked the driver to let us out early, because I feared for our safety."

"Well, I'll be busted. So that's what it was all about."

"What do you mean?"

"We had this one carriage stolen two days ago, then it reappeared last night. I thought it was kids, but it sounds like they was running a false taxi. Probably didn't realize the carriage was broke." He walked off, and I followed. Then he turned back to me. "Who all was driving?"

"Two gentlemen, one in brown, the other in white."

He shook his head. "I knew those two were up to no good. Came skulking around, said they wanted to buy a carriage. When I told them they weren't for sale, they left, but something didn't feel right. I went on a walk-around and they were standing across the field back there smoking cigars.

"They didn't seem to be doing anything other than smoking so I went on my way … then when I went back a couple hours later, the carriage was gone."

I frowned. "They didn't say who they were?"

The man shrugged. "The one in brown said his name was … something odd … he gave a card or I would have called the constable right off. I did call when the carriage went missing, and when it appeared, but they said the name on the card was fake." He took a pile of business cards from his chest pocket and began sorting through them. "You want to talk to the constable too?"

"No." I took a step back. "I don't want police involved; I'm a quadrant-lady. Please, all I want is to look for my friend's locket."

"Never you fear, mum, I'll help you." He paused, then said, "Here it is!" He fished out a card. "Frank Pagliacci, it says … never heard a name like that before. The constable called on me this morning, said there's no one in Bridges registered by that name." He glanced over at Katherine. "You, girl, keep away from them horses. Stay with us."

"But I like horses," Katherine said.

"Yeah, well, they don't like you. They're not puppies, they're work animals. Come on, now, come along."

Katherine came along, pouting.

The stable-man brought us to where the carriages were being repaired. A large, newly-mowed field of straw lay next to the repair area, and a stand of trees lay beyond that.

"That's the one." I pointed at a carriage. "See how the wheel is leaning?" It had a divot out of one wheel, just as the driver said.

"Well, good luck to you. If you need anything else just holler."

When the man had gone, I told Katherine, "Keep watch, and tell me if anyone comes by."

"Why?" Katherine said.

"It's a game my Mama used to play with me. Tell me what you see, all the people who walk past, any birds, animals, everything. I'll tell you what I see, and whoever sees most wins."

"You won't see anything inside that old thing."

"Yes, well, it's true, you'll probably win. Let's play anyway; it'll help pass the time. Maybe I'll find my friend's locket, and maybe you'll see something good."

I opened the door to the carriage. From my handbag, I took out a cylindrical case, much like a tiny hat case, which held nested circles of brass and glass an inch in diameter and in height. I unfolded it by sliding the nested tubes so that it looked like a small spyglass, several inches long. When you turned it, the lenses gave magnification of a variable degree, to the thousandth power. The magnification spyglass cost a great deal. But it came to good use in cases like this.

I inspected the door frame and the footplate. A white powder lay on the footplate and inside the door frame. When magnified, tan flecks lay in the powder.

"I see a red bird, and a string of ants," Katherine said.

"What kind?"

"The little black ones."

"I see brown carpeting." I laid the spyglass aside, opened my handbag, and took out a small envelope, which once held buttons. I also took out a stiff eyebrow brush, which I used to brush as much of the powder as I could into the envelope.

Picking up my spyglass, I climbed into the carriage and examined the cushions. Several hairs lay there: brown straight hair and black hair; but not black and curled, as one might expect from a Diamond, but black and straight. Could these be David's? I took out a second envelope and put the hairs into it.

"I see a tabby cat."

"I only see cushions. You're ahead!"

A gray string lay on the floor of the carriage; I put it into the envelope with the hairs. Then I lifted the cushions, finding a penny but nothing more.

I walked to the driver's area. A button lay on the floor of the foot rest: wooden, carved with an eagle's head, a wisp of brown thread attached to it. I put the button and thread into the envelope with the hairs.

"A boy is walking far off by the trees," Katherine said.

The mechanisms underneath the carriage were marvelous: springs and gears which made the ride perfectly smooth. They reminded me a bit of the mechanisms under the rusting steam automobiles back home. Air loved to look at them.

I scanned the ground around the carriage, but found nothing. "You win!" I folded the envelopes and the magnification spyglass and returned them to my handbag.

"You didn't find the locket?"

I acted dejected. "I don't see it anywhere."

"Let me look." She climbed all around. "I don't see it either."

"I bet she dropped it before we got in the carriage. I guess I'll have to go look there." I smiled. "Come, I'll get you a sugarplum."

The Encounter

As it turned out, Katherine's treat cost a penny, and we parted ways, with another warning not to tell. She was so excited with our secret fun I thought she would either blurt out the whole affair or never tell a soul.

Molly would see my being here as an escape. Roy would love the idea of insulting the Harts in this way. I would know whether Katherine was trustworthy.

Perhaps I was beginning to think like Roy after all. I wasn't sure if this was a good development.

I walked around the Plaza until I reached a storefront, with words engraved upon the front window in gold:

> Anna's Medicaments
> Potions, Medicines, And Salves Of All Sorts
> Supply To Hospitals And Clinics Our Specialty

Anna Goren: an apothecary, the woman who packaged and sent my morning tea after it was formulated and sent to her. She supplied the physicians on Market Center and much of Bridges.

Anna had brown skin and long brown hair which curled every which way, piled on top of her head in an untidy bundle. She wore a purple linen dress covered by a white cotton apron, and fussed about a room full of bottles, jars, and beakers, which were in turn full of pills, powders, and potions of all sorts.

She glanced up when I entered. "Mum Spadros! So good to see you! How can I help?"

"Would you look at these?"

"I'm ready to close for luncheon anyway." She shut the door, locked it, and turned the sign to "closed." Then we went to her back room, which was mostly taken up with testing equipment. Copper pipes with brass fittings came down the walls, leading to larger copper and glass cylinders with various labels. "Whatcha got for me, dearie?"

I took out the envelope with the powder in it and put the closed envelope in her hand. "If you could tell me what this is, I would be most grateful."

She opened the envelope, peered into it, smelled the contents, then set up a row of glass tubes in a pine and brass holder, putting a bit of the powder into each. She held up what appeared to be a lorgnette-style opera-glass. The handle and frame was brass, and it had large black lenses. "Shield your eyes."

I did so.

Then she dropped a match into the first tube. A flash of white light and a familiar smell wafted forth. "Just as I thought," Anna said. "Party Time."

***

I ate luncheon with Anna at a small table in her back room as she did one test after another. She sat for a moment, took a bite of her sandwich, then said, "Oh!" with her mouth full, jumping up to do another test.

I laughed. "You are like a Jack-in-the-box."

"When I think of something, I must investigate! How else will I know?"

Anna helped me more than once with strange substances I found while on cases, never asking for a cent. Her payment was to know, and to understand.

"I have it!" She flopped into her chair, a curl of her hair coming out of its bundle to fall beside her face. "This particular Party Time," she took a drink of her tea, "is the sort found in a factory, before it is cut and sent to the distributors. The Party Time itself is pure!"

"Oh?"

"Yes, unadulterated by any chemical normally used before distribution. However, it contains wood chips. Party Time in bulk is often stored in barrels; I imagine that the barrel broke, and shards of wood got into the mix. Where did you find this?"

"On the floorboards of a stolen carriage."

"Ah," Anna said, as if that made everything clear. "Dirt and shoe-polish and carpet-fiber mixed in. Now I understand!"

"Would you test these as well?" I opened my second envelope and handed her the threads. She snipped a tiny piece from each and lit them afire, then handed the larger portions back to me.

"The gray is wool; the brown is cotton. Both from a man's jacket, if I'm not mistaken. A seamstress could tell you more."

"You're wonderful, Anna." I planned to leave then, but recalled the Inventor's words.

"Is something wrong?"

She wasn't an Inventor, nor did she ever work on the Magma Steam Generator that I knew of. But if anyone could find the solution to this, Anna could. "I have a problem that perhaps you might have some insight into." I explained to her the issue with the pilings and the Magma Steam Generator, as best I knew how.

I had never seen her frown before. "This is a serious problem. I will consider it carefully."

"Why is it so serious? Can we not just use candles? Cut trees for warmth?"

"Oh, my dear girl," she said, "lights and heat are the least worry. This is no natural city; the whole of it is a construct, a mechanism. Its entirety, from the aperture to the river, runs on power. Life would be most unpleasant without it."

I had no idea. "Can you help?"

"I don't know, dearie, but I will try my best."

"Thank you for everything." I glanced at her clock. "I must go. I told Mr. Spadros I would be back for tea."

Anna smiled. "Ah, yes, the husband. How happy that I was never burdened with one!" She came over, took my face in her hands, and kissed my forehead, as she always did. "Off you go, my dear. Have a lovely evening."

I felt pleased for more than one reason. The Diamond Family had only one Party Time factory, disguised as a shoe polish factory. This must be where they held David. The factory did make shoe polish, but only to hide the barrels of Party Time behind in case the Feds came snooping.

Some zeppelins carrying Agents had unfortunate accidents, one involving a surface-to-air missile. Now the Feds seemed to be afraid to enter the city. Even though Party Time was illegal, the courts were mostly bought, and half the police were on it themselves, so not even they wanted the Feds around. If it weren't for the Bridgers — and of course, the Families — Party Time wouldn't be illegal at all.

I tried Party Time once — it felt a bit like being drunk, without having to down a few bottles to get there. Despite its frivolous name, Party Time made the Spadros Family a fortune: production, distribution, and marketing of Party Time in the Spadros quadrant was at an all-time high. Tony's father Roy planned to expand our territory outside the boundaries of Bridges itself.

But the Diamonds didn't make much Party Time themselves. Since they controlled the prison, they preferred to push for harsh sentencing of those hapless souls caught with Party Time and without a big enough bribe (or good enough Family connections) to escape. Then they charged the prisoner's quadrant a fortune for care and upkeep. It was a sweet set-up.

A ball came across my path, and a small boy ran to fetch it. I squatted to pick the ball up. "Here you are."

A young woman with light brown skin and blonde curls came up." Tell the nice lady thank you, Master Roland."

"Thank you." The boy was exquisite: brown skin, black eyes, black ringlet curls, a beautiful smile. He reminded me of someone.

"You're welcome." I smiled. "He's beautiful."

The woman beamed. "And such a good child, too."

This must be his nanny. I stood and put out my hand. "Jacqueline Spadros."

She took my hand and curtsied. "Octavia Diamond, mum, so nice to meet you." She beckoned to the boy. "Come along, Master Roland, it's time to go home. Let's see if Miss Bessie has had her calf yet."

"Hurray!" The little one skipped along beside her, and they held hands as they went.

***

On the way home, I stopped at Madame Biltcliffe's dress shop. Several well-dressed women browsed the wares, none of whom I recognized. Madame was returning a roll of cloth to its rack when I entered. She glanced up, surprise on her face. "Mrs. Spadros —!"

The women turned to me and curtsied.

"— How can I help you?"

I smiled. "I stopped by to ask about some cloth I saw in another shop. I would love a dress made of it."

The other women turned back to their browsing. Madame came over and took my arm. "Wonderful! Come to my office."

We went to her office, and she took a ring of keys from her waistband and unlocked it. Her office smelled freshly painted, and the window was new. She must have noticed my puzzlement. "Ah!" She put her hand to her forehead. "I am forgetting to tell you. Never have so many customers been here! Before the New Year, someone broke the window and came in."

"What?"

She nodded, closing the door. "The place, it was a mess!"

"Was anything missing?"

"Not a thing."

"Did you contact the police?"

She laughed. "I have been in Bridges long enough to know those results. Scandal for you, and policeman after policeman asking for money 'to speed investigations.'" She shook her head with a smile. "The window had a crack; it needed changing. So it's done, with less bother."

I showed her the threads and button. "Yes, your friend is right, from a man's jacket. I would say, hmm, five years old? This button company no longer does business."

Ah. Interesting. I took up the items and went to the door, opening it. "Thank you, Madame, you've been very helpful!"

"A pleasure, Mrs. Spadros. I'll order the cloth for you at once."

Clever woman, indeed.

During the taxi-carriage ride home, I thought about the button. I should have asked Madame what company made it. But a jacket maker who wished to economize, with clientele on a limited budget, might use older buttons for quite some time. I would have to investigate this later.

Why would someone break into Madame's office, then take nothing? I wasn't sure what information of value she might have there. Measurements?

Yet another item which made no sense. I put it aside.

I exited the taxi-carriage a few blocks away from home so no one would see I didn't arrive in a Hart carriage, and considered my plan as I walked.

I needed to learn the precise location of the Diamond Party Time factory, then obtain a set of blueprints. This meant a trip to the Records Hall on Market Center. The most difficult part would be to learn whether David still remained at the factory.

But that could wait for later.

I joined Tony in his study for tea.

He seemed anxious. "How was your luncheon?"

"Wonderful!" I remembered my time with Anna. "I had a lovely time."

"I'm so glad." Tony sounded relieved.

"Did your day go well?"

"Quite. The quarterly reports were ready. We took in over $3,000 during Yuletide."

I stared at him in shock, remembering the night long ago where I was captured for the promise of a dollar.

Damn my father — I never did get that dollar.

"I felt surprised myself. But I suppose all those pennies at the roulette tables and slot machines add up."

Why would anyone throw their money at the slim chance to win more? It seemed a foolish luxury.

"You seem distracted," Tony said.

Hmm. What to tell him … "I heard an unusual name today. Have you ever heard of a gentleman named Frank Pagliacci?"

Tony shook his head. "Doesn't sound familiar. Could be one of the new families over in the Clubb quadrant. I read in the newspaper the other day about the trials of people who move to Bridges from other cities."

The article seemed frivolous, but Tony enjoyed such things, especially involving the upper classes. "Is it so different there?"

Tony shrugged. "Depends on the city. Customs are different, wherever you go."

Mrs. Bryce spoke of debtors' prison. Depending on who you owed, you might be shot, but thrown into prison? It seemed a poor way to get your money back.

"Perhaps you might not like to answer right away, having just returned, but I'd like to visit City Hall."

I almost laughed. The Records Hall, exactly where I needed to go, was next door to City Hall.

"We're going to remodel the casino, and I need to speak with the officials there." He paused for several seconds then shook his head. "No, I should never have asked … it will take much of the day … and will be much too tedious …"

"No! I would love to go."

Tony seemed surprised. "I had no idea you enjoyed the place."

Those offices were dreary, but this was a perfect opportunity to find the blueprints to the Diamond Party Time factory.

Thinking of the Diamonds reminded me of the article about the new regulation, and I mentioned it to Tony.

"I hadn't noticed it. The Diamonds must be very pleased."

I chuckled. "My thoughts exactly. But what an opportunity to win the favor of our people. "

"What do you mean?"

"Pay the fines for anyone caught up in this law. This will encourage them to tell us of any police harassment, and make them love us more."

Tony beamed at me. "I have such a brilliant wife. I'll have the men pass the word."

Doubtless leaving out that it was my idea, but no matter. In that, I was like Anna. I delighted in having worthwhile ideas more than receiving praise for them. "If we're lucky, the other Families won't consider this for a while. We might even gain ground."

Tony became quite excited at that prospect, and took out paper and pen, making notes there at the table on how to make best use of this scheme.

Almost as if this whole thing were a game.

At least it was better to win ground by making the people love us than by violence in the streets.

"When did you plan to visit City Hall?"

Tony put his pen down and sighed. "I got word right before you arrived. The Clubbs have put a carriage-search on everyone going in and out of their quadrant."

I stared at him in shock. "What?"

He nodded. "So of course, all the other families are doing the same, and putting watchers on the river, in case this is a ploy to distract us from a Clubb attack. The lines going into and out of Market Center will be horrendous."

"Whatever could have caused them to do that?"

Tony shook his head. "The Clubbs are secretive. It could be their granddaughter Calcutta running off again, for all we know."

I doubted that. The look on Regina Clubb's face when she saw me ... "Well, I have nothing planned tomorrow."

"We should leave as early in the day as possible, after morning meeting, perhaps, and have luncheon on Market."

***

The next day, after a long wait to cross the bridge to Market Center, we reached City Hall. Tony told the coachmen to stay on the island

and gave them leave to visit the tavern. "You may put your drinks and luncheon on our tab."

I glanced back as we went to the building steps, and Honor tipped his hat. I felt touched by his thanks.

Tony didn't look back once.

Gardena was right. I wasn't a Spadros, not really.

Tony reached into his breast pocket, retrieving a long list of what he needed and who he must see today. I felt certain I could find what I needed while he was occupied.

The Hall had white walls with thick, dark wood borders around each of its equally dark doors. A floor of black tile led to a set of black wooden stairs with black banisters, edged in brass. We climbed to the fourth floor, and went to a door marked, "Permits."

I turned to Tony. "I'd like to view the paintings here and in the Records Hall while you're engaged. Shall we meet in front?"

"Certainly. In an hour, for luncheon?"

Was it noon already? As if in answer, the clock tower began its chiming. I nodded.

I waited until he went inside. I then descended four flights of stairs, hurried outside, and walked over to the Records Hall. On the inside it looked identical to City Hall.

The map room on the second floor held an ancient brown-skinned man with white-glazed eyes behind a black marble slab desk. "May I help you, miss?" A three-year-old boy played with dolls on the floor in the corner.

"I'd like to see a map of the city." I pitched my voice like that of a young girl's and attempted Mrs. Bryce's accent. If the old man thought I was young, he might let me see more.

"Come, come this way." We went down a long hall to an archway. The huge room beyond was full of brown wooden bookshelves. He crossed to the bookshelves, then turned left.

He shuffled along with his right hand on the bookshelves until we came to an oak table with a huge book on it. The book was bound in dark green leather, which was cracked at the spine. Across from this table sat a small-scale map of the entire city.

This map sat on a round table six feet wide, with a domed dust cover. The populated area was the size of a dinner plate; the rivers, the width of pencils; the island, a penny in the center. "Maps of the whole city. What quadrant are you from?"

"Diamond. My mother and I just moved here. She's next door getting her permits."

"Ah, yes." The gold band on his left ring finger glinted as he turned pages one by one. "These pages show the city quadrants, or you can look at the whole city, with the countryside and all, over at the dome-table." He gazed through me. "You look as long as you like. If you need anything else, let me know."

"Oh, yes. I almost forgot. I promised my mother I would draw for her." I saw the factory at once, with the number 3123/67, and a building near it. "Where might I find the blueprint area? She needs to rebuild ..." What was the name? I peered at the ancient map. "The Omaha building. I'm to make a copy."

"Right this way." He shuffled along the long row of ancient books. At the end of the row, he turned, his arm out. Five stacks down, he turned right, into a row of black-bound volumes. "It's not often we get newcomers to Diamond. I was born there in Diamond, way back when old Caesar Diamond and his pack was shooting up the area, back in Eighteen and Twenty-Seven." The old man cackled. "Big Cassino and the Beer Card Boys, that's what his men called themselves. You ever hear of them?"

"No, sir." A newcomer wouldn't know about them.

"I remember running after their carriages as a lad, when they rooted out the Wheelcard Gang. Those was exciting days."

He moved along, his hand running across the books. "Here we go, Plat 3123/66, the Omaha building. All the blueprints you need." He took out the book, shuffled back the way we came, and set it on a large table. A row of quills and inkwells sat in the center. "The paper for your copies is there." He pointed to a shelf past the table.

"Thank you, sir."

"It's what I'm here for." A bell rang, far out front. "Let me know if you need anything else."

He shuffled off. Once he was out of sight and sound, I hurried back, got out the book for the factory, took it to the table, and scanned through the pages, listening for the old man's return.

I pulled a small notebook from my handbag and made notes and drawings.

Canisters of materials … supply rooms …

Entryways … front, back, side …

Locker rooms …

Various levels … the layout of the building …

The basement … where the boy was kept. The most likely place, anyway.

I heard brisk footsteps, from far down the hall and around the corner, coming closer. Not the old man's.

I returned the factory blueprint book to its place and myself to the table, but intuition told me not to stay there. I hid behind the bookcase just in time. Jack Diamond's shaved head peered around the corner with a concerned, inquisitive expression on his face. He looked so much like his twin brother Jonathan that for an instant I forgot to be afraid.

What could Jack possibly be doing here?

"You're sure?" Jack said. The old man's shuffling footsteps came closer.

Alarmed, I hurried to the end of the first set of stacks, across an aisle, then past another long set, looking for an exit, but there was none. A short, thick bookcase of oak-stained wood with more quills and paper blocked my path, and I crouched behind it.

"Yes, sir, she was right over there at the table. She pretended to be a girl, but my eyes ain't that bad, sir. A full tall woman she was, wearing red like all the ladies are these days, and one of them feather hats. Something didn't seem right."

The footsteps began to move to the table, which would put them in view.

I needed a distraction. I took off my hat, which held two feathers in it, and pulled one of the feathers off, sticking it in the books so its top peeked up past the edge. Then I put my hat back on and moved out of their view.

"Any idea who she was?"

"No. She said she was new to Bridges, just moved into Diamond. Her accent was a bit like from Dickens … but her coloring, she looked like a Hart to me. And she knew the Omaha building. Most everyone in Diamond calls it the Smith building, on account of the bank that was there before your daddy shot Mr. Plafond Smith dead back in '87. No one's called it the Omaha since the Bloody Year," he gave a short laugh, "long before you were born. The Harts captured that part for a while there."

Oh, no. No wonder he became alarmed.

"Well, isn't that an old book? She could have just read the name off the page." Jack chuckled. "We're not in the old days anymore, Swan. There's going to be outsiders here."

"I suppose you're right, sir, but I didn't want to take chances. Not with all that's going on."

"You did right. Lucky I was next door."

"I smell her, she went this way." Swan shuffled along my trail.

I was gathering my skirts to move on when Jack said:

"What book is this? It was out farther than the others."

"That's the Mayer building, sir, right next to the Smith one. It's gonna be tore down soon."

I took off my hat again and peered between the top of the books. Jack stood frowning, book in hand. On his small finger, a silver ring with a clear stone glinted. "What could she have possibly wanted with this?" Then he glanced my way. "Look!" He patted Swan's arm. "There she is!" He rushed towards me.

I glanced to my right, appalled. I forgot about the feather! Gathering my skirts, I crawled along the long thick bookcase until I reached its end. I hurried past the gap to the bookcases just in time to avoid him, and was hidden by the bookcases between us.

I heard whispering at the far end, then, "Got you!" A sound as if someone leapt forward, then, "Damn!" A pause, then Jack let out an exuberant, approving laugh. "She's tricky!"

Swan laughed. "Most are, sir."

I rushed on tiptoe to the archway. Jack's voice came from the far end of the stacks, "Hey!"

I heard the click of Jack's white patent-leather shoes coming towards me as I fled the map area, panting. I ran down the hallway past the little boy, who waved at me and giggled.

I hurried down the stairs, through the front lobby and out the front doors, putting on my hat as I pushed past a host of ladies wearing various shades of red.

I forced myself to walk down the front steps, heart pounding.

Just before the last step, I glanced back.

Jack opened the front door, peering around as the sun broke through the clouds. I turned my head so he wouldn't see my face … and immediately bumped into someone.

"My apologies!" the man said.

"Master Blaze Rainbow." I kept my back to the door as people streamed past us. Clouds darkened the sky.

He took a step backwards, off the stairs. "Mrs. Jacqueline Spadros. Fancy meeting you here!"

I glanced at the door; Jack Diamond was gone. I took a deep breath and forced myself to smile. "A pleasure to see you again."

"A pleasure to see you too! What are you doing here?"

"My husband is at City Hall, so I thought I would amuse myself by looking at the paintings in the lobbies." I stepped off of the stairs and moved around the corner towards City Hall.

Morton followed. "So what did you think?"

"Dreadful. Most disappointing." They truly were, unless new ones appeared since the last time I viewed them.

He moved beside me. "I'm sorry to hear that. Did you happen to visit any offices while you were here?"

"Why, Master Rainbow, I would almost think you were garnering information. But a gentleman like yourself would never be so crass."

"I have offended you."

"Never. Rather, you have impressed me with your tenacity. I'm sure it was no accident, us meeting here." Clearly he had people notifying him of my whereabouts, which meant spies either at the Spadros bridge, or more likely here on Market Center.

I changed my assessment of him: perhaps he was one of the men following me, either he or an associate.

Morton tipped his hat. "You're most perceptive, madam. Then do you now know where the boy is held?"

I stopped in front of a large floral display, where we could be seen from neither the Records Hall nor City Hall, and faced him. "I believe I do."

"Would you be willing to share that information?"

"Why should I do that?"

Morton looked exasperated. "My employer will only pay me if I rescue the boy myself."

I smiled. "You have an interesting dilemma."

"As do you. The carriage-search. You can't get into the Diamond quadrant again unnoticed."

I hadn't considered that. "Are we to take another ride in your yacht, then?"

He smiled. "You have given me the quadrant. I will give you a ride in return, but I must accompany you."

I felt irritated at myself. "I might let you do that, for a percentage of your fee. But Zia must be aboard the yacht, and I will hire the carriage." I didn't trust a man who grabbed women in alleys, and I certainly would not get into any carriage that he hired, maid or no maid. "You've already admitted my information has value."

He chuckled. "Damnable woman," he whispered. "Very well, ten percent."

"Sixty."

"Twenty."

"Fifty."

"Thirty."

I felt amazed that the man bargained with me. "Forty it is then." He must have been either desperate or had no intention of giving me anything. At the time, I gave a fifty-fifty chance of the latter. "When shall we take our adventure?"

"I'll send another invitation in the post tomorrow."

"Splendid." I gave him my hand, which he shook.

Just then, Tony came walking up. "Master Rainbow! So good to see you."

Morton gave Tony a handshake, and tipped his hat to me. "A pleasure to see you as well." He checked his pocket-watch. "I'm afraid, though, that I'm late for an appointment — I must be off." He moved down the street and disappeared into the crowd.

"What was that about? I saw you shake hands."

I chuckled. "Apparently I made a fair impression upon Mrs. Helen Hart, and Master Rainbow has agreed to suggest another meeting with her."

"Really? How kind of him. I'm glad that you and Helen Hart are getting on so well. We should invite her to tea. I've thought our families should become better friends."

I took Tony's arm as we strolled along past the Records Hall. "Did you get your work done?"

"Most of it. One of the men I wished to see has fallen ill. I made an appointment with him for later this week." It began to rain, and he opened his umbrella over us. "But now, it is high time for luncheon."

While we ate, I thought about Jack Diamond, back in the map room. He sounded, acted ... normal, even reasonable. But Gardena said Jack had his lucid days.

I shuddered to think of such a horrible malady. But I couldn't let sympathy for Jack's plight cause me to let my guard down.

When we returned home, I sent a note to Master Rainbow at the address on his card, asking him to arrange a meeting with Mrs. Helen Hart for tea at the Spadros Women's Club, which like the others, had a boathouse.

I also sent notes to my contacts, inquiring after this Frank Pagliacci. I wished I had men of my own, as Tony did, to keep watch on Jack Diamond's whereabouts. That encounter was much too close.

The Question

After dinner, Tony read in his study by the fire, while I sipped sherry and thought.

There were too many questions.

Why were people so interested in my activities? Morton practically confessed to following me. Mrs. Clubb had lookouts for me. Jack had the map room watched.

Although … Jack Diamond didn't know it was I in his map room, or he wouldn't have stopped searching so soon.

I smiled, wondering what he did think. Some woman from Hart quadrant sneaking around, pretending to be an outsider, asking about a building next to his Party Time factory.

Oh, dear. Sooner or later he would make the connection. I hoped Jack didn't increase the guards around the factory.

Having the blueprints would help a great deal. But even assuming Morton was serious about accompanying me, we knew nothing about the guards and their number.

These blueprints fascinated me, yet I knew nothing about the mechanisms they held. This led me to a second question, which perhaps Tony might answer. "How is Party Time made?"

"Hmm? Oh, it's a series of chemical steps." Tony put a bookmark in his book, then went to his desk for paper, taking a fountain pen from his vest pocket. "It begins as a plant: its leaves are crushed and treated." Using his book as a base to write upon, he began to draw, and I peered over his shoulder in excitement.

But he began speaking of things I didn't understand. He drew lines and letters as he talked, making many shapes, and arrows which went from one shape to another. I wanted to know, so I felt discouraged and frustrated at not understanding his words, which gave me little insight. Neither Roy nor Molly gave me this information, or even knowledge of the notations Tony made.

"I'm impressed with your knowledge." I felt mortified by my ignorance of something so vital to the Business. Perhaps Roy considered a Pot rag too ignorant to learn this.

My eyes stung at that thought, but I took a deep breath and forced the feelings away, keeping my voice light. "It looks quite complicated."

Tony put the paper aside, then capped his pen and returned it to his vest pocket. "I've never made it myself, but I must know how it's made, so I can oversee the workers and give advice if needed." He paused for several seconds. "A few of these reagents can be explosive if mixed in large amounts."

"Why do you mention that?"

"If the men who attacked intended to kill me, they could have set the factory to explode when we entered. Or shoot me in that ambush, now that I think of it. Six men, aiming at me ... one of those bullets would have hit true."

I felt horrified. "So why attack with pipes instead?"

"That is the question. To distract us?"

To distract us. From what? What were they really doing?

The fire crackled. It struck me how quiet Roy had been these past weeks. "What has your father been doing?"

"I sent him to find our missing guards," Tony said, "with strict instructions to torture no one, but to bring any suspects to me."

My heart began pounding in fear at the prospect of speaking to Roy in that manner. "You have courage."

Tony shook his head. "I almost died the other day." He paused, then spoke slowly, gazing at the floor. "I can no longer allow my life to toss in the wind, as if I had all eternity."

He straightened, staring straight ahead. "And I refuse to be dictated to by a man who holds neither love nor respect for me, but enjoys finding ways to cause me pain." He turned to me with determination in his eyes. "If my father wants me to become his heir, he must pay me heed. Otherwise I will take you and leave Bridges, and he can find another heir. I will no longer be treated like a child in my own home."

Tony risked his life … confronted Roy Spadros … for us?

A burden lifted from my heart, and I felt as if I saw my husband for the first time. Tony was no longer a boy frightened of his father, who I must protect out of fear for his life. Somehow, without my knowing it, he became a man, with the strength to stand up to a man who terrified an entire city.

I took his face in my hands and kissed him, my heart full. Then I gazed into his eyes; this was the first time I felt real love for him. "I have never felt such pride in you. You are truly a man worthy of respect."

Tony took my hands and drew me to sit upon his lap, and this night, I don't recall thinking of Joseph Kerr once.

When I woke, I regretted that. I felt I had betrayed Joe.

It made no rational sense. Yet I wasn't happy. Joe wasn't happy: I could see it in his eyes.

I didn't want to love Tony.

I never wanted to love Tony, and when the servants left me alone for a moment, I wept in frustration at the cage I was in through no fault of my own.

Why couldn't Tony be repulsive, or cruel, or evil? Why couldn't I hate him for what his father had done to me?

***

There were two notes in my mail. The first read:

> Mrs. Helen Hart presents her compliments to Mrs. Spadros, and will have much pleasure in accepting her kind invitation to luncheon at the Spadros Women's Club on the 30th of January.

Which was two days from now.

The note was, again, not quite Mrs. Hart's writing, so I took it to be from Morton and Zia.

The second note had no return address and read:

Dock 21

This appeared to be in Morton's handwriting, on the same paper as the first note. I put the notes in my dresser and locked it, then returned to my seat and pretended to read the newspaper.

So we were to rescue David Bryce, if possible, in two days.

This was bigger than any case I had ever done, and much more dangerous. I took a deep breath and put the paper down, trying to stop my hands from shaking.

Morton planned to sail across the river to the Diamond quadrant. Putting on Zia's uniform would be a good disguise. Getting to the Party Time plant would be easy, once I was in the Diamond quadrant proper. Getting into the plant itself would be more difficult.

David Bryce might be injured, or afraid, and we had not met since he was two years old. How might I win the child's trust? How would I get him out of the building if he couldn't walk? What doctor could I bring him to — if he needed medical attention — that would be discreet? What would I say to Mrs. Bryce if he was dead, or so badly hurt that his life was in question?

Not knowing Morton's true motive frightened me. Could I trust he merely wanted to rescue the boy? What if his goal was to put me in a compromising situation?

Jacqueline Spadros, captured infiltrating the Diamond Party Time plant. That would send ripples through the city even Roy wouldn't be able to solve.

"Your bath is ready," Amelia said.

I let Amelia undress me. "Do you remember the first time I was brought here?" Amelia was a scullery maid then; I suppose she never thought she would rise so far.

"Yes, mum."

"I had never taken a bath. I thought you tried to drown me."

Amelia's eyes widened. "Well, that explains why you fought."

It was a revelation: I fought, and I was right to. This made me feel strong.

The Traitors

During luncheon, Tony said, "My appointment with the man at the Records Hall is day after tomorrow. Would you like to accompany me?"

"Mrs. Hart and I will be having luncheon that day."

"Oh." He sounded disappointed. He seemed very much like Katherine then.

"There will be other times."

"Well, yes," he said. "Will you be having luncheon here, then?"

The Harts had never come to Spadros Manor, as far as I knew, refusing every invitation. This I found odd. Even if they despised me, to refuse Tony's invitations could be construed as an insult. "No, we'll be meeting at the Women's Club."

Tony nodded. "Probably for the best."

I glanced at the servants, who were pointedly not watching us, and decided to save the obvious question for another time.

I pondered our conversation the night before, and the question left unanswered. Was the attack on Tony a distraction? A distraction from what?

The boy and the men, held in the same place. What was the connection? Who was Frank Pagliacci, and what was his connection to Jack Diamond? To hear the stable-man tell it, Frank Pagliacci was in charge. I knew little of Jack, other than what Jonathan and Gardena told me and what I observed. But Jack Diamond didn't seem like a man who allowed another to command him, even in pretense.

Tony said, "Would you like to go for a stroll?"

I didn't, really, but I had no reason not to. "Of course."

We walked through our garden, past the flower mounds Gardena plucked from, and around again. The days seemed ever overcast, the sun a pale ball in the sky, when we saw it. "Do you feel the weather has worsened since we were children? It seems to continually threaten rain of late."

"What troubles you?" Tony said.

I shook my head. "Nothing."

"Forgive me, then, but it seemed at luncheon ..."

I went back over my train of thought, and much of it, I couldn't talk with Tony about. "Oh! I was thinking of the Harts. Why do they refuse our invitations to visit? It seems rather rude."

Tony chuckled. "Yes it does ... but I'm sure they have their reasons. My guess is they don't wish to be accosted by my father."

I laughed. "I hadn't considered that!" I didn't want to see Roy either. I felt glad Tony banned him from appearing uninvited.

We walked on for a while in silence. "Last night, you said perhaps this attack was meant to distract you."

"Yes," Tony said, "but I can't think of from what."

I had a sudden thought: what if the attack was to distract **me**?

"What is it?" Tony said.

"It occurred to me that we may be viewing this the wrong way. What if these events have been meant to **test** us? Our defenses, our information sources, our thought processes, our methods of attack. How the Business functions with you incapacitated. Who we trust and who we do not."

A prelude to something else?

"Wake up," Tony said. "I never considered this. A spy. An Associate?"

"That, spies in our household," I said, "or a spy amongst your main men."

"Or all three," Tony said. He turned, hurrying to the house, and I followed far behind. Who might fall into all three of those categories? Pearson came to greet him, they exchanged words, and both went inside.

When I entered the house, all was a-flurry. Tony seemed a different man, giving orders in a firm voice, too low to hear unless you stood nearby.

I remained a few paces away, watching as he spoke with one of his men after another. He turned and gave me his hand. "Come with me."

We went into his study. He closed the door behind us, and took my hands in his. "You see things I do not. My father was right to trust you."

I stood in shock. Did this mean Tony hadn't trusted me until now? I could sleep with a man I didn't love, but surely you couldn't sleep next to someone you didn't trust.

Tony brought me to the chairs by the fire and we sat. "I have felt uneasy since my men were rescued. I'm having them brought here to account for themselves. Never fear; they will be bound. Don't speak; I would like you to listen and watch. Tell me what you see."

I nodded, feeling nervous about this.

Tony rang for Pearson. We ordered drinks, and I asked for my cigarettes.

The reports of his men recounting their journey in a carriage together yet ending up at different places had bothered me. At the time, I blamed faulty memories of the situation.

Pearson returned with our drinks on a silver tray, which he tucked under his arm as he lit my cigarette.

"Thank you, Pearson," I said.

He bowed and left.

Tony smiled at me. "Thank you for being here."

I squeezed his hand, my heart too full to speak. Whether he trusted me before no longer mattered. He did now, and this meant a great deal.

A few moments later, a knock came at the door. Tony let go of my hand. "Come in."

Four of his men dragged in two men who were bound hands and feet, with hoods on. These men they placed on their knees, and removed the hoods. They were blindfolded and gagged. These men were young, perhaps younger than Tony and I. Both had light skin and brown hair but one was taller and painfully thin. I didn't know them; with the blindfolds on it was difficult to tell who they were in any case.

Tony said, "You betrayed me, of that I'm sure. I don't wish to turn you and your families over to my father yet, so I will give you a chance to confess. The first one to do so will live."

I immediately saw the error in Tony's plan, but I thought better of speaking, especially in front of his men.

Tony gestured; two of his men took the man on the right away, who struggled and made urgent noises, while a third followed, opening and closing the door for them.

The man remaining was the thinner of the two. He hadn't tried to speak since his companion was removed, yet tears streaked his face and blindfold.

"Remove his gag," Tony said.

The man said nothing.

"Well?"

Silence.

"I see. You don't wish to confess. I'm disappointed in you, Duck. But perhaps Crab will confess, given time. My father trained my men well. When they —"

"No!" Duck said. "Don't hurt him! He did nothing."

"He did nothing? How do you know he did nothing?"

"I just know."

"Do you confess then?"

"Not if you're gonna kill him, I'm not."

Ah, as I thought. Tony had gotten himself into difficulty.

"Oh, well," Tony said, after a moment. "I suppose I can just turn the both of you over to my father, then."

"No! Please, Mr. Anthony, no!" Tears began to course down Duck's face again. "I beg you, don't let Mr. Roy hurt him."

Tony glanced over at me with surprise on his face. "What is Crab to you?"

Duck said nothing.

"Very well, I'll speak with him then." He spoke to the two men standing: "Move him ... let's see, over there." He pointed to the far corner of the fireplace. The men moved anything which Duck could use to free himself and left him kneeling, still bound and blindfolded, on the hard stone.

Tony took cotton from his pocket and put a pinch in each ear. "Hand me your pistol." One of his men did so.

Tony held the gun in his left hand. "If you make a sound," he pulled back the hammer with the gun pointing at the ceiling, "I will shoot you."

I stared at Tony in shock. In the house?

Duck had been sniveling, but instantly went silent.

Tony said, "Bring Crab in."

Crab was shorter and heavier, his hair, thin at the temples. The men brought him in, and Crab knelt with a defiant air.

"Remove his gag," Tony said. "Well, Crab, what do you have to say for yourself?"

"What do you want to know?"

"When my father finishes with Duck, who takes his body?"

Crab sat with his mouth open. "Why are you doing this?"

"Because," Tony said, "you betrayed me. Duck told us all."

A strangled noise of outrage burst from Duck's throat. Tony's arm lowered in a relaxed, almost lazy motion as he shot the man in the leg — but not before I and his men hastily covered our ears.

Duck screamed in agony and fell over onto the carpet.

Crab's face around the blindfold went white. "You bastard! Duck! Duck!"

I felt terrified. What if Tony missed? In this small room, the bullet could have hit any of us on the ricochet.

Duck slumped to the floor. Tony gestured for his men to take Duck out, leaving a plate-sized puddle of blood on the gray stone.

"Duck! Speak to me!"

"He can't talk to you anymore," Tony said loudly, "but you can still save yourself. Tell me true, now: what happened that night?"

"You're a fucking monster, same as your father."

Tony sighed. "You're trying my patience. But I'd rather not have my father tear your tongue out just yet. Duck is not dead; he merely fainted. I'll get him help, but you must help me in return."

Crab began sobbing. "Thank the Dealer … please help him."

I felt sorry for Crab. I suppose I shouldn't have, but I did. I hated to see anyone cry.

Over time, Crab gradually became calmer. "I'll tell you what you want to know."

***

Crab, Duck, and Bull (the man Tony executed at the Grand Ball) joined as Associates at the same time. This wasn't an accident; they had known each other since they were boys, and not in a platonic sense, either.

A man came to them at the Grand Ball after they learned about Tony's order, when it was too late to save Bull, and offered sympathy. This made Duck angry at first, but then the man asked if they wanted payback. "All we had to do was distract the others, get them to walk away from the door, and he'd pay us $100 each."

Tony and I stared at each other. Where did this man get that kind of money?

But at the appointed time, ten other men arrived, shot their buddies, and took them to a warehouse in the Diamond quadrant.

Tony stared at Crab, appalled. "Good heavens, man, why did you not tell me this before?"

"He said Mr. Roy would torture us and our families to death if we confessed, because we betrayed the Family. Then when he let us go he upped the ante. We had to spy wearing the clothes he told us to. Brown gentlemen garb —"

So they followed me, at least some of the time.

"— If you asked about our imprisonment, we were to lead you astray and talk about a little boy, who he described to us."

I gasped, and Crab nodded. "I thought you were there, mum. Mr. Anthony doesn't smoke. Anyway, there was no boy. I'm not sure why he wanted us to say so."

If I hadn't seen the boy struggling to free himself, I might begin to doubt his existence.

"Tony said, "Did this man give a name?"

"Frank Pagliacci."

Tony and I stared at each other in shock.

Tony said, "Give him a chair and take off his blindfold." The men released Crab's hands but not his feet, tying him around the waist to the chair.

We sat there, Crab and I, staring at each other.

"What else did you do for this man?" Tony asked.

Crab shuddered, as if remembering a scene he wished he did not. "Every day we wrote what you both did, what you said, where you went —"

I twitched, startled at the thought. How much did they find out about me? Did they know about my disguises?

"— who you met with. You have good taste in dressmakers, mum, but yours takes too long to make a dress. My mother could make one in half the time."

I felt relieved that he was unable to follow me further.

Tony frowned. "That's none of your concern. What shall I do with you? You've lied to me, spied on me and my wife, and who knows what else?"

"Nothing else, sir, I promise. If I would have known this man was so false … ahh." Crab put his face in his hands. "What did I expect? I betrayed my Family, we both did … we never meant it to go this far."

"I know." Tony turned to his men. "Bring him to his friend, and guard them well. I'll have further orders shortly."

"Yes, sir." The men took Crab, closing the door behind them.

Tony rang for Pearson, then turned to me. "I'm sorry you had to see that."

I shrugged. I assumed that was what he wanted me there for.

Pearson came in. "We'll be taking tea in here," Tony said. "Have a girl clean up the blood."

After a brief glance at the fireplace, Pearson bowed and left.

"What do you think?"

I stared at Tony. About shooting a gun in the house? About being followed? About his men spying on us? "About what?"

"About the situation before us."

I took a deep breath and tried to focus, considering the matter. "Perhaps this can benefit us. Assuming no other spies remain, Frank Pagliacci doesn't know these men are ours again."

"Do you think we can trust them?"

"Duck? No, but he won't be going anywhere soon. Crab, now … him we can trust to do what we ask."

Dr. Salmon came over to treat Duck's wound. While he was upstairs with Duck, the maid cleaned the hearth. Soon after, Pearson came in with a letter for Tony.

Tony read the letter, his face stern. "Has a Constable Hanger been here?"

"Why yes. Twice, about a woman wanted in a kidnapping. He seemed to think I knew her."

Tony frowned. "Well, he got a warrant to search the home of one of our maids at the Country House. Why would he do that?"

Fear stabbed at me. Had she done what I asked and destroyed the letters? "I don't know. What happened?"

"They found nothing. How dare he step onto my property, question you without my leave, and search my servant's home? That is one fellow I would happily turn over to my father."

He's angry, I thought. Surely he doesn't mean it. "What will you do?"

"I'll talk to the Chief of Police when I'm on Market Center. This nonsense will stop."

A knock at the door. "Come in," Tony said.

Dr. Salmon came in, Sawbuck with him.

"How is he?" I said.

"Resting. I was unable to locate the bullet, but it should work its way out in time. I've dressed the wound and dosed him with pain medication. I left more with his … friend, with instructions."

Tony nodded. "You did well."

"I'll return tomorrow to check on him," Dr. Salmon said.

"Ten," Tony said to Sawbuck.

"Yes, sir?"

"Get Crab back down here, I want to talk to him."

"Right away, sir," Sawbuck closed the door behind him, returning a few minutes later.

Crab had been cleaned up and appeared much more willing to talk with us.

Tony said, "What does this man really look like?"

Crab's description of this Frank Pagliacci could match several dozen men at the Grand Ball that night, and several dozen more of their retainers: brown hair, brown skin, wearing a "dark" tuxedo, and "very good looking."

"What color tuxedo?" I said.

Crab shrugged. "I don't do well with colors, mum. Never did. It runs in the family. Maybe ask Duck when he comes to?"

Later we sent Crab to ask, then heard Duck shouting, "How in the hell am I supposed to know what color his fucking clothes were? Maybe you'd know if you hadn't been staring at his fucking arse the whole time!"

I laughed. "By the Shuffler!"

Tony shook his head, not finding it funny. "Duck's in pain, and medicated. I'll have Sawbuck look through the guest list and the list of retainers, and see who might fit this description."

Crab returned red-faced, and we set him with a charge: continue to report to Frank Pagliacci, but report what we told him to. If Frank Pagliacci asked, he should say we sent Duck to the countryside. Crab agreed readily when we told him we would hold Duck to insure Crab's good behavior until this man Pagliacci was either caught or killed.

We moved the men to a room on the top floor, locked their windows, and stationed men outside of the Manor and outside their door. Then we sent word to Duck's family that we needed him in the countryside; he would send word when he could.

"Duck's Ma and Pa don't care about him," Crab said, "only one who'd care is his brother, and he's too young to come here."

After dinner, Tony and I retired to our rooms, and spent many hours talking. It felt exhilarating to help in such a practical way with the Business, and I wondered if this was what Roy meant for me to do all those long years ago.

The Preparation

That night went no differently than any other, and I woke at Honor's knock feeling drained and weary. One more day — and one more night — to endure before I could try finding David Bryce. I sat numbly sipping my tea, watching the rain fall outside as servants, horses, and dogs trudged in the mud.

What was I doing? Was this worth it?

Perhaps I shouldn't trust Morton at all. Perhaps it was wiser not to go out tomorrow, to find a different way to the Diamond quadrant, not use his help.

I could meet up with a madman, a strangler, who might do the same to me. I could find myself delivered to Jack Diamond — who might be one and the same — by this Morton's hand, and might very well meet my end. Perhaps I had no need to put myself into peril tomorrow. I could simply tell Tony where David was and then … what?

No, Tony couldn't save the child, even if he believed my information and didn't care how I got it. Could Tony, of all people, get into the Diamond quadrant unnoticed? Even if he did, for him to go to the Diamond Party Time plant and rescue David … I would have to go also, if only to identify the child.

Jacqueline Spadros, I thought, you're being a coward.

I considered little David Bryce, Air's brother, alone. Or worse, in the company of a madman who had already strangled his older brother — perhaps even in front of him. I felt ashamed.

If I wanted to get the child back, using Morton's offer of help was the best way I had found so far, and I needed to move soon. I couldn't wait for another opportunity. Otherwise, I could be chasing rumors of David's whereabouts forever. But I wasn't going to blindly assume Blaze Rainbow intended to protect me, or even had the same objective.

When Amelia arrived with my newspaper, I stared at it, feeling I missed something, something important. I pushed my tea and toast aside, then I put the newspaper on the windowsill, to get it out of the way.

"Amelia, bring me pen, ink, sealing-wax and writing-paper, five sheets."

"Yes, mum," she said.

"And ask Madame Biltcliffe to send the corset I asked her to make me."

"I'll send a note right away, mum."

When she returned with the items I asked her for, I wrote a letter addressed to Madame Biltcliffe:

> If you do not hear from me in three days, go to the police. In my dresser is further information. —JS

I put the letter in my pocket. Then I wrote everything I knew about the case so far, including my speculations about Morton: three pages worth. I folded and sealed it, locking it in my dresser. The fact I needed to do it felt terrifying. Afterward, I felt relieved.

Tony went into his study after breakfast, accompanied by Sawbuck and several of his other men, doubtless plotting about Frank Pagliacci.

I went to Crab and Duck's room, a guest room above the parlor; one of Tony's men stood guard.

"Morning, Mrs. Spadros."

"Good morning. May I speak with Crab?"

The man opened the door. "You want me to come in?"

"It's not necessary." I glanced at Crab, who sat in a chair beside Duck's bed. "I'll only be a moment."

"I'll be right outside," the man said, and closed the door.

I rarely went into the guest rooms, but they were much like the rest of the house: white furniture, gray tile. Duck snored softly, his face pink. Crab's eyes were bleary, his clothes rumpled. I drew up a chair and sat. "When are you supposed to report in?"

"Tomorrow, after luncheon. I go to the river promenade, and signal if I'm not being followed. If he doesn't see anyone he walks with me and we talk."

Perfect timing for what I had in mind.

Might Tony and his men have planned to catch Pagliacci at this meeting? Would Tony risk a gunfight in a crowded place?

"What exactly did Mr. Pagliacci tell you to say about the boy?"

Crab thought a moment. "He said to say that the boy was ten, with dark hair and eyes. Also to say he tormented the boy, and the boy would cry for his mother. He said, say it just like that."

Interesting. "How were you to say he tormented the boy?"

"Whispering to him. We were to make it sound horrible."

What could this man be about? Was this a game to him?

I had an idea. "Mr. Spadros will tell you to report to Mr. Pagliacci tomorrow, and give you words to say. What I would like you to also say is that you mentioned the boy, but we care nothing about him."

Crab's eyes narrowed, then he nodded.

This would either cause Pagliacci to relax, or he would become suspicious and return to Diamond at once. But it would be too late. With luck, Morton and I would have the boy and be gone before Pagliacci knew we were there.

If Tony's men played this right, they could capture Pagliacci once he left the promenade. If David were a pawn, or held important information, Pagliacci might focus on securing David rather than on watching behind him. "Thank you for your help."

Crab seemed worried. "Duck's face feels hot."

***

Tony and his men were eating luncheon in the study, but I asked Pearson to call the doctor.

Dr. Salmon arrived an hour later to examine Duck. He later asked to speak with Tony, then left, returning with a male assistant and two large basins.

Tony's men moved Crab to another room while the doctor worked. We heard Crab griping all the way in the dining room. Duck howled in pain from time to time, accompanied by Crab's sobbing screams. It made for an unsettling dinner.

When Dr. Salmon came downstairs, he looked grim. "Your man has a severely infected wound and diabetes mellitus."

"What's that?" I said.

"The sugar disease," Dr. Salmon said.

I felt shocked. How had the man lived this long?

"I removed a great deal of infection from the wound, along with the bullet, which went too deep to find yesterday, and washed the wound with whiskey. Astonishing how much purulence his body generated in 24 hours. I've given him medication for pain and fever. But he needs close attention, and may not survive."

"I'll have rooms set up for you and your assistant," Tony said. "Whatever you need. We must not lose the man." Duck was our only hold on Crab, who was our only link to Frank Pagliacci.

Tony went to the men, and I followed. Before he got to Duck and Crab's room, I took hold of Tony's arm. "We must tell Crab."

Tony shook his head. "We can't tell Crab how serious this is until after he passes this message along. He must believe Duck has a chance to survive."

"At least let me go with you. He might believe it from me."

Tony shook his head. "You are a woman, unused to hiding your emotions. If you're there, he will see the truth in your eyes."

If I denied it, I told Tony that I hid my emotions on a daily basis, destroying what little trust he held for me.

Tony went to the door and shook hands with the man on guard. I stood nearby as Tony went inside, leaning my head back against the wall.

"Ho, Crab, how is he?"

"I might ask you that, sir."

"The doctor retrieved the bullet: it's a good sign."

"I'm grateful." I heard low murmurs back and forth for quite some time. In the middle, it sounded as if Crab were crying.

I didn't know how to feel. Crab betrayed the Family, and the penalty was death. Yet Tony killed a man Crab loved for no good reason, then shot another for even less reason, who might now be dying. Crab was no dummy; surely he saw the conflict of interest Tony faced when telling him anything.

Then Tony said, "How are you to mark all is well?"

"I use this kerchief here. This red one. He said, use red to show all is well."

"This isn't red, Crab, it's brown."

"But … it's the one he gave me." Crab wasn't sure.

"Then use that. Nothing must alarm him."

The door opened and Tony came out. "Guard them well."

***

Someone pushed me out of a carriage. I fell on the rough cobblestones. Strangers gathered around me. My knees burned.

"Fine dress for a Pot rag," an older girl said, yanking on it, laughing as it ripped.

I struggled to my feet.

"Combed hair and everything, ain't she fancy," a man said. He spat in my face. "Too fancy to whore for the likes of us."

I ran from them, down a long passageway, a flight of stairs, a maze of machinery, searching for something.

The dark shape of a man followed me in the shadows, coming closer each time I looked back. A diagonal of light crossed Jack's face. A dagger glinted in his hand. Terror filled me. But I moved so slowly …

"Ahhh!" I woke, my heart pounding.

Tony was already gone, but Amelia had not been in yet. The drapes were shut, only a pale line showed that dawn was near.

I lay back in bed, taking deep breaths as tears filled my eyes.

Oh, to have a night without dreams.

I curled onto my side. Tears wet my pillow. Sometimes, I felt Jack Diamond made good on his promise to make my life hell just by being in my nightmares.

I never returned to sleep. While I drank my bitter morning tea, I took the invitations and notes from Morton and compared them to the false note sent to me on Madame Biltcliffe's stationery. The writing didn't match.

I felt glad the writing didn't match. But I couldn't deduce who wrote that first note. Frank Pagliacci was a prime suspect, or perhaps some female associate with a good eye for copying.

I realized I should have investigated the false note and the break-in at Madame Biltcliffe's shop before doing anything else. If I had done that, I might have discovered Frank Pagliacci's identity sooner. Perhaps Herbert and Stephen's deaths could have been avoided. Now it was too late.

Morton wasn't Frank Pagliacci. But it didn't mean he held honorable intentions towards me. What if Morton was an accomplice, pretending to help me in order to bring me to Frank, Jack, or both?

What if I was caught?

I pictured Jack in my dream, with a knife, ready to do his worst. Or perhaps Roy, if I survived. Roy would be furious; a slap would be just the beginning. I could say Morton kidnapped me, or lured me there on false pretenses.

No, I decided, I wouldn't let it go that far. I had no wish to be tortured by either of them. I would have my six-shooter with me, and keep the last bullet safe.

Jack Diamond wouldn't capture me alive.

***

After the morning meeting, Tony went to his appointment. I asked Amelia to choose a luncheon dress for the Spadros Women's Club, suitable for boating on Mrs. Hart's yacht.

"I have just the thing!" Amelia chose a blue wool crape dress with dark blue buttons.

While she tightened my corset and got me into my dress, I thought about many things:

Why did Frank Pagliacci want us to know he held David? My only answer was the child was bait for a trap.

I didn't like this idea much, but I could find no other reason to do what Frank Pagliacci was doing. This was why I told Crab to pretend we cared nothing for the boy. This would force Pagliacci to …

Oh, no. What if he killed him?

"Are you well, mum?" Amelia said.

"Yes, I'm quite well." Morton and I would arrive before Crab talked to him. David would be safe, assuming he was still alive.

"Your package from Madame Biltcliffe is on the dresser."

"Would you wrap it as a gift, please, Amelia?" David had to be alive. I couldn't let myself think he was dead. Someone would have found his body by now had Pagliacci killed and dumped the boy, as he did with his other victims. It was a thin hope, but all I had to go on.

The idea that Frank Pagliacci did this to distract me rather than (or in addition to) Tony still lingered. I had no evidence for this, nor could I deduce why the idea stayed with me. But when an idea stayed with me, I never ignored it.

It suggested Pagliacci already knew or knew of us.

Between Tony and I, enough people disliked us to fill a ballroom. But someone who hated us enough to beat Tony, to kidnap and murder children, just to distract us? From what?

I shook my head, puzzled.

"You're worrying on something, mum, I can tell," Amelia said. "Anything I can help with?"

I laughed. "I'll let you know if I think of something."

I thought of the Red Dog cards, and of what I told Tony, that perhaps these actions were to test us.

Bait for a trap. Distraction from something else. Tests. "I have a puzzle but not all the pieces."

In the end, though, did the answer really matter? Right now, all I cared about was finding Air's little brother and bringing him home safe.

"Well, mum, my little ones always lose some of the pieces in their puzzles. If you know the picture, it makes it go faster."

That made me stop. What was it I thought of earlier, when I spoke with Tony? A prelude to something else. But what?

"Sit down, mum, and I'll get your boots on you," Amelia said.

The bell rang downstairs, and Pearson answered it. Soon Pearson's heavy tread came to the door; he knocked as Amelia finished tying my boots.

"Come in," I said.

"Master Jonathan Diamond calling," Pearson said.

"Wonderful! I don't need to leave for a while yet."

"Very good, mum, I'll seat him in the parlor."

"Pearson, let Dr. Salmon know we have a visitor. I don't want Duck and Crab howling with a guest here." I picked up my letter to Madame Biltcliffe and handed it to him. "Would you post this for me?"

"Certainly, mum."

Jonathan looked much better today, and walked without his cane. "How beautiful you look! Do you have time to see me?"

I smiled. "For you, always. Would you like some tea?"

He smiled. "I would."

I rang for a maid. We sat across a small table, facing each other as she brought us our tea.

Jonathan wore a dark brown corduroy suit with brass buttons. How many thousands of men wore brown today?

When the maid left, I said, "How can I help you?"

"I wished to see how you fared. I'm afraid I wasn't very good company last time."

The room was warm and comfortable. The sun peeked through the clouds, shining bright in my face. I felt an enormous temptation to stay here, spend the day with Jonathan, and forget David altogether. "I'm so glad you came by. I could use some counsel."

Why did I bring this up? I instantly regretted it. But I suppose I needed reassurance that I wasn't insane, risking my life for a boy I didn't know.

Jonathan nodded, more at ease. "I would be glad to help."

What could I say now? "I have a … hmm, how to say it …"

"Simply say it."

The sun went behind the clouds. I gazed into Jonathan's eyes and felt foolish, even flustered. I never felt this way around him before.

"Suppose … there were a task … you felt was right and honorable, that would help someone, but it put you at some risk."

My hands lay on the table, and he leaned forward, placing his hands on mine. "And you couldn't pay someone to do this?"

I shook my head, glancing away. "No, I'm the only one with enough knowledge of the situation to do a proper job."

He shrugged, and leaned back in his chair. "The answer seems obvious, unless there is some aspect you haven't told me."

I laughed. Of course there was, but I couldn't say that. Even so, I felt relieved, as irrational as it might seem. "You have helped me immeasurably."

"Well, I'm glad I could be of help, although I don't feel as if I've done anything." He almost sounded annoyed.

I had the sudden feeling he wanted to tell me something, but could not. "Jon, what's wrong? I'm glad to see you, but why are you here?"

Jonathan gave me a level look. "I thought you might need actual assistance."

"In what way?" I felt baffled.

"There have been odd rumors of late," he paused. "Screams coming from Spadros Manor." He reached across the table and touched my face. "You've covered it, but your face was bruised the last time my sister and I visited." He took a deep breath. "Is your husband treating you well?"

I stared at him, astonished. "Is that what you think?" A laugh burst from me. "No … no. Quite the contrary. Tony has been wonderful. We have visitors … one has fallen quite ill and is beside himself. He is finally sleeping."

"This explains the doctors." Jonathan shook his head, resting his arms on the table. "I'm sorry; it's just that …"

"I know. Tony is Roy's son, but he is certainly not Roy." I patted his hand and placed it on my unbruised cheek, feeling a surge of fondness for him. "Never fear; if that ever happened, I would tell you."

Relief crossed Jonathan's face. "I am truly grateful."

The sun came out again, and Jon's face fell into shadow. I closed my eyes, enjoying the warm sun on my face. For a moment, I had another temptation: to tell Jonathan everything, to ask for his aid in entering the Diamond quadrant and wresting the boy away from his brother.

But how could I use him to defy his nature, as I had tried to do with Vig? Jonathan loved his brother Jack, in spite of Jack's madness, and would defend him. Jon might not believe my story. He would want me to wait while he investigated it, allowing Frank Pagliacci to harm or even murder the child. I might lose my dearest friend over this, and for what?

As I told Jon, this was my task, and I would do it.

A knock at the door; I became aware of how this might appear. I leaned back, taking my teacup in hand, and Jonathan let his hand fall to the table. "Come in."

Pearson entered. "Your carriage is ready, mum."

I heard Jon blowing his nose behind me.

"Thank you, Pearson." I turned to Jonathan, who faced the window. "I must be off. Walk with me?"

He smiled, but his eyes were red. "With pleasure."

"Are you well, Jon?"

He folded his handkerchief in his pocket, clearing his throat. "Of course, my love. Nothing to fear. A bit of dust, perhaps."

I took Jonathan's arm as he escorted me to my carriage. Before I climbed in, Pearson handed me the gift-wrapped maid's corset, then returned to the house.

After I sat inside the carriage and the door closed, Jonathan said, "Do your right and honorable deed, if you must, but take care. I would have nothing harm you."

It was such an echo of my words to Tony the night he went looking for the kidnapper, hurt as he was, that I felt touched. "I am going to luncheon." I snapped open my fan and fanned myself. "I should manage not to harm myself too badly there." I grinned at him.

He laughed, slapping the carriage to signal the driver.

I waved as we drove away, then turned to wipe my eyes. I had never lied to Jonathan before, ever.

How I wished I could tell him the truth! But he would never allow it, and would surely have me followed if I persisted, or worse, follow himself. I could never forgive myself if harm came to him on my account.

I leaned back into the carriage cushions and closed my eyes. Today, I thought, this would be over, one way or another.

I was a fool.

The Trap

The Spadros Women's Club was elegant in its own right, with piano black paneling trimmed in silver. Black roses lined the walkways. Dock 21 was close by, and there again was Zia.

She smiled shyly, gesturing for me to follow her onto the gangplank and into the yacht. The girl might be deaf, but she was quite pretty.

Morton sat at the table downstairs in the oak-paneled galley, loading his revolver. Today Morton wore a dark brown business suit and a dark brown Derby hat. He holstered his gun and rose when I came down the stair. "Good afternoon, Mrs. Spadros."

"Good afternoon, Master Rainbow."

Morton insisted I remove any makeup and jewelry, and cover my hair. "Your portrait is everywhere. This outfit is little disguise if someone recognizes you."

With a shock, I realized he was right. Was that why Constable Hanger kept visiting? Had someone recognized me?

Morton frowned when he saw the yellowing bruise on my cheek, yet said nothing of it.

I changed clothes with the maid, putting on the maid's corset Madame Biltcliffe made and Amelia wrapped. I placed my clothes and jewelry into a dress bag Morton obtained for the occasion, with zippered pockets for small items. I felt impressed with his planning.

I didn't know if I would get an honest answer, but I had to ask. "Why are you helping me?"

"My employer would like this conspiracy of kidnapping and murder to end, and the boy returned to his mother. So our goals run along the same path. It's most efficient to help each other, don't you think?"

That sounded too easy. "May I ask who your employer is?"

"I'm afraid I can't reveal my employers' names, just as you avoid revealing yours, and for similar reasons. But my present employer wishes you no harm, as far as I can tell."

"Then I am relieved. It is imperative that I do nothing to bring scrutiny upon either myself or the Spadros Family."

"Be assured, madam, that as far as I am concerned, you were never here."

Feet ran along the pier, and a boy's voice called out, "Message for Blaze Rainbow."

"Ah, good." Morton went up the stairs and out of sight, the boat creaking with the added weight as he stepped onto the deck.

I heard the boy speak, but not what he said.

"Are you sure?" Morton sounded incredulous. "Okay, thank you." He came into the cabin looking grim. He and Zia had a spirited conversation: anger lay in her face as she gestured wildly.

He turned to me. "Let's discuss the plan before we go any further."

"After you tell me what just happened."

Zia turned away, hand to her face.

"I just received some disturbing news," Morton said.

A surge of fear. "Is it about the boy?"

Morton shook his head. "No, not about him. Think nothing of it." He gave Zia a quick glance, then stared at the table between us.

"What are you going to do?"

"Let me see what your plan was first, then I can decide," Morton said.

I had the feeling Morton didn't want to talk about his dilemma in front of Zia. I also felt she wasn't his maid, but something closer.

"Very well." I opened the small notebook with my sketches

of the factory.

"How ...?"

I smiled. "The plans are public record. As to how I found the building, that shall be my secret."

Morton said nothing.

"There is a door round back, which goes to the worker's areas: washrooms, lockers, equipment, and so on. Past that is a stair down to the basement. The boy is likely held there."

Morton frowned, which made me nervous. "Very well. I promised to help you, and I shall, for as long as I can."

***

Morton and I untied the thick golden ropes which bound us to the dock. Once we cast off, Morton gestured for me to approach him where he stood near the wheel. He handed me brass and leather-bound binoculars. "There are watchers on the Diamond side of the river for just what we plan to do. So we can't simply go across."

I peered through; men on the opposite side peered back at us. I returned the binoculars. "What shall we do then?"

"I'll show you." Morton turned the boat towards Market Center, moving along the wide river with several others.

The day was pleasant, if overcast, and the wind favorable. Soon we passed under the bridge between Diamond and Spadros closest to Market Center. Morton then turned the boat right to circle the island.

We passed under the same bridge Tony and I crossed so many times to and from Market Center. I thought of New Year's Eve, and what Tony said up there.

Tony and I had a life together. Perhaps I should forget about Joseph Kerr and stop living in the past like Jack Diamond seemed to, before it drove me mad as well.

"Would you go downstairs and get a brown suitcase with a brass star on the corner?"

Zia paced back and forth inside the cabin, wringing her hands. She ignored me as I searched out the suitcase. At first I thought the suitcase would be too heavy to lift, yet it was light. When I emerged with the suitcase, Morton was removing the last of the white sails, which he folded up.

By this time we had passed out of sight of Diamond, and Morton began hooking blue sails to the mast. "Open the suitcase, then help me with these lines." Blue cloth filled the suitcase, so thin you could see through it!

It was then I noticed that everything on the yacht had been white: sails, decks and lines.

Zia peeked out, curiosity evidently overcoming her distress. Morton made hand movements and she took the blue cloth out of the suitcase. Starting at one corner of the stern, she draped it along the outside of the boat, like bunting.

Once we raised the blue sails, we made much better time around the island, traveling under the bridge to the Clubb quadrant. The bridges, unlike those in the postcard, were white: desperate men peeled away the gold leaf long ago, if in truth it ever existed. "I never realized Market Center was so big."

"It's fortunate," Morton said, "because it allows the watchers on the Diamond shore to forget us." He smiled. "But this will distract them altogether. Follow me."

We went aft, and Zia was tying the blue material onto the other side. She then went forward, towards the bow.

Morton and I moved a bench far away from the stern wall. He opened a compartment in the floor next to the stern wall, lifting the floorboards up by hinges to fold onto the deck.

He climbed into the compartment and unhooked a board shaped like the inside of the stern wall. This board attached to the lowest part of the stern by hooks, and at the railing by hinges. We raised the board over the side using long hooked poles, the board just clearing the rudder mechanism. When this board dropped over the stern wall, it clicked into place, covering the stern.

"The *Finesse* is now the *Action Card,*" Morton said. "No one is searching for that boat at all."

We walked towards the bow. Zia was at the wheel, and we went under the bridge to the Hart quadrant as if on vacation.

Morton took out a cigarette and lit it. "I'm sorry, here." He held his cigarette in his mouth while he offered me a cigarette, which I took, although perhaps I shouldn't have, and lit it for me.

So far, the day seemed enjoyable. But I didn't let Morton behind me, nor did I forget what I was doing. I walked into a trap. I could very well die that day.

Zia and Morton exchanged gestures after he tied the boat to the dock, and she seemed calmer. After a peck on Morton's cheek, Zia returned to the boat, and went inside.

Morton must have noticed my curious gaze, for he said, "My younger sister."

Master Gentleman Morton's dark brown private coach waited at the docks in the Diamond quadrant, complete with driver and footman. Morton tried to get me to enter, but I refused, hiring a public taxi-carriage which came down the street a few moments later.

We sat across from each other. Silence seemed the best choice.

"You don't trust me; I don't blame you. It was abominable of me to lay hands on you the day we met, and I deeply regret it."

"Then why did you?"

"I don't know." The way he said it told me that this man was new to his job, fearing his task was impossible, afraid he ruined the opportunity to gain me as an ally. "I … I never played a rough man before."

I almost laughed. Is that what he thought of Pot rags? "I don't trust you, true. For all I know, you could be the murderer."

Morton stared at me, aghast. "Murderer? I assure you, madam, I'm not!"

"And so a murderer would say. However," I said, with a sigh, "I must return David Bryce to his mother if I can, for reasons I will not share with a stranger. And so I must ride with you, and let you accompany me."

Morton didn't speak for several moments; his eyes, nose, and cheeks turned red, and he looked less certain of himself. "I believe this is a trap."

I stayed silent, hoping he would say more.

"Do you know a man named Frank Pagliacci?"

Now perhaps I would learn the truth. What should I reveal?

I decided to be as honest as possible. If he played me false, this might put him at ease, and he might let some information slip. "He is the man who kidnapped the boy and holds him now. He killed two of my husband's men and kidnapped two more, blackmailing them into spying on us. I also believe he strangled your Stephen and the older brother of the child we seek."

When I told him the last part, Morton stared at me, horrified. "This whole thing felt wrong. I have met this man; he's ... a consummate liar. He almost had me fooled."

"What did he tell you?"

Morton then told his story, slowly and with much hesitation. He was hired to discover who created false Red Dog treys then blamed their villainous deeds on the gang. While on his investigation, a trusted friend introduced him to Frank Pagliacci. This man passed himself — quite convincingly, from Morton's descriptions — as part of the district attorney's office.

"I felt suspicious ... I didn't understand why he would want to help me."

By then, Morton learned of David's disappearance from Clover. His employer became alarmed at the news, and asked him to retrieve the boy.

But Frank Pagliacci claimed no child was missing: he paid a woman to tell this story. They asked Morton to pretend to assist me in finding the boy. In exchange, they would give him access to a man who had the information Morton needed.

This man, who Morton never met, would talk only if he met with me. Pagliacci claimed this pretense of a kidnapping was necessary to lure me to the meeting. A police detective joined them, but only to corroborate the story.

Why would anyone need to lure me anywhere? Because it was someone I wouldn't want to meet with otherwise? I couldn't think of anyone who fit that description, except perhaps my father. Or Jack Diamond.

Ah. That made sense, frightening as it was.

I considered Mrs. Bryce, her barren rooms, her empty plate, and her dead son. "I have spent a great deal of time with this woman, who I have known since childhood. I am confident that if they paid her to concoct this story, the pay wasn't nearly enough."

"Their reasons made no sense," Morton said. "A man going to the police with information in exchange for meeting you. Though you ran an independent business, he couldn't meet you? Because your husband was so jealous?" He glanced at my face.

I touched my cheek. "It's not what you think." I sighed, melancholy at my failure with Thrace Pike. "It's a long story."

Morton peered at me, then shook his head. "None of it made sense. They were insistent on their tale and plan, though, and it seemed to make sense to my friend, so I let the matter drop. But I began to check their story.

"The second man was a detective once, but had been let go. He now works as a private investigator."

Oh, dear. A Bridges detective would have to do or be something quite extreme to rate dismissal.

Morton took a deep breath. "The most alarming part of this was that they refused to tell me where the meeting was to be. I would receive word to be at a certain place and told what to say. That is why I was in Diamond, and why I didn't rescue the boy. At the time, I didn't think he was real. But when I saw his mother, so frantic and hopeful, I began to doubt their story."

"And then there was Stephen."

"Yes." He paused. "I never met Stephen, but from the way Clover took the news ..." He shook his head. "When you told me you sent Stephen to find the boy, and then to see his portrait in the paper ... murdered ... I knew this was real. Something was horribly wrong."

Morton sat for a moment. "I could get no confirmation that Frank Pagliacci was who he claimed to be. So I sent a messenger boy to bring a letter to the man. A test, to see how he would reply. The messenger told me the office lay empty. I knew then this was a trap."

I frowned. "Why trap us?"

"I'm not sure they wished to trap me, although I can see several reasons they might wish to. I'm certain they wish to trap you, but for what purpose it's unclear." Then he sat bolt upright, his voice full of dread. "Zia."

No surprise here. "You must decide what to do for yourself."

Morton stared out of the window, his face pale. He kept one hand to his chin, the other tapping his fingers and checking his pocket-watch. We clattered along in the taxi-carriage, the horses' hooves ringing on the cobblestones.

Several minutes went by. I felt relieved that Morton didn't turn the carriage back. Frank Pagliacci could have been returning to kill or move the boy soon. "Did you follow me?"

"I did, the day you went to the train and the bar. Once I met you in the Pot, I knew you dressed as a shop maid. It was easy to deduce where you might obtain a uniform without much trouble."

"I was to meet Stephen there at the train." I felt somber. "He never arrived."

"The police found him. I wish now that they'd kept him; perhaps he'd still be alive."

The driver brought us round back of the Diamond plant, a few streets away. "Please wait for us here," I said. The driver glanced at Morton, who nodded. The driver took out a cigar, lighting it as we crossed the street.

The sun emerged from the clouds, and I moved towards the factory. "This way." Morton followed.

Few people walked the streets. We were too close to the slums for the homes to be other than those of the lowest day-wage servants. This hour, most were at work in the better areas as temporary help, shop girls, and the like.

A black brick building mortared in gray stood at the far right intersection of two alleyways. At the corner, a gray wooden door stood at the top of a short staircase with a gray metal railing.

An ancient wooden sign above the door said:

Diamond Shoe Polish
Since 1874

A

m

an sat smoking on the back stair, while another stood guard, revolver in hand. Neither saw us, with our alleyway cloaked in shadow.

Morton took out his pocket-watch and examined it. "My guess is that the man on the porch will go off break in a few moments," he whispered. "I will then draw the gun-man away. Go in when the way is clear."

I grabbed his arm. "Why are you really helping me?"

Morton turned to me. "Why do you care?"

"I need to know." I needed to know he hadn't sold me to Jack Diamond. Or to hear him say it, even if he lied.

Morton took a deep breath and let it out. "Perhaps it's to prove you've misjudged me." Then he gazed away with an introspective smile. "Perhaps I'm just a sucker for a pretty face."

I hadn't expected that answer.

"Or perhaps," Morton said, "I just can't walk away when a boy may be in danger."

I nodded, humbled. Morton returned the way we came.

A few moments later, the man on the back stair threw down his cigarette and stepped on it, then went inside. A horn sounded inside the building.

I heard a trash can thrown against a wall, then gunshots, both from my left. The man with the pistol glanced up and down the street, then moved one slow step at a time towards the commotion. More gunshots, then hoof-beats.

Was that my carriage? Had Morton abandoned me to rescue Zia? I might have no way to escape.

But the way was clear; I had to go now, or go back.

I crept from the shadows, peering around. Seeing no one, I crossed to the stair and opened the unlocked door.

Inside was a long white hallway, its sides filled with boots and overcoats. This led to a white kitchen, which held a full trash can and dirty pots in the copper washbasin to the right. The room smelled of recent cooking. Across the room was a locker area, painted gray.

I saw no exit from the locker room, so I went straight on through then turned right. White-clad workers tended huge intricate machines past the large windows to my left. I kept myself low so they wouldn't see me.

I went through a tan room which held equipment and an enormous black room full of barrels, stacked high enough so I couldn't see over them. Large lights glared from the ceiling, which seemed several stories up.

I almost stumbled on a man checking the barrels, but I crouched down before he saw me. He wore white, but the white of a factory laborer: white shirt and overalls, with dark brown work shoes. The man's brown skin matched his hair, which hung in curls, and he held a notebook, writing every so often in it.

I felt a touch on my shoulder, and startled, I turned, ready to fight or flee. Morton stood behind me, and I sighed with relief.

He put a finger to his lips and gestured for me to follow. He led me around a stack of large wooden boxes which screened us from view of the workman and we crouched down again. "Where to now?"

I checked my notes. "This way," I whispered.

We went down a long gray hallway. Several of the bulbs above us were burned out, but there was enough light to make our way. We came to a door, which Morton opened.

An unlit oil lamp hung on the wall beside the door. Morton lit the lamp with a match from his pocket, and we hurried inside, closing the door behind us. The light revealed a flight of steps leading down a white stairwell.

Morton drew his revolver and went first, one step at a time. I followed. A black metal railing lay along the wall to our left. Another began once we cleared the ceiling, with supports for the railing every few yards.

Lamps hung from the low ceiling of a large windowless white storage room. The room held rows of the same wooden boxes, stacked waist high.

The room was silent except for a faint rhythmic squeak, far off. Morton lit each lamp in turn, searching the area shown before lighting another.

Far in back of the room, a dark shape moved, huddled in the left corner, surrounded by boxes. Morton lit another lamp. A child, barefoot, curled into a ball, arms around knees, rocking.

I approached him. "David? David Bryce?"

He gave no sign he had heard, so I moved the hair away from his face. I stopped, shocked at the torment in David's gaze. "This is he." I held his little face in my hands, so much like Air's, and grief overwhelmed me.

Morton took David, murmuring, "What have they done to you?" But the boy didn't answer. Morton glanced at me. "Let's get him out of here."

We hurried through the long room towards the stairs. It seemed Lady Luck smiled on us. We found the boy, and he was alive. All we had to do was go through the deserted storage rooms to our waiting carriage.

This might just work.

When we were ten yards from the staircase, a man spoke from the top of the stairs. "He's on his way."

My heart began racing in fear. Who was on his way? Frank Pagliacci, or Jack Diamond?

I gasped in horror as footsteps descended. We were trapped.

The Fight

A light-skinned man wearing a black vest and jacket and a black Derby hat came down the stair. He pulled a gun from his pocket in a relaxed manner, pointing it at us. "Now, now, folks, don't do anything foolish." He moved down the stairs and into the room, putting a row of boxes between us. "Come on along, now, let's go."

I collapsed to the floor with a sigh. Morton looked down and I winked at him.

"Don't shoot." Morton held up his hand. "Let me help her."

"Go ahead," the man said.

Morton knelt, laying David on the floor. Then Morton drew his gun and shot towards the man. I covered my ears just in time. David screamed, hiding his head in his arms.

A shot rang out from the other side of the boxes an instant later, then a thud. The room fell silent.

"That was hardly honorable." I was half-joking. After all, it was what I hoped he'd do.

Morton appeared unamused. "Fuck honor. We need to get this boy out of here."

I stared at the bullet hole through the box just above my head. It didn't seem real.

"What's going on down there?"

I gathered my skirts and peered out. The stairs creaked with the weight of several men descending. We took cover, pulling David behind the boxes.

The first man stuck his head out from the corner where the ceiling met the stair, then withdrew. He then came down the stairs in a crouch, another man following, both scanning the room.

I held my gun with both hands. They were targets. Roy stood over me, shouting. When the men were almost to the bottom of the stairs, I pulled the trigger.

The blast was so loud it surprised me, but I hit the first man square in the chest. Elation swept over me. I did it!

The man screamed in pain and fell down the stairs. Blood spattered and streaked on the white wall behind him.

The second man's eyes widened in shock. He raised his gun, but I was faster. He clutched his chest, slumping down the stairs onto the other man.

Morton stared at me in amazement.

I yelled, "Look out!"

The man running down the stairs fired at Morton and missed.

I didn't. This man tripped, sliding down the stair, landing just above his first companion. The stairwell was smeared with blood.

Morton ran for the stair, pointing his pistol up it.

Morton shot twice more. Gunshots and screams came from the stairwell. Two men fell into view, ending on top of the others. Morton returned to us. "The others went back to the hall." His words were so soft I almost didn't hear him.

"I've never shot anyone before." I know I spoke, but I could hear little even from my own mouth. But I felt I could fight the whole world. My pulse thumped in my ears, and the lights seemed too bright.

"You did well."

I saw no windows, vents, or openings of any kind. "They won't keep coming down those stairs. We must find a way out."

"Stop shooting," one yelled from the top of the stair, "we just want to talk."

"I'm done talking." Morton appeared to be speaking normally, but it came out as a whisper.

I put my mouth near his ear. If I couldn't hear him, perhaps he couldn't hear me either. "We can't get out unless they think we surrender." I counted our shots: six. "They don't know I have a gun." I holstered my gun, but didn't secure the latch.

Morton didn't say anything. When the men finished counting too, five of them, all light-skinned and wearing black, came downstairs with guns drawn. Morton made a show of putting his gun away and his hands in the air.

"You goddamn bastard," a heavy-set man yelled at Morton, face red, "I should shoot you right now. The deal was no guns."

Did they think we were stupid?

Then he waved us along. "You're lucky he wants you alive. Get the kid and let's go."

I felt terrified. "He" wanted us alive? Who wanted us alive? What horror waited for us? My nightmare of Jack Diamond with his dagger flashed through my mind.

David lay on his side, curled up, hands over his ears. I took him in my arms, and he seemed too light. We moved toward the stairs, towards the damp smells of blood and filth. I hugged David to keep myself from screaming as much as anything else.

Morton let me go first. One of the gun-men went ahead, climbing backwards through pools of blood. A man lay on the stair face down, moaning piteously, a bullet hole in his back.

Gore dripped down the wall beside me. The man on the stair moaned and sobbed, his gasps coming slower with each breath. Terrified of him grabbing my ankle, I forced myself to take another step up the stair.

I thought of Air, and Herbert, and poor Mrs. Bryce. I gazed at the little boy in my arms, his large dark eyes, so much like Air's, staring up into mine, peering into my soul.

I gazed into those dark eyes, and I knew that this child's life — or death — was up to me. Five men with guns held us. Who knew how many more awaited us at the top? No one was going to rescue us. No one even knew we were here.

I had to get this child home, even if it meant my death. There had to be some way to escape. I couldn't let this boy fall back into Frank Pagliacci and Jack Diamond's hands.

I would not let David die because of me.

The man ahead of me stopped at the door. He kept his gun on me, but his eyes on Morton, holding the door open with one hand. As I passed him, I took several slow steps down the empty hall.

I had an idea.

I slowly turned, laying David down by the wall with a sigh. Then I knelt on the floor beside David. The man gave me a glance but kept his gun towards the open door.

Morton came round the corner and into the hall, hands raised. The man at the door had his eyes fixed on Morton.

I pulled my gun.

Morton's eyes widened and he dropped to the floor.

I shot the gun-man in the head. His gun fired as he slid down, gore streaking along his path. Blood spread from the dead man's head towards the staircase.

The men downstairs were in an untenable position; if they came up the stairs, they would be shot. But we couldn't reach the dead man to shut the door without being shot ourselves.

Morton scurried to our side, panting. "I will hold the men back." He began reloading his gun. A dark wet area stained the back of his right sleeve. "Take the boy and go."

"You can't hold four men off yourself, unless you brought a whole box of bullets."

Morton sat in thought. He took a penny from his pocket. He flung himself towards the open doorway, shooting as the coin clattered past the men.

A scream came forth, along with the sound of something heavy hitting the stair and thumping down it. He rolled towards me as a return shot missed by a wide margin.

When he reached the wall, he panted, "three."

Morton was inventive, I'll grant that.

I couldn't help but notice the slow thick drip in the stairwell.

"You must go," Morton said. "If they make it past me, you won't be safe."

I realized the wisdom of this: one of us would get killed at this rate, and not even I wished this on myself or David. Gratitude filled me. "Thank you."

"Heh," Morton said, taking off his jacket. "Never thought I'd hear that from you. Go on. I'll catch up."

I picked David up, rushing down the long hallway towards the room with the floodlights. Several shots rang out behind me. I crouched to the floor, fearful that one of the men had made it into the hallway.

I glanced back but could see no one. David held his arms over his head, his eyes squeezed shut.

No one seemed to be in the room with the lights, so I started past the stacks of boxes. A gunshot came from above and to the left, just missing us. Dropping to the floor, I dragged David to the left over next to a row of boxes.

That was too close. I felt short of breath and shaky.

"IF YOU MOVE I WILL KILL YOU," a voice said over a loudspeaker. The sound seemed to be coming from all around us.

David shrieked and covered his ears with his hands. I held him close, sharing his terror.

The voice was distorted. "THIS IS THE ONLY WAY OUT."

I heard more shots from the stairwell behind me. After a few seconds of silence, frightened shouts, then a door slammed.

Morton hurried to us, crouching. Red stained his left arm.

"Are you okay?"

He laughed. "Door's locked, that should give us a few minutes." He began to get up.

Terror surged through me. "Wait —!"

Another bullet whizzed past, knocking off Morton's hat.

Morton cowered next to me against the boxes, jacket in one hand, eyes wide. "What the hell?" A trickle of blood rolled down the side of his face near his hairline. Morton's hat rolled over on the floor, and it had a gouge in its crown and a hole in the brim.

"I'm pretty sure it's Pagliacci." He sounded nothing like Jack. "Wherever he is, he can see us."

"I KNEW YOU'D COME WHEN I TOOK THE BOY. I COULDN'T BELIEVE MY LUCK WHEN I SAW HIM. I PICKED HIM JUST FOR YOU."

So he did know me. Few people knew about that night, about what happened, about Air. About how much he meant to me. I closed my eyes and hugged little David, overcome with emotion. My mind ran through the faces in the crowd, Roy's men ... who among those people would do this to me?

"I'm out of bullets," Morton said. The blood trickling down his face dripped to the floor.

"I'M IMPRESSED. YOU THOUGHT TO TRAP ME INSTEAD ... IT WAS A GOOD TRY." He did sound pleased. His test seemed a success, at least to him.

What sort of madman was he?

"IF IT WASN'T FOR CRAB'S FUCKING RED HANKIE IT WOULD HAVE WORKED. I KNEW HE TALKED WHEN THE FOOL GOT THAT RIGHT." He laughed.

How dare he mock a Spadros Associate? Heart pounding, I searched for a spot where I could see between the boxes. According to my sketches, an overseer platform lay up and to the left. Pagliacci must be there. The glare of the lights made it difficult to see him.

I had the urge to ask about Pagliacci's motivations, but thought better of it. That would just give away my position, and I had as good a view of him here as I ever would.

"I HAVE YOU, AND WHEN THEY COME FOR YOU, I'LL KILL THEM, ONE BY ONE. DO YOU LIKE MY PLAN?"

I considered the question. This man was not only mad, but an amateur. He believed Morton wouldn't come armed. He had no idea I came armed. I counted ten of his men so far. If he had many more, where were they? And where were Jack's men?

Surely he didn't think Tony or anyone else would come to rescue me alone? The entire Spadros quadrant would compete to invade Diamond. They would tear this building to the ground.

So Frank Pagliacci had a grudge against the Spadros Family. Him and most of the city.

This made his alliance with Jack more plausible. But the boys' murders seemed an afterthought, a way to amuse himself, just as he used David and our men.

A shadow, far up, walked back and forth, and the way he moved seemed familiar. I shielded my eyes from the glare of the floodlights, trying to get a good shot. I had two bullets left. I would only get one chance.

"STAY THERE. MY MEN ARE ON THEIR WAY."

Pagliacci leaned over the railing. The shadows around him lightened, showing dark clothing and relatively pale skin.

The men in the basement began crashing against the door.

We had to get out of here. Now.

The world became silent. The sounds of failing hinges, Pagliacci's mad boasting, David's rocking, Morton's bleeding, all vanished.

I saw the man on the platform. He was only a target.

I took a deep breath, then shot just as he moved. He screamed. A tremendous crash far below, then silence.

I felt astonished. I did it.

Morton held his gun aloft. "Run!" I grabbed David and followed. As we raced down the hall with the windows, the white-clad workers screamed and fled.

A dark-skinned man in white stalked towards us from the front of the building. Panic struck me.

Screaming in terror, I caught up to and passed Morton.

When we got outside, Morton said, "Keep moving, Pagliacci's men are here." He sounded alarmed.

I took a deep breath and handed him my gun. "There's one bullet left."

He took it, gratitude in his eyes. "Round the corner, cross the street, then three blocks right. Look to your left."

I hoisted David on my shoulder and fled. Several shots came from behind me. When I got to the corner, I went round it, across the street, then right as Morton directed, but no carriage sat there.

Terror punched me, hard. I looked to my left: a torn newspaper wafted down the street. Morton had abandoned me.

Tears of fear and disappointment filled my eyes. I took a deep breath, and blinked them away. He did say he would help as long as he could. I moved away from the factory, not knowing where I was going.

My ears rang and I felt shaky, but the boy seemed light. I carried him as fast as I could run until exhaustion caught me and I had to slow to a walk.

I set us down on a cracked wooden bench, panting, until my breathing slowed. My hands trembled, and I held my face with my hands, fighting the urge to vomit. I kept glancing around even so, terrified of seeing armed men appear.

After several minutes, the nausea passed, and I peered at David. His eyes stared into emptiness. He sucked his thumb, rocking, curled into as tight a ball as one could at that age.

"David?" I brushed his straight black hair away from his face. "David, I'm Jacqui. I'm taking you to your Ma. Can you walk?"

Peedro Sluff grabbed my arm and yanked me in front of him. "This is my daughter."

Roy Spadros let out a cold, cruel laugh, claiming victory over his mortal enemy. "You're sure about that?"

Fear crossed Peedro's eyes, which turned into determination. "If she goes, I go with her."

Air yelled, "No!" He dashed towards me, terror on his face, broken bottle in his little hand.

Peedro Sluff squeezed my arm so hard it hurt as he turned towards Air. "You're not ruining this for me."

Air leaped at Peedro, stabbing the broken bottle into Peedro's upper chest. "Leave her alone!"

"You little shit!" Peedro shrieked, "You cut me!" He pushed Air away with the gun in his hand, and the gun went off.

David stopped rocking and stared in my eyes. I saw Air the instant he was shot, the moment he looked at me with those dark eyes that peered into your soul. The utter pain in his eyes, the knowledge his life was over, the emptiness, the longing. I put my arms around him and began to weep.

"I'm sorry," I sobbed. "I'm so sorry … I should never have gone there … I just wanted to help."

I don't know how long I sat there. I cried about everything: Air's murder, my lost life, what could have been. I cried until I couldn't cry any more.

And this little boy who had gone through so much put his hand on my shoulder to tell me it would be all right.

It was a while before I could speak.

I put my forehead on David's. "Can you walk?"

He gave no answer, so after wiping my face with Zia's apron, I picked him up. He seemed much heavier now.

I walked, arms aching, until I found a taxi-driver who would take me to the Spadros quadrant without payment in advance. Zia's pockets were empty.

The whole trip, David said nothing, did nothing but rock, curled up there on the bench seat. "Your mother sent me to find you. I'm taking you to a doctor. Are you hurt?"

The boy said nothing.

At the bridge into Spadros quadrant, the driver said, "She's taking the boy to a doctor. Looks like he needs one." The guard took one look at David and waved us through, to my relief.

Dr. Salmon didn't seem surprised to see me appear in maid garb, carrying a child. The doctor paid the taxi-carriage then sent a messenger to fetch the boy's mother. We stood there, somewhat awkwardly.

I thought I might not have another chance to ask, so I did. "Mr. Roy Spadros told me that he has known you since he was a boy." My voice sounded too quiet, and buzzing filled the room.

"Yes, indeed."

"So you've known Mrs. Molly Spadros for some time."

"I have."

I was unsure how to proceed. "How did they come to marry?"

He smiled. "What do you know of her background?"

I wasn't sure how much he knew of mine. I shrugged. "She told me she came from the same place as I."

He nodded, then peered at me for a moment, evaluating me. "Yes, she did." He paused. "I first met her as a … young girl, really. She was sixteen. Mr. Acevedo Spadros called me to the Pot, wishing me to ensure she had no illness."

I felt confused. "Mr. Acevedo?"

"Yes, Mr. Roy's father. The man was in his late 40's, if I recall … yes, his 50th celebration was later that year. But oh, he was smitten. I have never seen two people so in love." His lined face lit with the memory. "When she came of age, he brought her into the quadrant, set her up in a little grocery over on 2nd street. I believe a fabric store is there now."

A shock went through me at his words. "Why in the world would she marry Mr. Roy?"

"You know what Roy is," Dr. Salmon said, his tone bitter. "I was never privy to their reasoning. I suppose they felt it a good way to move her into the house, to have their affair in front of Mr. Acevedo's wife without anyone knowing." He shook his head. "It's a miscalculation I'm sure she regrets."

My vision blurred. I couldn't imagine the pain Molly must have gone through, losing the man she loved. And to such foul murder, betrayed by his own men. Men he trusted, men she probably trusted as well. Then to be yoked with Roy Spadros ….

Dr. Salmon gave me his handkerchief. "As I told you before, she's a strong woman. I admire her a great deal."

And suddenly, I did too. She had been harsh with me at times, but only to make sure I survived. To live with Roy Spadros so many years and still live must have taken all the ability she possessed. "I have underestimated her."

The doctor smiled. "Many do. I hope one day the two of you become friends."

Through our entire conversation, the boy stared, sucking his thumb, rocking back and forth, as if his world were gone forever.

Once his mother arrived, the doctor examined the boy. "It as if he hasn't had a finger laid upon him —"

"Was he —?" Mrs. Bryce said, and it was clear from her tone what she meant.

"No," Dr. Salmon said, shocked. "No abuse of **that** kind …"

Mrs. Bryce sighed in relief.

"... he's malnourished, but that can be rectified in time."

"Why is he acting this way?"

"He suffered severe mental trauma, which may take time to heal. It's common in these cases for a child to regress to a former age. But gentle care over time will give him a feeling of safety. Eventually he'll come to his senses." The doctor smoothed David's hair. "You're safe now. Your mother will take good care of you."

But the boy never said a word. So we brought him home — it took all the money Mrs. Bryce had on her to pay for the taxi-carriage — and laid him in his bed.

"The police will come when they discover the boy is here," I said. "Don't trust them; don't let anyone near David. Tell your neighbors to watch for those men who took him. If David speaks, even one word, contact me at once. Our lives may depend on it."

"I'm so grateful," Mrs. Bryce said. "You brought my boy home, as you said you would. I'm in your debt."

I shook my head, feeling bleak. It might have been kinder for all involved if the boy had been found dead, instead of in this terrible condition. But I tried my best to smile, and made my way outside.

Mrs. Bryce lived on 2nd street.

Spadros Manor was on 192nd.

I had a long walk home.

When I got three blocks away, the rain poured down, and me without an umbrella.

The Vow

As I walked up Snow Street in the lightning storm, sodden and discouraged, I thought about the Masked Man.

Ma thought I slept. But after Eleanora took Air's body, the Masked Man entered our quarters. I peeked through the gap between the too-small door and its jamb. Ma told him everything.

"Well, this is a situation," the Masked Man said.

"She's gonna ask," Ma said. "What do I tell her?"

"You know very well what to tell her." They went out of view and sound.

After he left, I heard my mother sobbing, and the memory brought me to tears as I walked that rainy street ten years later. It was the first and last time I ever heard her cry.

I never saw him again.

The rain poured down. A carriage pulled up beside me. Major Blackwood leaned out of the window. "Madam, would you care for a lift?"

I stared at him while a footman came round. Then I thought, what the hell, and got inside.

"Spadros Manor," Major Blackwood called out, and the carriage lurched into motion.

"Thank you," I said.

The round old man smiled. "Always glad to be of assistance, my dear. I almost didn't recognize you with that get-up on, but I had a time when I was temporarily snow-blinded when I was in the military, and I learned to take note of the way people walk as a means of identifying them. It is like a habit to me, and I was riding along and saw you and thought to myself, Major Blackwood, that is Mrs. Jacqueline Spadros walking in this hellish weather, and her without so much as a coat! Why, it wouldn't have been gentlemanly of me to just let you —"

"I appreciate your help. I would also appreciate you not speaking of this matter further."

"But of course, my dear. I wouldn't think of it. I remember when I was in the military, the scrapes I got into ... you know, once when I was in the academy, I lost a bet, and was forced to walk home wearing a DRESS!"

"Scandalous."

"Quite! So I know the value of good and discreet acquaintances."

This man has done me a service. I underestimated him as well. The thought humbled me. "Thank you. This means a great deal." I paused for a moment, considering all the possibilities. "Would you be available for Queen's Day dinner? I have a cancellation ... if it wouldn't be too much trouble."

Major Blackwood beamed. "I would very much enjoy the pleasure of dining at Spadros Manor. Very much so."

It took me a few minutes to persuade Major Blackwood to leave before I had gotten inside. He finally did after I told him my husband would be vexed if he learned I rode in a bachelor gentleman's carriage unescorted. This pleased the Major no end.

When I went around the back, Rocket began to bark. I rushed into the house, keeping him outside as I locked the door. I managed to sneak into my bedroom and get into dry house clothes. Right as I exited the closet, Tony walked in, leaving the bedroom door open a bit.

"Good heavens, I thought you were with Mrs. Hart!"

"I was, and we had luncheon, and we went boating, but then the storm came up, and we were drenched! Fortunately she had clothes I could change into to return home. Pearson must not have heard my knock with the thunder, because I had to go round the back to get in."

Tony laughed softly and took me into his arms. "You poor dear. What a day!"

Rocket came bounding into the room, barking, the stable-boys and maids chasing behind, and shook water everywhere.

"Get that dog out of here!" Tony said. They dragged Rocket off, howling as he went.

And so it was done, and no one was the wiser. I went downstairs later and told Rocket what a good dog he was. Both Pearson and the doctor looked at me strangely for a while, as if not sure what to think. I never explained to Dr. Salmon why I was with a traumatized boy and his mother wearing the blood-spattered dress of a maid. But he never asked, and to this day has never said a word about it.

Pearson never missed a knock or a bell, no matter what the weather. He must have felt a deep sense of personal failure at missing mine, especially since I had a terrible cold for the next few days. He was especially attentive to any bell for months after.

Poor man — but it would have been suicide to appear at the front door in a maid uniform, much less tell anyone where I was that day.

***

We ran laughing down a glorious moonlit alleyway, then leaned against a wall.

Air put his head on my shoulder. I put my arm around him, feeling safe and at peace as we gazed out at the wide plaza before us.

Snow glittered on old Bridges: the soaring curved lines of the 'scrapers and mansions, the majestic statues, the stately fountains. Beautiful sleek steam automobiles chugged through the streets, while ladies in flowing gowns strolled past.

Air's face was full of wonder. "'Tis pretty, here at night."

***

Tony and I were wakened by a gunshot.

We rushed towards the sound in the pre-dawn light, to find Tony's man standing aghast. Duck was dead, peacefully, as if asleep. Crab had put a gun in his mouth.

We stood there stunned until Tony's man picked up a note, which had fallen to the floor:

> I am sorry to disturb your rest, but I can't bear to see another sunrise. I will do this one last service and spare you the trouble.

"I asked too much of him," Tony said, his face stricken. "I killed everything he held dear."

"It's not your fault." In truth, I wasn't sure, just as I wasn't sure about Herbert and Stephen. Or David.

"Where did he get the gun?" Tony said.

Sawbuck came up behind us. "Must have been when the doctors were with Duck. We put him in Mr. Roy's old room. Mr. Roy must have had a gun hidden in there; we never thought to search Crab afterward."

We stood there listening to Crab's blood drip on the floor.

Sawbuck said, "May they be dealt better hands next time."

Tony leaned against the door frame. "I have lost four men, four more are badly injured, two horses had to be put down, a whole shipment lost … Frank Pagliacci has much to answer for."

I didn't know what to tell him. Was the man dead?

I shot him. I heard him scream. I saw him fall.

***

We buried our men. I had Zia's uniform cleaned, pressed, and sent to the address on Blaze Rainbow's card. A few hours later, I happened to be downstairs when the bell rang. "I'm right here, Pearson, I'll answer."

A tear-stained messenger boy of about twelve stood with Zia's package, his bicycle on the ground. "There's no such place, mum. I asked, and they laughed at me."

No such address.

I took the package. "I'm so sorry they laughed. I'm grateful you tried, and that you brought it back." I put my arm around his shoulders and had Pearson find him a treat, which seemed to make them both happy.

So Morton didn't live in Hart. Who was he? Why give a false address? Did he even work for the Harts, as he claimed?

Perhaps he really was Blaze Rainbow, an investigator hired to find David and solve the mystery of the false Red Dogs. We both got much more than we bargained for on this case.

But why abandon me and David before we got away safely?

I suppose I no longer needed his help, and perhaps Zia needed him more. I couldn't fault a man for going to the aid of his sister. Joe would have done the same for Josie. But the fact that Morton took the carriage and left us irked me. And he didn't pay what he promised, either.

A few days later, a large package came with my belongings. Included were my cleaned gun and my wedding ring, neither of which I thought I would see again. The package was without a sender, a postmark, or even a note. "Amelia, who brought this?"

"I don't know, mum. Pearson said it wasn't the usual messenger boy; this one was much older, with an eye-patch."

***

David constantly rocked, curled into a ball, sucking his thumb, just as I found him. He refused to sleep in his bed, hiding underneath it all night. His thirteenth birthday came and went. He grew taller; a few hairs sprouted on his chin.

Mrs. Bryce brought in another doctor to examine the boy. No injury, no evidence of violation, but his mind .... Whatever happened to him, David Bryce refused to talk, to walk, to do so much as feed himself, as if he became a babe again.

Sometimes I visited, just to let Mrs. Bryce do her shopping. I sat with the boy as he rocked, asking, "What did he do to you?" Just like the time I asked before, and the time before that, he gave no answer.

I vowed to find the answer. Frank Pagliacci might be gone, but I had no doubt that Jack Diamond was involved in this boy's ruin, if only to offer that villain sanctuary.

I was tired of his threats, tired of his madness, tired of being afraid.

Jack Diamond needed to be stopped.

This would not end until one of us was dead.

~This ends Chapter One of the Red Dog Conspiracy~

The Queen of Diamonds: Part 2 of the Red Dog Conspiracy

Appendix

The History of Bridges

1400 AC (After the Catastrophe): Benjamin Kerr charters the domed garden city of Bridges as a neo-Edwardian city-state with the North American Federal Oversight Authority.

Over the next 300 years, the Kerr family becomes a benevolent hereditary monarchy. Around 1700 AC, mismanagement and greed causes the rich/poor gap to widen. Corruption increases, and gangs begin to form in the swath of slums outside the opulent city center known as "The Pot of Gold."

Around 1750 AC, many crime families emerge, engaging in racketeering, extortion, bribery, etc. Wrought-iron fences are raised to keep the hungry from coming into the wealthy areas of the city. A religious group called the Dealers, based in the Cathedral, raise charity houses outside the fence to help the poor.

1799 AC: The Alcatraz Coup begins.

Opposition leaders dynamite the bridges on each side of the Pot. Hungry mobs, backed by Opposition forces, storm the Pot of Gold, while Kerr loyalists retaliate in force. Bombing, cannon, ray fire, and torching leaves the Pot of Gold a ruin.

Many flee to the countryside or leave the city. The first Polansky Kerr and his family, unable to flee after the zeppelin station falls to the Clubbs, go into hiding.

Bridges falls into deep financial straits, and Party Time use skyrockets. A radical religious group called the Bridgers begins lobbying for the drug to be made illegal, linking it to the decadence of the Kerrs.

Once made illegal, dozens of gangs take over factories and begin converting them to production of the drug. All-out war over the distribution and market share of Party Time begins.

Four Families emerge, who seize the four quarters of the city. The Families are led by Caesar Diamond, the first Acevedo Spadros, Charlie "The Cowboy" Hart, and Johnny Clubb.

The Four Families

(Those members named so far)

Spadros

Motto: We never changed our name

The Spadros family has been in Bridges since the raising of the dome, being among the original laborers brought in to work on the project.

Patriarch: Roy Spadros (wife: Molly, daughter: Katherine)

Heir: Anthony (Tony) Spadros, age 22 (wife: Jacqueline)

Inventor: Maxim Call

Retainers:

John Pearson, butler (wife: Jane, daughter: Mary)

Jacob Michaels, manservant

Amelia Dewey, lady's maid

Peter Dewey, stable-man

Skip Honor, day footman

Blitz Spadros, night footman

Dr. Salmon, private surgeon

Rocket, a bomb-sniffer dog

Poignee, kitchen maid

Ottilie, kitchen maid

Treysa, kitchen maid

Business:

Sawbuck (Ten Hogan), Tony's right hand man

Crab, Associate

Duck, Associate

Bull, Associate

Diamond

Motto: Diamonds protect their own

A large group of immigrant workers from the South African diamond mines settled in Bridges in the early 1500's AC. Proud of their unique identity, this disparate group of families began to call themselves "Diamonds" and exclusively intermarry.

Patriarch: Julius Diamond (wife: Rachel)
Sons:
Jack Roland Diamond III (Black Jack), age 26
Jonathan Courtenay Diamond, age 26, his twin brother

Daughter:
Gardena Diamond, age 24

Retainer:
Daniel, a manservant (deceased)

Others:
Octavia Diamond, a nanny
Roland, a small boy

Hart

Motto: Ready for anything

Descended from Appalachian and Chinese workers, Crispin Hartmann led one of the early street gangs of the early 1700's. This gang called themselves the Harts and were one of the major players in the looting and other unpleasant acts seen during the Coup.

Patriarch: Charles Hart (wife: Judith)
Heir (and Inventor): Etienne Hart (wife: Helen, daughter: Ferti)

Under protection:

Joseph Kerr, age 23
Josephine Kerr, age 23, his twin sister
Polansky Kerr IV, age 87, their grandfather
Marja, their housekeeper

Clubb

Motto: A golden harvest

Clover Banditerna was a worker on a farm near the zeppelin station until the Alcatraz Coup. Seeing an opportunity, he and his fellow workers called themselves the Clubbs Of Justice and seized the zeppelin station, along with the controls to the aperture.

Knowing that no one could go in or out of the city without going through them, the group charged exorbitant rates and became extremely rich.

After the Coup, Clover Banditerna changed his name, calling himself Johnny Clubb.

Patriarch: Alexander Clubb (wife: Regina, granddaughter: Calcutta)

Heir: Lance Clubb, age 23

Other players

<u>Spadros quadrant</u>:
Eleanora Bryce, a widow
Herbert Bryce, age 16, her son
David Bryce, age 12, her son
Nicholas (Nick, Air), her son (deceased)
Madame Marie Biltcliffe, a dress shop owner
Tenni, age 17, her shop maid
Vig Vikenti, a saloon owner
Gypsy gal, a working woman in Vig's saloon

<u>Market Center</u>:
Bridges Daily, a newspaper
Acol Durak, the editor
Thrace Pike, age 20, a reporter (wife: Gertie)
Swan, map room caretaker (Records Hall)
Anna Goren, an apothecary
Constable Paix Hanger, a policeman

<u>Other</u>:
Jacqui's Ma, a brothel owner
The Masked Man, rumored to be a quadrant money-man
Ely Kerr, a drunkard
Major Blackwood, an old Army man
The Red Dogs, a children's street gang
Stephen Rivers, age 15, a "chip"
Clover, age 18, an "ace"
Morton, their trey leader/Blaze Rainbow, a gentleman
Golden Bridges, a tabloid
Frank Pagliacci, a scoundrel
Zia, a maid
Peedro Sluff, a Party Time addict

Acknowledgments

A novel is, by necessity, a team project. Many people have helped me along the way, and I'd like to thank them. I appreciate the willingness to read a partially finished book and the wonderful input given by Andy Loofbourrow, Bekah June, Sharon Lee, Samantha Ashpaugh, Tasha Reese, and David Bridger. I also want to thank Dennis McDonald for his support, advice, and example in self-publishing, Erin Hartshorn for her generosity and meticulous proofreading, Anita Carroll for her gorgeous cover art, and Jerry Bennett for his boundless enthusiasm. You inspire me.

This book would not be what it is today without the hours spent by my son Corwin Loofbourrow reading and re-reading my many edits and haranguing his mom to make my work the best it could be. Thank you.

About the Author

Patricia Loofbourrow is a writer, gardener, artist, musician, poet, wildcrafter, and married mother of three who loves power tools, dancing, genetics, and anything to do with outer space. She also has an MD. Heinlein would be proud.

You can follow her blog at http://www.jacqofspades.com and find her on Twitter (@Jacq_Of_Spades), Tumblr http://red-dog-conspiracy.tumblr.com/ and The Jacq of Spades Facebook page.

Note from the Author

Thanks so much for reading *The Jacq of Spades*. If you liked the book, please contact me, or leave a review!

The Queen of Diamonds
Now Available
In All Formats

She just wanted an easy case ...

Private eye Jacqueline Spadros, recovering from her harrowing experiences the week prior, wants nothing more than a simple, straightforward case - preferably one the Spadros Family won't find out about. Aristocratic jewel merchant Dame Anastasia Louis, aka "The Queen of Diamonds," seems to be offering the perfect arrangement.

But Jacqui can't leave the madman "Black Jack" Diamond's crimes unpunished. And the more she learns, the more she begins to believe that this particular job wasn't such a good idea after all ...

www.ingramcontent.com/pod-product-compliance
Lightning Source LLC
Chambersburg PA
CBHW030359310726
48979CB00001B/363

* 9 7 8 1 9 4 4 2 2 3 0 4 5 *